WHEN

JONAH

RAN

To Aleta
♡ you!
For God so
Loved the
World...

Rachel

WHEN
JONAH
RAN

A Novel

by

Rachel S. Neal

Lena Charles Ink
Printed in the United States

To Uncle David and Aunt Vi,
For decades of love

PROLOGUE

The old woman licked the last drops of broth from her lips with a satisfied smack, then settled into the cushions that kept her thin bones off the floor. She was asleep before I could tuck the hides beneath her chin. Unable to walk for a year now, the tolls of her life were coming due. I brushed brittle tendrils of gray from her forehead with fingers gnarled and tender, aged like the woman's, both of us an accumulation of time and the trials of living.

Above my head, the ceiling creaked under the weight of the man who walked there, repairing the roof. I looked up, instinctively. Protectively. His children had children of their own now, and yet he would always be my baby.

"Mother?" He called through a finger-wide crack, his face momentarily blocking the stream of sunlight that poured through and warmed the old woman's face.

The blue-veined lids snapped open, eyes bright and alert. In unison we answered, "Yes?"

JONAH

Silence.

Sparrows chattered from olive branches in the valley below, crickets played the last strains of their morning lament, and a bullfrog bellowed from the streamside. That was all. There was no voice from the heavens.

Lifting my hands, I prayed again. "O Lord, fill my ears with wisdom. Plant an unquenchable fire in my soul, a passion for your righteousness. Give me the words to speak. You chose me as your voice to the children of Israel, and I have been obedient. Use me again, tell me what to say."

Silence.

Kneeling before my stone altar, I waited until the first rays of morning struck the pinnacle of land where I sought divine interaction. Sunrise in Gath-hepher was swift once it started, and soon I was bathed in light. I waited for a response until the last shadow was chased from the hilltop, then rose to my feet.

God hadn't come to me in the coolness that preceded dawn. He had delivered no words of wisdom or judgment or council. Daily, my knees fell to this same patch of earth, my hands lifted to the same heavens, my heart poured out the same cry.

And daily, my God did not respond.

A prophet, yet my lips, my ears, my soul, all were empty.

Brushing off my knees, I turned away from the altar, taking the winding trail from the summit toward home. Further prayer was useless. If God wasn't going to speak, I wouldn't waste his time, or mine.

It's not as if I wanted to become a prophet. It was God who initiated that call, whispering words of urgency to me in the night, giving me a message for the king of Israel. Then he lingered, waiting to see what I would do with the divine invitation. Accept a position as a human voice for the Most High, or decline? It wasn't forced upon me. Had I chosen to believe it was merely a dream, or bluntly refused to carry the role, I could have done so.

I accepted, understanding it was a lifetime commitment. At thirteen years of age, my mouth delivered a profound message to the ruler of my people. As the prophecy was proven true and my nation's borders expanded, I was enrolled in the School of Prophets. Formally trained in our history, I was expected to dispense wisdom and judgment, and fill the gap between my people and their God. For three decades, this had been my duty.

I'd had three decades of prosperity since then.

Three decades of power and influence.

And three decades of profound silence. No words of great importance had come to me since that time as a boy.

Veering onto a narrower path, I headed to the pasture. What had I done wrong? Where had I gone astray and angered God? I kicked a stone from the path and sent it careening into a tree trunk. Never once had I missed a morning of beseeching the heavens. Even in sickness, calling out and listening. Listening. Waiting.

"When shall I put in my wheat crop, Jonah?"

"Which merchant will give me the best bargain, Jonah?"

"Ask your God for the rains today, Prophet, but not tomorrow because I have to travel."

Six days a week, the people found me at the city gate and flooded me with their petty issues and mundane questions. Only on the

Sabbath did I refuse to entertain their concerns, the overt work of smiling and exhibiting patience beyond what the Law allowed, in my opinion.

The advice I dispensed was common sense. Not that my input had no value, it was just so painfully ordinary. When I gave my 'Yes' to the Most High, I expected to do more than sooth the anxieties of the prosperous or ensure a fair trade of livestock. For each man I helped, there were countless others left to suffer the fate of the courts. If anything, the injustice was growing. I had done nothing of lasting value.

Disobedience was still rampant among us, despite my efforts to see its end. The children of Abraham weren't chosen for covenant with the Lord God because they were innately righteous. They were chosen to be *made* holy, to be set apart. And they didn't want to be. They were troublesome when it came to the laws of Moses.

God's justice seemed remote, his punishment for sins a forgotten reality. Mercy had been poured out over and over again, and now it was expected. There was little fear among the people of God anymore.

Sin flourished. It wouldn't be tolerated in perpetuity. We were vulnerable, discipline hovering above each prayer to a foreign god, waiting permission to descend. The consequences would eventually be meted out.

"The Lord will strike Israel, uproot and scatter her because of her sins." This prophecy from Ahijah was one I feared as more than a call to righteousness. It was a threat.

And so, I fell before the eyes of the Most High each morning. I loved Israel, the land, and I loved Israel, my people.

I thought God did, too.

Why couldn't my touch heal the blind and raise the dead? Where was the fervor of Elijah flowing through my veins, the passion of Elisha burning words of repentance in the hearts of men?

All that filled my soul was annoyance and disappointment. My role as a prophet was simple to summarize in one word: unfulfilling.

"Why do you not speak to me?" I yelled, my face and fisted hands lifted to the cloudless sky.

God didn't respond, and honestly, I hadn't expected him to.

MICHAL

"Neh! Neh! Neh!"

The insistent wail of a newborn broke the stillness of morning, carried across the courtyard on the breeze at dawn's first light. I allowed the pail of grain in my hand to plunk to the ground and hurried to the entrance of my home.

A woman's heart can't repel that cry, the very nature of the sound drawing up a tenderness from a well of emotions that have been gathered and stored, poured out and replenished time and again in her lifetime. It didn't matter that the cry came from a child I hadn't delivered from my own womb. They were the ones who needed me the most.

The baby was cocooned in a basket outside the wooden gate, skillfully wrapped in cloth so only his face was exposed, red from the effort of making his displeasure known. The back of my hand on his cheek felt warm despite the cool tinge to the morning air. He hadn't been waiting on my doorstep long.

As I anticipated, the infant appeared to be alone, not the first to arrive like the prophet Moses in a tiny ark of reeds. I swept my gaze over the landscape, towards the shadows in the tree line and stone fencing of the sheepfold. Somewhere out there, a pair of eyes watched over the baby. A mother's, or sister's perhaps. This carefully bound babe came with the ties of love still attached.

"Yes, tiny one, I hear you." Seeing no one, I took the bundle inside and rang a bell to alert Timna, my mother's widowed sister. Seated on a bench, I separated the babe from the rough-hewn cloth and found not a boy, but a perfect baby girl within, two weeks old at the most.

I released the breath I'd been holding. There would be no burial, no funeral this time. The abandoned infant was strong in spirit and body.

"A girl child?" Timna's knees crackled as she entered the room and knelt, providing her knobby finger to the squalling babe. My husband Jonah's status was well known, as was our doorstep, a sanctuary for these children who had been turned away by their fathers.

"A healthy one. An addition to Lydia's family, don't you think?" My daughter was still nursing her last son, her fifth boy in a row. She could take another babe and provide the nourishment.

Timna swept long braids of hair over her shoulder as she nodded her approval. "A daughter at last. She'll be so pleased."

"I didn't see anyone else outside." I handed the baby to Timna and spread the swaddling cloth over my knees, then the other warm coverings, seeking an indication of the newborn's identity. The weave and patterns often pointed to tribes within the region, and even once, to a nation far beyond the Hebrew borders.

Rarely did I know for certain who had born the baby entrusted to us until later. A woman's eyes speak loudly when they pine after a child cradled to another woman's breast. Love, sorrow, and gratitude are intertwined cords not readily broken. Hidden among the many faces in the markets or festivals, she'll listen to the cries, look into the faces, to find the child she gave away, to see for herself that her child is loved. In a small measure, it assuages the guilt that refuses to release her soul.

That need for a mother to find her peace was a hope that I clung to. In every market or gathering, with the passing caravans and travelers, I watched. I wanted to find the eyes of one mother in particular.

"From the south by the make of this weave, tribe of Issachar," I said. "I'll get her a rag soaked in goat's milk, then take her to Jonah for the blessing right away. I want to present her to Lydia before I make the bread. This little thing is hungry enough to take to a new mother without a fuss, I believe. She'll be satisfied and asleep before long."

The last baby I kept for myself was Ethan, seven years ago. He had arrived in the care of travelers, a small band of foreigners who delivered the boy to me then disappeared from the region. His silky skin had been oiled with jasmine and wrapped in fine linens. Only a mark over his eye marred perfection, yet to Jonah and myself, the reddish blotch was a touch of the hand of God, for because of it, Ethan was ours.

Time faded the crimson spot, and faded my guilt. Ethan came wrapped in a secret that I had never revealed. Not to anyone. Not even my husband.

And I never would.

MICHAL

Jonah slurped down his stew, his attention seemingly on the bowls of food I placed before him, yet I wasn't certain he tasted anything.

"Jonah? Is something wrong with your meal?"

He startled, as if he hadn't realized I was still sitting beside him. "No. It's fine. Very good."

"Anything in particular on your mind?" I asked, as if I didn't suspect. It was a hot day in the month of Av and our pomegranates were splitting their skins already. It was this season many years past when Jonah intended to collect his chosen bride from her father's home and take her to his own. It had never been allowed to happen. The Assyrian raid that came as a whirlwind on Gath-hepher prevented their union. Miriam was taken from him. The cloying scent of rotting pomegranates hovered over the city afterwards, clinging to our sackcloth for the weeks we mourned the losses.

This time of year, when fruits are ripening, always came with the unwanted memories of that day.

"No. Nothing. Where are Ethan and Timna?"

"Staying with Lydia tonight. He said he wanted to play with the new baby, but I think Timna put that notion in his head. I think she wanted an excuse to stay over there and hold the little girl herself."

I waited until Jonah's blank expression became one of recall. "The baby I blessed this morning. Yes. She's with Lydia then, and our daughter was pleased?"

"Delighted to have a girl child without the pains of birth. It's a fine fit for her family."

My husband nodded and took his time lathering goat cheese on a chunk of bread. He was trying to be attentive to me rather than his own thoughts, and doing a poor job. I filled the growing pause. "And the counselling today? Anything of interest?"

Jonah sighed and turned to peer through the window into the darkening sky. In his forty-third year, he was easily as strong and fit as any of our sons. The plenty of our hearth hadn't led him to gluttony or sloth. As a boy, Jonah had been called from the land, but the land had not ceased to call his name.

If given the choice, my husband would work the fields and tend his animals rather than perform his duties as a prophet, preferring the sheering of sheep to shepherding the people of Gath-hepher. They drained his joy, yet he found it again in the mending of a fence. Picking up an axe or taking to the plow when he returned from town helped him maintain a balance.

My own position in Jonah's priorities was another matter. I couldn't seem to find a niche where he needed me. It was easy to feel like one of our servants on most days, performing adequately without raising or lowering his mood. I was simply there.

The sigh of a discontented heart escaped my lips before I could stop it.

My husband's eyes returned to mine. The deepening creases on his face told of both hours in the sun and of contemplating the concerns of others. "No. Nothing of importance was brought to my attention. The fields are doing fine, the lambs are healthy, no great worries in the region. Mostly I've been asked how to make the rich coffers richer. Do I buy one new field or two? That sort of thing."

"No one seeks God when all is well."

Jonah snapped his head up from where it had returned to his bowl, eyebrows raised.

"Other than you, of course," I was quick to say. "I'm sure you gave wise council. The small issues have importance to those who ask your advice."

The tightening line of his lips dismissed any further discussion. He stood, making his way to the window, looking toward the Plain of Megiddo and the mountains beyond.

I wished he could be content with the life he had. God no longer spoke, and it troubled him. The only time he really brightened anymore was when he was asked about the calling and prophecy of his past. It had been a glorious time for him, and it seemed he yearned for those days more keenly as the years passed.

Jonah's attention wasn't mine for the evening, so I gathered the dishes. He hadn't said anything about Miriam, preferring to be alone with her in his mind rather than sharing her memory with me. He had forgotten that it wasn't only his loss of a bride those years ago in the raid. Miriam, my sister and closest friend, was ripped from my life that day as well.

At least, one would think she was gone. While I didn't want our memories of her to be lost, I thought by now the pain in my husband's heart would have diminished enough to allow me in. I was a good replacement wife and he had no place to complain against me. Except that I wasn't Miriam. Staring at my husband's back, the truth of it fell once more in my gut like a stone weight. I never would fill her place.

The Law says "don't marry your wife's sister if both are still living." Jonah hadn't broken the Law knowingly. I don't believe anyone would have imagined Miriam would continue to be alive in his heart all these years later.

JONAH

Ripped profiles of mountainous terrain stood in stark silhouette against the horizon. Above the peaks, the inkiness of night was descending. I pressed my shoulder into the window frame as the stars emerged, intending to stand for only a moment before preparing for bed. At some point, I thought to ask Michal what the newest baby girl was to be called, so turned to inquire, but she had already left the room.

I was too awake to sleep. My mind was busy trying to wrestle with a problem I couldn't quite identify. Rather than feeling settled after a meal and eager to close my eyes, I stood and stared outside. The air itself was crisp, alive, quickening me. Relaxation wasn't coming, only restlessness.

My hand rested on the ivory knife handle attached to my belt, still sticky with the juices of the pomegranates I sampled from trees near the barn. Images of Michal's sister Miriam always flashed across my mind this time of the year. I didn't allow them to linger. The joy in the young woman's laughter and our innocent glances as we passed on the street were memories overshadowed by the Assyrian raid.

It was a day I didn't want on my mind. I couldn't save my betrothed from the hand of the enemy, their arrival too swift for me to have a plan in place, one that would have saved both her and Michal from their grasp. As men and women fell around me, I defended myself, trying to be on the offensive yet unable to stop even one of the attackers as they barreled through the city. The warriors were strong, and with only a puny knife, I couldn't stop them with their swords and benefit of surprise. I was of little consequence to help anyone standing in the path of the murdering hoard.

It was a day of failure, best forgotten. It did no one any good to speak of it, to jab the knife of guilt back into my soul again and again as if there was a way for me to change the outcome. Still, those memories haunted me, blamed me.

I didn't hold myself to blame for the entirety of the senseless slaughter, however. God could have prevented the attack. He could have warned me. Should have warned me. Of what purpose was my calling as his prophet?

Had I known, we, the men of Gath-hepher, would have been ready. Instead, the Assyrians took the victory.

I shook the persistent memories away, not willing to review and analyze them yet again. Thoughts of what I wished would have occurred and what I should have done differently didn't make sleep come more readily.

Stars covered the sky by the time I gave up on feeling sleepy and tied on my sandals. My restlessness had an element of anxiety, a growing sense that something needed attention Something needed fixed. I didn't know what, so went outside, intending to check on my sheep.

We lived near the end of a quiet road. Gath-hepher proper was to the right, where homes were side-by-side and blocks of merchants set up their trades. My fields and barns and pastures were to the left, and that's the direction I turned, but I didn't go among my flock or investigate the barn for something amiss. I followed the path to the crest of the tallest hill in the area, up the familiar switchbacks to the summit, a flat stone-paved patio with the altar of God in the center.

No one went up there but me now. In the past, it's where men were sent to find me if I wasn't sitting among the leaders of the village at a reasonable hour. They would find me there in prayer, because in those days, I thought the length of time I sought the Lord actually mattered.

I hadn't been there at night in several years. The stones were still warm from the sun when I sat on the bench to look out at the points of lantern light. Beyond my village, nestled among the rolling hills, Nazareth lay shrouded in sleep. Irregular cricket melodies rose from the grasses, then gradually fell away. It was calm, and if I hadn't felt an anxious stirring in my soul, it would have been peaceful.

I exhaled and looked over the land promised to Moses by God, confirmed through Abraham, Isaac, and Jacob. It was a divided now, my tribe of Zebulon and nine others banding together, with only Judah and Benjamin joining as one to the south. The Northern Kingdom of Israel and the Southern Kingdom of Judah, our lands were called.

Although Israel claimed the cities of Bethel and Dan as centers for worship, I knew that God placed his feet first in the temple of Jerusalem. The very heart of the Hebrew people was in the land of Judah. I didn't mention it to anyone, the topic too contentious, yet the scriptures made it clear. God chose Jerusalem as his dwelling place.

But it wasn't as if God never left the sanctuary. He encircled his people in both kingdoms of the promised land, walking in all her valleys, crossing all of her hills and deserts and streams. I was nowhere near Jerusalem's gleaming temple when God first spoke to me. It was here, in Gath-hepher, that he called me by name.

A prickle of chill coursed up my spine.

God had spoken to me on a night like this, one silent and still, the earth and skies holding a collective breath, waiting.

I rubbed my arms and looked at the star-lit heavens, aware that my heart was thumping in my chest, and that I too was waiting. Waiting for more, more of the Holy, more of the words that came from above and filled my ears and soul and mind in one blast of comprehension.

With no way to adequately explain how, I knew the Lord had returned to Gath-hepher. Hope rose from the depths of my soul. Perhaps my God had not forgotten me.

"I'm here!" I called to him, not wanting him to pass me by.

He didn't.

I was not alone.

Closing my eyes, I soaked up the inexplicable awareness. My chest felt as if it would explode from the intensity of the divine presence on that hilltop. I could feel what I could not see, sensed what I couldn't touch. Around me, in me, through me. He was part of me, yet so removed that I shuddered at my own unworthiness.

Desperate to flee the awesome presence and desperate to grasp for more, I was both barren and filled. I was starving and I was fully satiated.

Knees and hands hit the earth, then my forehead as I stretched my entire self out before him, trembling. Fear. Joy. Sorrow. Elation. The entire contents of my soul tumbled about, seeking refuge, or recognition. In that moment, I had nothing, and I had everything. I was nothing, and I was all I ever could be. At long last, my God remembered me, the prophet he had chosen.

He spoke without sound, yelling clearly while whispering gently. "Go!"

MICHAL

The morning light was creeping around the shutters when I awakened from a restless sleep. I didn't need to roll over on the cushioned pallet to know that I was still alone. Jonah never did come home after he left the house so abruptly. I assumed his mind was so consumed with Miriam that he couldn't rest.

I don't believe he intended to put her between us, and had heard many denials when I used to ask where his thoughts had landed. Subdued this time of year, rubbing the old knife on his belt and sighing, I can only imagine it's the past occupying his mind. My husband mourned the life he never had a chance to live.

Jonah refused to talk about that day, about our mutual loss of Miriam, or any lingering pain. He kept those memories to himself, as if sharing them would weaken the barbs. He resisted the healing that might come by letting her go, as if it dishonored Miriam somehow.

At least, that's what I believed. He didn't talk to me enough to confirm or deny my suspicions.

My father gave him that old knife he still carried. He had it in the market when the Assyrians came. It didn't save my sister. Was he waiting for a second chance to redeem his bride?

Jonah knew he needed to let Miriam lie in her grave. He, like everyone, stopped talking about the raid, not as if it never happened, but as if it hadn't torn the hearts of every family into bits. The incidents of that day were recorded in our history, the facts, not emotions, inked on the scroll. It was the way with my people, to mourn, then relegate the pain to the shadows and step out in the light to live again.

I couldn't simply choose to forget, nor did I want to. As it pierced my heart to remember the last time we saw her, Miriam was my sister and I wanted her to remain with me, so I made myself look back. I felt it honored her by doing so, the not forgetting. The fierce pain of those memories had dulled, as only time can prove itself as a healer in that regards, yet the images remained vivid in my mind.

The Assyrians had been raiding towns along our northern and western borders for years, so we shouldn't have been surprised when we heard the first screams. We were though, believing the territory of Zebulon was far enough removed to be safe, or at least to be central enough to have a warning of an attack coming this direction. Gath-hepher had no such warning. It was the middle of the day, and they thundered in. I was bartering for honey cakes, two of them, one treat for me and one for Miriam.

My fifteen year-old sister paid no attention to the commotion. When I dropped the coins in my hand and grabbed her arm, she was looking across the stall to a handsome young man, Jonah, her betrothed. Not permitted to address one another in public, she toyed with the fringe on her golden colored head veil, chin tipped down and eyes flirting above reddening cheeks. He had yet to see the invaders, his eyes locked to Miriam's, and for that briefest of moments, no one else existed.

My screams brought Miriam and Jonah back to the market, mine and everyone else's as men on horseback, helmets and breastplates shimmering, spread among us like a nest of provoked hornets suddenly set free.

Curses in an unfamiliar tongue blended with those of the merchants and townsmen. Swords were slicing the air, piercing hearts. It was a blur of motion and sound, fast and incomprehensible.

Hands fell hard on my shoulders and pushed me to the street. I raised my fists to strike until I saw it was Jonah, white faced, knife gripped tightly. He shoved me with his free hand beneath an awning that had been sliced in half and now dipped to the ground. I rolled into its scratchy folds and gripped the edges, pulling it around me. In its confines, my breath came in quick pants, especially when I realized Miriam wasn't there with me.

I called for my sister from within the cocoon, revealing the safe haven so she could join me inside. Miriam was older than me, yet the protection reached both directions. She kept me from the harm of a snakebite as often as I pulled her away from the fangs of traveling vendors with their gaudy wares. We were the armor for one another.

My voice was swallowed by the chaos of battle. Miriam didn't answer. Stamping feet around my head, wails of fear and anger, of conquest and defeat, anchored me to the earth. I couldn't get up and find her. The worst moment of my young life was outside the safe arms of someone older and stronger than me. There were no whispered words telling me it would be all right. And it wasn't all right. Nothing was, really, after that.

What felt like eternity was no more than a few moments, the Assyrian raiders moving swiftly through town in a rampage, killing and plundering at will before the men of Gath-hepher could rally an army and try to fight back.

I emerged from the rolled canvas only when I heard my father calling. "Miriam! Michal! Miriam! Michal!" It was the first and only time I heard that sort of despair in his voice. Even a few years later, when my mother and newborn brother both died in the same hour, there was profound sorrow, but not the desolation of the day he couldn't find his daughters and feared the worst.

The market was in shambles. Stalls tipped at sharp angles,

pottery smashed and strewn, pigeons fluttering around mangled cages and crying for their mates. Fire was burning somewhere, an awful stench with acrid smoke. Men stood in the street, stunned. Others ran frantically with names on their lips, calling and calling. Some were lying where they had been killed, the gutters between the stone pavers stained red.

Father scooped me up as he had when I was a young child, squeezing me into his chest, pushing my face against his shoulder to protect my eyes from the horror.

But I had seen.

Over Father's shoulder was Jonah, himself bleeding as he hunkered near the old city well, face buried in a blood soaked golden veil.

THE FISH

"Go!"

The great creature of the sea needed no further instruction. The soundless voice of its creator had spoken, and it responded. No questions. No arguments. No stalling or negotiating. There was no place for reasoning or establishing value upon the sudden call to turn and follow a current towards the heart of the open waters. There was no choosing to obey, only hearing without ears and doing. That's the law of the sea and of the sky and of the dry land, for all created kinds, with one exception.

JONAH

"No!"

I raised the axe overhead and let the blade plummet into the fallen tree trunk. Drops of blood fell with it, blisters rupturing and burning in my unrelenting grip.

Anywhere but there, anywhere but that pit of despicable sin. I would not give the call to repentance. I would not give the Assyrians a chance to find favor in the eyes of my people's God.

I would not go to the city of Nineveh.

There were nations too vile for compassion. Those who practiced evil and fought against my countrymen deserved no mercy. They would never share in the eternal glories of the Lord Most High.

The axe head jammed in the wood. I yanked it free and delivered another blow. And another, splitting the splits until the trunk was little more than a large pile of kindling. Strength depleted, I sat back on the stump of the healthy olive tree I had destroyed, staring at the sky as the morning light crept up the hillside, trying to make sense of God's command.

"Go to Nineveh. Jonah, son of Amittai, go to Nineveh and prophesy. Warn them of their impending destruction."

Warn them!

How could the Most High ask that I place one sanctified foot in the unholiest of all nations? I would forever be unclean. The stench of sin would cling to my skin, filth coating the eyes of my memory and tainting my sight with images I did not want to see. I couldn't walk among their temples and not see the unclad priests and priestesses, I couldn't not see the butchering of the innocent, the profane manner of living. How could a Holy God expect me, his prophet, to go there? I would never feel righteous again. All the ritual purification couldn't remove that filth from my soul.

The Assyrians were brutal in their conquest of lands and kingdoms. The raid I had witnessed was petty vandalism compared to the all-consuming destruction its armies ensured. As if the vast region they already ruled wasn't sufficient, from the sea to lands beyond the Tigris River, with fertile fields and pastures. No, it wasn't enough. Their forces wanted God's chosen land, and lands to the north and east too. Hordes of soldiers descended on the enemy cities, striking down men in the fields and children as they slept. They took women and herds for themselves, plundering and destroying, leaving burning heaps in their wake. No one remained untouched. The unfortunate man to enter the city afterward found smoldering ruin and piles of the dead, stacked by Assyrians as a monument to themselves.

Nineveh was the black heart of these Assyrian people. I despised them with every sinew of my being. Let God display his hand of wrath against them.

Let them be wiped from the earth.

Let them burn in a rain of sulfur like Sodom. No one walking the streets of Nineveh deserved anything less.

PERSIS

Thunder echoed from the gray covering of clouds, chasing the downpour into the streets of Nineveh, tiny rivers flowing between the square stones and merging, filling low spots with small ponds. I bunched my long tunic up in both hands and leapt over one before finding relief beneath the roof of the nearest shrine. Young Ba'hiya jumped the puddle as well, her nine year-old legs intentionally falling short and landing with a splash.

"Ba'hiya!"

My charge's delighted grin turned to one of horror as if she hadn't known where her feet would land. She splashed her way to my side, thoroughly drenched. "I'm sorry Persis. Don't be mad."

I glanced around the shrine, relieved none of the other patrons paid us any attention, then pushed long strands of hair off her forehead, tucking them behind her ears. "No fears," I whispered. "I'm not going to punish you." The girl should be allowed to play, to enjoy the temperaments of the weather. It wasn't her place, however. A child of her status had to conform and I had to insist that the childish manners be eliminated.

A loud grumble fell from the dark sky. I allowed the girl to cling to my arm, knowing it was my own fear she reflected when the skies howled. Why I still thought a thunderstorm signaled something more horrific to come, I didn't know. Great floods were the tales of other nations, yet they stoked unrest in my heart. I feared the annihilation of the Assyrian people, feared judgment from a hand more powerful than the empire in which I lived.

"Is Ishtar angry?" Ba'hiya asked.

I breathed in slowly. "Perhaps. Or one of the other gods. But rain isn't necessarily punishment, even though the clouds sound angry. What would happen if there was no rain?"

"We would have no crops and the river would dry up. There'd be nothing to eat or drink in time."

"So rain is also a blessing from the gods. You must always seek both sides to fully understand. One day you'll be expected to give wise council, and to show no fear."

Ba'hiya released my arm and linked her fingers together in front of her ribs while pulling herself erect as she had been instructed to do time and time again. "It's the screaming part I don't like. The god bellows and sounds hateful."

"I understand about the thunder." I held the same posture as the girl, displaying only the calm of one who has no tremor of uncertainty, one who has the blessings of a goddess upon her shoulders and therefore the security of one in the arms of the divine. Too bad it was a lie.

Fear was my companion. No one had immunity to the whims of the elite. In favor one day, executed the next. What one owned could be easily taken and given to another, be it cattle or coin or concubine. Always, the threat of instability. And always the threat of punishment. The fine living I had today could be gone before sunset if I was found to be unsatisfactory.

Punishment from man, punishment from the gods. Yet there was one whose power I feared most of all, one whose wonders I only heard as whispers – the god of the Hebrews. From his word, it was said, the land became land and the waters became waters. From his hand, dirt became man with breath and life. He gave Israel rules and expected them to be sanctified, set apart. He did not like the sins of other lands.

He could not like the Assyrians.

Fortunately, that deity didn't live here. I hoped his days were so busy tending to his chosen ones that there remained no time to gaze beyond the borders.

As a child, I hadn't had these fears. I didn't realize the potential for man to hate man so vehemently, or to never find satisfaction in what he owned, always a quest for more. More power. More possessions. Inflicting more harm, more injustice. My world had grown colder as I aged. I didn't want Ba'hiya, of any of the wards in my care, to know of man's cruelty or a god's vengeance. I could protect them only so long.

Frankincense clung to the moist air in the small enclosure, pots of it smoking from the altar of Dagon. The fish-god's onyx eyes looked out into the torrents and seemed to smile. Beside the carved image stood a man, thick of flesh, soft featured and covered in ornate robes. He fixed his gaze on Ba'hiya, her damp indigo garment clinging to her skin. His hungry expression was common in these shrines.

The girl was of age to be immersed in the religion of the land, and for that reason I had been told to bring her to one of the gods again today. She had not yet been chosen by a patron or one of the priests, but I didn't want the leering man to make the offer. The same repulsion I always felt in such situations rose up and filled me with defiance. I had brought the girl and waited, so had fulfilled my duty. No one told me I had to wait more than a minute or two.

I took Ba'hiya's hand in my own. "Let's run home from here," I said. The undignified display would be reason for punishment if my husband found out. I was willing to suffer the consequences. It was worth protecting the innocent girl one more time.

MICHAL

"Michal."

I jumped back from the voice in the courtyard, unaccustomed to a male presence near the cooking ovens at that time of morning. My bucket of grain clattered to the stone floor. "Jonah?"

My eyes surveyed the sky for signs of foul weather, the only reason my husband would be here and not at his altar already. Even as I birthed his children, he was on the hilltop. With Adin, our firstborn son, I tried to delay the inevitable arrival so Jonah would be near. That was foolish. My mother and her sister Timna both chastised my attempts to hold the babe inside while I groaned in agony.

Jonah knelt in the shadows, rising when I approached. I couldn't help but gasp at his appearance. Can a man gain a decade of life overnight? His eyes were heavy, rimmed in dark shadows, hair and beard peppered with sawdust. Yesterday's work tunic bore the signs of dirt and blood in its wrinkled folds, and both palms were wrapped in linen bandaging. He smelled of sweat, reeked of discontent.

"You didn't come home last night." I said it as a statement. I wanted an explanation. I wanted him to tell me he was trapped by a bear or overtaken by bandits or that he got lost in the hills. I wanted anything other than what I suspected, that his yearning for Miriam was unbearable. That the longing for the life he wanted was too much, and he had been tormented through the night with his memories.

Jonah shook his head and examined his hands. Spots of blood seeped into the fabric wrappings.

"Where were you?"

"Forgive me, Michal. I couldn't sleep. I chopped wood instead." He turned to the horizon and looked beyond his pastures.

"Is it because of Miriam?" I couldn't stop myself from asking. I wanted him to know that's what I thought, and allow him to convince me otherwise. Pretending was meaningless.

His reaction was one of genuine surprise. "What? No. Of course not. Nothing to do with her."

It felt like truth. "What happened to your hands?"

"Just blisters." He examined the bandages, avoiding my eyes. "I'm going to Bethel today."

The city of Bethel was both beloved and a source of pain for him. His training as a prophet was in Bethel, with Amaziah the priest. He cherished those memories as well, a young man in his prime under God's favor, under the king's favor, and under my father's favor. But the ways of Moses had not been deep-rooted, even there. Rebellion rode beneath the customs and formality of religion. The worship of the Most High had become more corrupt since his days in training and for this, Jonah's heart grieved.

"Why today?"

On the floor was the bundle of provisions he was packing when I entered, enough for the long day's journey. Jonah had no difficulty acquiring additional resources as he traveled. No one would dare deprive King Jeroboam's favorite prophet of anything requested.

"I need to see Amaziah. It can't wait. I..."

He caught my eyes and I could see his indecision. After a moment, he turned away. Whatever weighed on his mind wasn't going to be shared.

I sighed with little attempt to conceal it, crossing my arms over my chest. "You promised Ethan he could go with you next time."

Jonah paused, then finished rolling the dried fruit cakes and unleavened bread wafers into a parcel. "Not this time. He'll understand."

The bond between my husband and youngest child was strong. Jonah was a good father and Ethan could never get his fill of his father's attention. "He'll be disappointed."

"Next time. I have business to see to, important, and I need to be on my way."

I didn't remind him that his growing son was also important, even with the responsibilities that lay beyond his own family. Instead, I stopped Jonah from leaving right away to do what a good wife does. "Let me tend your blisters first, and fetch you some respectable clothing while you wash that sawdust from your hair. If you show up in Bethel like this, they'll think Elijah has returned."

My husband's lip twitched into a weak smile as he walked toward the well. The rest of him, his eyes, his shoulders, his walk, spoke of a burden he was determined to carry alone.

JONAH

"They'll think Elijah has returned." I shook my head again at Michal's words as I slowed the chariot. The tail of a small caravan blocked the road as it made the turn toward Joppa. Nearing the end of their journey, the farmers were eager to press forward. Donkeys, carts and men rattled around the bend in a dusty line. I came to a stop and watched it pass.

If my wife only knew how her comparison irked me. Elijah had been obedient to God, fervent in his role as prophet. A bold, irritant to the king, he did what was asked of him, regardless.

But the Lord had never told him to go to Nineveh. God had me chained between a ravenous lion and a hornet's nest. If I went to the camp of my enemy, I'd please God but incur the wrath of my people. If I didn't go, or for that matter, even tell anyone what God had commanded, I would anger God but remain true to Israel. True to myself.

If. If I didn't go. If I disobeyed the creator of the heavens. It was hard to imagine myself even considering the notion of blatant disobedience. Hadn't I preached against the very thing for years? Hadn't my words been constructed to lift the holiness of God and seek the repentance of the sinful? How could I even conceive of saying no?

But Nineveh. How could I say yes?

It wasn't fair. The years of loyalty and seeking wisdom meant nothing? I was to be the pawn of some mad game?

Michal's expression when I told her I was leaving flashed in my mind. She didn't understand, naturally, but she had already judged me. It was worse this time of year, that undeserved harshness, when she remembered keenly that I had not saved Miriam from the warriors. Not telling her that God had spoken wasn't intentional, but I saw disappointment written in her face before I could even begin to express my torment, so I kept it to myself.

She wanted to be supportive. I intended to discuss the matter when I returned from Bethel, after I had resolved my own dilemma and chosen a course of action. Or inaction.

Snapping the reins when the dust had settled, then grasping them tightly to keep my balance, I resumed a southward progression. Behind me, six armed horsemen kept pace. Mouth of God or not, there were men along these roads who wouldn't mind a share of the king's favor for themselves. A fine hewn chariot, black stallions, and the robes of a nobleman would make a handsome take.

I preferred to travel alone. I hadn't in years, not since it became obvious my original prophesy was indeed divine. King Jeroboam had been successful in restoring Israel's boundaries from Lebo Hamath to the Dead Sea, as the trembling young Jonah predicted. The first of my chariots arrived when the kingdom made its first expansion, followed by livestock and vats of wine, and rugs from distant nations. With each wave of progress, I had been blessed with reward. Now the chariots only arrived for exchange once per year. I was known by them, and travelling in anonymity was impossible.

The speed of travel by this method was worth the accompanying entourage. There were enough prophets in Bethel to warrant God's presence. Surely, I could catch his ear while there, and receive a new command, or a retraction of the one I had been given. There were no other alternatives that I could see. I couldn't go to Nineveh. I couldn't not go.

MICHAL

"We have to hurry, Mother!" Ethan tugged my hand, trying to lead me more quickly through town. "They might leave before we get there. Pleeeeeease."

The boy was a physical reflection of his adopted father, the same lean build and strong muscles, the same natural agility, and the same pressed lips when frustrated, as my son was wearing right then. In spirit, it was my sister Miriam I saw in Ethan. He shared her eagerness to taste something he'd never tasted, see something he'd never seen. Delighting in unscheduled adventures, not worrying beyond the moment at hand, he had a lightness of heart that I had not been blessed with.

Today, it was camels that Ethan had to see. For Miriam, it had been a cinnamon from Egypt to sample, gourds from Ethiopia, or perfume supposedly gleaned from some remote island blossom. Haggling as expected, questioning the quality of every item that caught her interest, still the merchants made much profit when my sister had money in her belt.

I released my son's fingers and gave his hair a finger comb, a futile attempt to make the unruly curls behave. "Go on then. I'll catch up."

The boy rewarded me with a smile that made his entire face brighten before he dashed off, eager to see the large caravan that arrived in the night from Damascus, now settled on the outskirts of the city. Disappointment in his father's unforeseen absence was replaced by the excitement of the inevitable herd of camels that accompanied the wagons.

"You and your sister used to run after the caravans like that."

I turned to the chuckling voice behind me. Caleb had been friends of my family since before I was born, our families living on adjacent land for generations. A friend of my older brothers, he had often accompanied us to market, and often rescued Miriam from buying some worthless bauble at an outrageous price. I had once assumed they would marry one another, but Jonah's family asked for her first.

Caleb pulled a small empty cart behind him, his limp noticeable. The affliction had grown more pronounced over the past year since his wife's death to high fevers, the sorrow draining his strength in more than one form.

"No donkey?" I asked, slowing my pace so he didn't have to work as hard.

"Hoping to buy one today. Ahab is too temperamental in his old age to hook to a wagon any longer. He's not tired of resisting my efforts to make him mind, but I am."

"And yet you love that stubborn beast. You've never laid a whip on his back to make him behave, have you?"

A faint blush rose on the man's cheeks above the graying beard. He laughed as he spoke. "Well no. I suppose not."

I knew he hadn't, he wasn't that sort of man. "So, you're the donkey pulling the cart, and Ahab is, where? On your bed catching up on his sleep?"

Caleb's laugh came from deep in his belly. It was the infectious kind, one that made passers-by smile for no reason.

"I brought a cart along to test the animals before I buy," he said. "Once the merchants leave, no refunds. That's how I ended up with Ahab, looking fine and peaceable here, not bucking the harness alone, then fussing like a mother bear when I got him home and put him to work."

We kept an even pace, allowing others to scurry around us as they went about their tasks. The morning was clear and I felt no need to hurry, especially as we neared the old city well. I couldn't walk past it and not be reminded of the day I lost my sister, my eyes turned every time to that spot on the ground where Jonah wept into her veil. I did so again as Caleb and I passed, then jerked my head up and swallowed the sting.

"She loved the caravans, didn't she? I hear there's more glittery jewelry than the last few that have come through. Makes me think of her."

He didn't have to say her name. He knew where my thoughts were compelled to travel, no matter the season or if I pretended otherwise. When Jonah and I passed this spot, we talked of the weather or the price of wool.

I smiled, grateful that this friend understood my need to keep Miriam alive. It wasn't her fault my husband couldn't fully love me. As much as I needed Jonah to bury her, I never would.

"Fabrics do too. Silks and linens." He stopped to pop a kink from his knee, rubbing it until the ache had eased.

"I can't remember her wearing anything plain by choice. Even her cooking apron had colorful stains."

Caleb glanced at my brightly hued tunic, striped in crimson and indigo. "She liked to dress you up, do you remember?"

An old tunic I could get dirt on without being scolded was more to my liking as a child. Bare feet were always faster than sandaled ones, and jewelry just got caught on tree branches.

"I do. I hated it because she scrubbed my skin first. I even spit on her once to make her stop." With the memory came the regret of fighting, although I knew it was silly. We were normal sisters to squabble once in a while. Still, I hated that I had ever spoken harsh words to Miriam, ones I could never take back or apologize for saying.

"She intended to buy cloth that day, to make me a coat," I said. "She was the one getting married but she shopped for me, wanting to do something to lift my spirits."

Caleb put his hand on my shoulder and squeezed just once before anyone witnessed the inappropriate action. He wasn't a relative, so had no business touching me, yet the fleeting gesture filled a place within me that was hollow. It was a reassuring touch of awareness, the simple hand on my shoulder communicating that my feelings were understood, my thoughts and memories important enough to acknowledge. In the brief interaction, he gave me value.

JONAH

"Please, just a shekel for a widowed daughter of Abraham." The old woman grabbed my cloak and held it in a tight grip. "My family land was taken from me, and my children sold into slavery," she said. "Have mercy." She fell to her knees but didn't release her hold.

I stopped reaching for my coin pouch when I saw where her sleeves had fallen back. The crossed scars on her arms were the mark of Baal worship. From the building where she had come, I heard the wails, priests and patrons screaming out as they cut their own flesh in homage. The simple home had been converted into a temple just steps away from the one dedicated to the Lord God.

And no one seemed to care. Pagan worship competed for dominance among my people and it appalled me, the boldness more alarming each time I traveled. Even more so, the indifference.

I yanked my garment from the woman and stepped aside, allowing her curses to curtail any bit of pity I may have had. She used the cry of injustice to raise tribute to a foreign deity and I would have nothing to do with the abomination to my own God.

A handful of men stood near the gates leading into the temple courtyard, pouring fragrant oil over the surface of a smooth stone, repeating prayers and leaving tribute with the priests who stood nearby. Our ancestor Jacob used a stone here as a pillow the night of his vision, when he saw a stairway connecting heaven to earth at that precise location. 'This stone will be God's house,' an inscription read.

The stone itself was said to miraculously transform, and therefore had the powers to heal. In truth, when one sacred rock was stolen, another from the quarry was simply heaved into its place. When the coffers were low, I suspected the priests had a hand in making the current relic disappear so it could be renewed, and filled with fresh anointing.

I bypassed the slippery rock, entered the courtyard and picked a path through the merchants to the temple steps. As usual, I hesitated before entering the stone structure, needing to swallow the bite of guilt that arose when I stood before the carved doors. The only temple where I knew for certain the Lord God maintained a presence was in Jerusalem. But that was down in Judah. One could not be in Jerusalem and not feel a difference. There was a magnification of the shekinah, I felt, the glory of God, only in that most sacred of all places.

This temple was established by King Jeroboam I, after our nation split into two kingdoms. I had never expressed the opinion to anyone, even with my status as a prophet, that perhaps this elaborate un-ordained shrine was an offense to our God.

How could I? We weren't welcomed in Jerusalem when our tribes were at odds. Regardless, under King Jeroboam II's payroll, I was expected to be seen at this worship center, regardless of how I felt about it.

The rectangular room was nearly empty. The priests scurried about in their duties, disappearing in and out of the fragrant incense clouds that permeated the air. Of similar design as the one in Jerusalem, the differences were subtle. I doubted anyone could point them out. Instead of one table of showbread, there were two, and six golden lampstands lined the perimeter rather than just one. On the back wall, a similar thick curtain separated the people from the presence of God.

In theory, anyhow.

Behind the opulent crimson drape was nothing more than an idol constructed from the elements of the earth. Not that the golden calf residing there wasn't impressive. The height and breadth of a real animal, polished daily, it was dazzling. Amaziah had shown it to me and the rest of my class in our early days of training. He meant to inspire us.

I was not inspired. The awe of God's presence was stripped from me that day. I couldn't find it afterward with the same innocent eyes and hopeful heart I'd had as a youth, called into service. When the divine was revealed as a product of my own mortality, it took me years to realize that what I'd seen had nothing to do with the Lord I served.

Long shadows fell across the room before I rose from my prostrate position on the floor and left the temple. In the hours of seeking, I had heard no new commands, no rescinding of the previous one. There was nothing but my own inward screams, begging for a task that took me anywhere but Nineveh.

God had sealed his lips once again.

JONAH

"Were you frightened?"

I shifted my hips on the cushion and leaned forward to scoop a chunk of bread in the bowl of stew, pulling it out loaded with choice morsels. Amaziah sat across from me at the low table. No longer officially in charge of the young prophets in training, he had not relinquished his power over them, and had arranged for the young men to dine with us. Their questions were the same as others had asked of me over the years.

I ate the food in my hand, then responded. "Frightened? Yes!"

This response always brought laughter. The stern history recitations rarely allowed for the prophets to be human. I, not yet one of the ancients, had no intention of feigning a fearless heart that did not react as any other man's. "Yes. The words of God were firmly engraved in my mind and I knew without doubt they were not my own thoughts, but that didn't remove the fear of facing the king. One word from him and I would have been imprisoned, or killed. I had to pass many guards and checkpoints to enter the palace, then the throne room. Each time I stated my purpose, I was ridiculed. I think they allowed me audience with the king for sport."

"Was he kind to you?"

"At first he was irritated. Wasting his time. Then he saw my fear and realized I wasn't there as a troublemaker. I told him good news, fortunately. Israel was to expand her borders according to the Most High. He questioned me repeatedly after that, specifically how I knew I heard from God and why did he speak to me, and who was my father and was he a prophet, and on and on."

I paused, waiting for one of the eager pupils to ask why God did choose me. It was a good question and a good lesson. I liked to tell them the truth, that I was no one, that I had done nothing to warrant God's call except love the land and people of Israel. I had no lineage of great significance, no dreams of speaking for him, no special skills to set me apart. The call was unexpected, and proved that God could see within a heart and find the man he wanted.

But that was not the question that followed.

"What if God told you bad news, that the kingdom would be overrun, what then? Would you have said 'yes' to the calling?"

The heavy pit of fear opened up inside me again. I had pushed the last few days from my mind, not wanting to think yet of the latest word from God. Now the issue was on my plate. Was I only a willing prophet when it suited my agenda? Only willing when the message was one I personally agreed with? If God had asked me to confront the king with a message of doom, would I have done so? And what of the message I had burning on my mind now?

The room grew quiet. I sucked in a slow breath then released it. The correct response to these minds just learning the ways of a prophet was to say that of course I would have done as God had asked, regardless. God speaks and there is no choice but obedience. "I don't know," I said instead.

Amaziah kicked me under the table.

"I don't know," I repeated, pointedly ignoring his pinched expression, "because it didn't happen. I was thirteen, barely a man, and prepared to work the fields for livelihood, not prophesy. I want to say that I would have been willing, but I can't say for certain how I would have responded."

"Nonsense. You would have been obedient. Just like you'd

respond favorably to any command now. You would've been punished for disobedience otherwise. Our God does not tolerate rebellion." Amaziah made a statement leaving no place to question.

I dropped my eyes from the fresh faces around the table, the pairs of eyes seeking a foundation for their own service unto the Lord. "Yes. Certainly." The lie did not come easily.

"God wouldn't have asked you if he knew you'd refuse."

I had no intention of correcting him in front of the pupils, even though he was wrong in his assumption. There was room for choice. As a boy, I had been given the opportunity to turn down the Lord's request to be his spokesman. I understood that without being told. It was a decision I never regretted, even after all the years of silence. At least, I hadn't regretted that decision until now. Today, I longed for my calling among the farmers and shepherds.

MICHAL

Brightly hued awnings covered the line of wagons snaking along the roadside. For Gath-hepher, this was a large gathering of merchants, the thirty or forty mobile stalls of goods and beasts and people only a small portion of the caravan they would join further on, where the road connected to the main north-south thoroughfare.

Behind the line of vendors were the beasts, some resting from their duties in the sparse shade, others for sale. At the far end, I could see a temporary pen with camels enclosed. That's where I would find my son. My dreams for him to attend the School of the Prophets as his father had were always put in question when I saw him interact with the ungainly masters of the desert, or any other furry four-legged creature.

"The finest beasts, sold here! Tame! Eager to work!"

Caleb stopped near the braying donkeys, his eyebrow raising at the notion that the well-fed beasts were eager to be harnessed.

"Damascan donkeys, my friend. Do you know of them? They are of royal origin!" The swarthy man was at Caleb's side, leading him away.

Caleb looked back at me and winked. I smiled back. The unfortunate merchant believed he had a poor ignorant farmer in his hands, one who wouldn't know a fine Damascan animal from a temperamental Syrian. Caleb would get a reasonable bargain, and the merchant, an education in matters of integrity.

I stood where he left me, watching him lower the cart and place his hands on his hips as he surveyed the donkeys tethered to a makeshift fence.

"Would you like to give your husband a free sample of my best product, the kyphi incense of Egypt?" The vendor stood at my side, tipping his chin toward Caleb. "It is rumored to make a man see his woman with the passion of his youth."

The implication made heat rise in my face. I pushed his offered sample away with more offense than was called for, and stepped away as if I had been insulted. I knew the mistake wasn't the man's fault.

Weaving among the shoppers and merchants, it was difficult to attend to the sights and sounds and smells. I couldn't wrestle my thoughts away from Caleb.

My father thought highly of his neighbor's son. I was surprised he arranged the betrothal between Miriam and Jonah rather than Caleb. No one could miss the light that brightened Miriam's eyes when the young prophet was nearby, of course, not even my father. When Jonah's father began negotiations, everyone approved.

Caleb and Beckah were married soon after I was given to Jonah as my sister's replacement. They had nine children, a comfort for him through the illness that took his wife. He had found a wonderful substitute for my sister, I thought. They had always appeared happy together.

I never considered him as a match for myself, mostly because he preferred Miriam. He looked out for me as a little sister. After the raid, he spent more than a year rebuilding the flock the invaders had stolen. When established again, he took Beckah as his wife. I attended their wedding banquet as the young bride of Jonah.

I stopped at a stand and admired the gold earrings, dangly ones with tiny bells that tinkled in the breeze, ones my sister would have wanted and my father would never have permitted her to wear. Would Jonah would have allowed her to do so, once married?

Caleb would not have been so impractical. He lived simply, preferring routine and the serenity of the land over the bustle of town. My sister would have struggled as his wife, but it would have been fine for me. Caleb's income would have been enough, and –

My thoughts were leading me on a path I knew was dangerous, wondering what my life would be like if I had married Caleb.

If. I shook the thoughts out of my head. There was no changing the current state of my life. I had a fine husband and had been surely blessed by God to carry Jonah's sons. Foolish pondering didn't change anything.

"Stop! Stay where you are!"

The command wasn't for me. It came from the end of the caravan line, where I expected Ethan to be waiting. I ran the final distance.

A small crowd had gathered around the camel enclosure. I looked for my son as I pushed to the front, knowing he wouldn't be anywhere but there. He wasn't hanging to the rails as I hoped, wasn't sitting on some stranger's shoulder for a better view, or even on the hump of one of the tamer creatures with a giddy delight and tightly held reins.

"Don't move!" The command came from within the pen, from a man in the midst of the dozen agitated camels. I caught my breath. These stomping and snorting animals had wounds in their flesh alongside scars in various stages of healing. They were not well treated, their friendly nature traded for one of defense. The man held a sturdy wooden dowel tipped in a metal point, keeping it between himself and the camels. He spoke not to them, however, but to the child in the pen among them.

Ethan.

My child stood in the center of the enclosure, his neck craned back to look up at the animals towering over him. One dropped its head to sniff at him, bottom lip tucked, a sign of its unease. Ethan didn't flinch as the nose came near his face, but his grin widened, then he giggled. The animal backed up and snorted, then puffed its cheeks, spewing foul spittle across my child.

Ethan laughed. His arms swiped at his head to clean off the residue.

Pressing my hands over my heart to control the beating, I prayed to the Lord God, screaming without a sound so the beasts wouldn't startle. Their hooves could crush my boy in an instant. Ethan wouldn't invoke their agitation intentionally, yet to him this was play, and I wasn't certain what he might do.

Fear has memory. As my heart pounded, I felt the fallen tarp surrounding me, taking my breath. I heard the stomp of warriors on cobbles, not hooves on the hard-packed earth. "No," I whispered, not willing to go back there. "Stay still, Ethan. Don't let them find you."

My father's voice wouldn't penetrate the fear this time, he wouldn't come to collect me and shield me in the protection of his arms. I made myself breathe deeply and release the air slowly. It took all my focus not to dash into the pen and snatch my boy from harm.

Two men now stood in the enclosure, barking directions in a foreign tongue and trying to guide the beasts toward one side. The camels fussed and resisted the prodding. They stamped at the dirt, snorted and spat.

A third man crept toward Ethan, and when he was close enough, pulled him back against his legs, holding him there. His lips were moving and Ethan was nodding.

A whistle from the perimeter drew the animals' attention. The man whistled a second time, then tossed an armful of feed into the pen. The beasts moved towards the grass. It was enough distraction for Ethan and his protector to back away from the danger.

That's when the scream finally left my mouth. "Ethan!"

The man lifted him over the fence and dropped him in front of me. I pulled Ethan into my arms as I was berated in a language I was grateful not to understand. The irritated words bounced off my back as I led my son away. Finding a secluded spot of shade, I pried my fingers from his arm.

Ethan wasn't holding back tears as I was. He rubbed at the finger welts I left and grinned at me, his eyes alight in wonder.

"Did you see me, Mother? Did you see how tall they were?"

My motherly scold, the reprimand every mother carries on her lips at all times, that all-encompassing, "what were you thinking and you must be careful and don't ever do that again" refrain, fell to the side for the moment. Ruffling Ethan's hair, I found remains of the thick, foul spittle, which I wiped on his tunic with exaggerated disgust. "Yes, and one spit in your face," I said, then allowed him to relive the moment for me from his perspective.

This child given to me loved life. I often prayed that the mother who gave him birth knew he was alive and strong. I prayed that she was alive and strong as well, and happy in her circumstances. If she was watching him today, I hoped she held no grudge against me for allowing Ethan to roam freely into the path of danger. The very notion made me glance around, looking into the faces of women, seeking the ties that bound them to my child.

Retrieving the baskets I had abandoned at the camel pen, and filling them with small clay pots of spices, I followed the skipping steps of my son toward home, twice catching him with a foot on a moss covered stone and the other poised to follow. I wondered what Jonah would think when he heard of his boy's adventure. My husband would discipline fairly, as he had with all our children. It was me I really wondered about. What would my husband think of me for allowing our son to scurry off like he did?

Jonah wasn't a man of quick temper. I knew this, and still I didn't want his disapproval. He never outright accused me of failing to meet his expectations, but I saw it in his eyes sometimes, that certain look that spoke of not being happy yet not wanting to stir the air with accusations. There was peace in our home for the most part, yet joy was elusive.

I allowed a sigh to escape. It didn't really matter if I was in all ways a woman of King Solomon's Proverbs. I watched over the affairs of my household and provided for the poor. I worked hard and brought my husband honor, and all the virtues in the list. The celebrations I planned were executed flawlessly, even though the very thought of entertaining taxed my spirit. Jonah was expected to be hospitable, and for him I scrubbed and peeled and baked and smiled. Miriam, an eager hostess in our mother's wake, would have been proud.

As blameless as I tried to be, I couldn't truly say that I was my husband's friend, that our hearts were connected by threads, interwoven and not easily broken. He came to me for advice at times, and trusted me with his children, yet didn't seek me out for comfort, or with the heavy concerns of his day. His greatest fears and disappointments were kept from our discussions. Part of him was never allowed to be seen.

And part of me was hidden as well. My negligence in monitoring Ethan closely was because I was in no hurry to leave Caleb and his easy way of listening to words I didn't speak. I could never explain that to my husband.

I had no place to complain. I had a good life. It was selfish to think I deserved more.

JONAH

"The old priests believe that the enemy of Israel will be her ruin, as the 'rod of God's wrath.' The Assyrians, perhaps?" I broached the topic with a forced calm to my demeanor.

Amaziah and I sat beneath an avocado tree on a padded mat. The lush garden was tucked behind the temple in Bethel, worked by the students, and enjoyed by the priests. The beautiful young woman bringing us a pitcher of wine was neither pupil nor teacher. She and Amaziah held each other's gaze long enough for me to grasp the nature of their relationship. I turned away until I knew she was gone.

I had not yet mentioned God's command to me, but instead spoke in general of the state of our nation, the state of our enemies.

The learned man rubbed his chin between his thumb and forefinger. Patches of skin were visible among the strands there, revealing decades of contemplation. He wasn't much older than me, obtaining the position as a teacher before he was twenty, confirmed as a priest a decade later. He wasn't a Levite as the Law required, yet it seemed to make no difference in his status. It was another rule that had softened over the years. At least he was a circumcised Israelite. Not all the priests in this region could claim the blood of Abraham.

"I'd like to believe we're strong enough to defend this land," Amaziah said. "If there were any serious threat, we would defeat any who attacked us. Our God won't allow his chosen ones to be eliminated. Chastened, I suppose. It's happened before."

"The famine in Elijah's day, that was a three and a half year long call to repentance. He's shown his hand of discipline without involving the Assyrians."

My mentor nodded slightly, his thumb rubbing the same spot on his chin, then stopping its motion. He looked at me pointedly. "Why are you so concerned about Assyria?"

I flipped my hand casually in the air, making certain my tone had no tinge of defensiveness. "Not just them. Any who oppose our ways. Any of our enemies."

Amaziah nodded again, no longer holding me with eyes that probed for secrets. I continued my line of thought. "I was thinking about the sins of Israel, and how God might show his anger. Would he show favor to an enemy, then turn them against us?"

My bold suggestion froze the man's expression, brows lifted, mouth agape.

"I mean, if our people continue in sin and another nation seeks to honor the ways of Moses..."

Amaziah's face relaxed, except for eyes that were once again narrowed and direct. It was a look feared by the students. "You are suggesting that God will break his promise to Abraham? That he would find sufficient fault to reject us and choose another people? A *pagan* people?"

"No, no. What I mean is, can others be chosen with Israel, or-" I threw my hands in the air. "I don't know what I'm asking."

"No. You don't. I can see that. You know quite well that God will never break his oath to the seed of Abraham. Nothing can change the covenant. Our sins are forgiven by our God, and they are nothing compared to those of Assyria. You know this, Jonah."

I nodded, and said nothing more of the thoughts running amuck in my head, ones that churned my insides. Ones that allowed my enemy to repent and find salvation in the God of Israel.

What I thought I knew about sin and repentance, punishment

and mercy, didn't make sense any longer, and I hadn't yet figured out how to formulate my confusion into a sensible discussion. At least, not without revealing why I was confused. My foundation had jostled since God had delivered his command to me. I no longer knew that I knew truth. God decided to change the game, and hadn't given me all the rules.

The priest sipped from a golden goblet, his eyes watching my expression. I did my best to appear nonplussed as I nibbled on the delicacies spread out between us.

"Has the Almighty spoken? Is he filling you with a message of destruction for his own chosen ones?"

"No," I said honestly, answering the second without responding to the first question.

"Good. Combatting the sins of our nation by frightening them with threats won't be effective. No one listens to a doom and destruction discourse with interested ears any longer."

My mentor preferred a gentle approach when addressing the transgressions of the Hebrews, a contrast to the specific failings he addressed with the students. Little leeway was given to those who broke the rules. Found sleeping during lectures, a student would stand the remainder of the day reciting his lessons to a tree trunk. Walking more than necessary on the Sabbath led to a week of crawling on hands and knees. Dismissal from the school came with too much questioning, too little resources, or when the priests had simply tired of any one man.

Outside the school, there was far greater leniency. The people of Bethel and those who came to worship at the temple didn't fall under Amaziah's strict expectations. He over-looked a good portion of the grievous rebellion along with the petty infractions. Mercy and blessings were dispensed freely, with or without repentance.

Rebellion against God wasn't of less importance than rebelling against the priest. Amaziah controlled what he could and put the remainder in the Lord's hand to judge, he'd told me once. It wasn't his responsibility to cast stones. He was wrong about that, I felt, but respected him too much to argue the issue.

"The Promised One will be from Israel. We know the One who will be our salvation will come from among our people, born in Bethlehem, of all places. And this has not occurred. No enemy can defeat us, therefore. The Prophecy has not been fulfilled." Amaziah popped a deep purple grape in his mouth, discreetly spitting the seed into a linen cloth.

"Why the concern over this matter, Jonah? You came to Bethel with a burden and I'm not certain yet what that is exactly."

I spit my own seeds into a cup, aware that I hadn't even tasted the fragrant juice of the last dozen I'd eaten. As much as I wanted to share the news that God had at last spoken to me again, I still couldn't. Once I said it out loud, I had to act upon it and I was certainly not ready for that. Especially not knowing what that action was going to be.

"Shalom!"

Both of us turned toward the greeting and the man striding up the path in our direction. My companion groaned beneath a fake smile. "Not again. Bear with me, Jonah. This young man believes himself to be one of us. I need to be civil, of course."

The priest rose and took the man's pack from his shoulders. "Amos, my friend. Sit with us."

The sun-weathered man was younger than he first appeared, half my age I guessed as we were introduced. Dressed in simple, unadorned garments, worn sandals, and several layers of dirt, he and Amaziah were quite the contrast.

Amos took a long drink from the flask I offered, then propped himself on one elbow. As he shifted, a cloud of dust rose, then settled back over him.

Amaziah coughed into his fist before he addressed the man. "So, Amos, what brings you up from Judah? Those southern tribes kick you out for good this time?"

The newcomer tossed five grapes in his mouth at once and proceeded to answer as he chewed. "It was God again, Teacher, putting a message on my heart for my northern brothers. The worship here of handmade idols must be forbidden."

"You're a prophet?" I asked, aware of my mentor's face stiffening with the question.

"He has not been to our School, or any of the others." Amaziah's opinion of the man was obvious. If Amos detected the disdain, he didn't acknowledge it. "His profession is as a shepherd, and a sycamore dresser from down near Tekoa. He ventures up to Bethel when he feels like expressing an opinion."

Amos sucked in a sharp breath through his nose, puffed his cheeks and sprayed grape seeds into the air. I flinched. The young man winked at me as I brushed off the one seed that landed on my shoulder. "Not my opinion. I am sent with words not my own," he said.

"Yes. Of course. And are you arriving today or is this a bundle for departure?" Amaziah asked as he started to pat the man's belongings, then seemed to think better of bringing up another brown cloud.

"Going home. I was sent to Gibeah. Wanted to see you before I left the region. It's an honor to lay my eyes on the Prophet Jonah. I'm glad I detoured."

The words felt sincere. "Thank you, Amos. Tell me, do you consider yourself a prophet?"

He shrugged. "I hear from God. I say what he tells me to say in the town he tells me to visit. He's tired of the rebellion, the worship of Baal on the high places. Even here in your city, Amaziah, incense is burned before Nehushtan. The bronze serpent of Moses is worshipped! Why do you tolerate the compromise? Tear the temples down, and stop feasting off the poor. Where is the justice? There must be repentance or God's hand will come down and-"

"Enough!"

I flinched again, this time at Amaziah's rebuke, the harshness unforeseen. Amos, who had risen to his knees and was speaking with great animated gestures, dropped back down to sit. And to stuff more grapes into his mouth. "Thorry." He said. "I know you hate it when I thpeak like that."

"Maligning others will not bring their repentance." Amaziah sounded like his old self, controlled with a hint of condemnation, as if his words were the Law itself and everyone should know them.

"I interrupted your discussion. May I ask what deep well the two of you were draining? Teach me something useful. Powerful." Amos grinned at us, waiting like a dog knowing a bone will be tossed his direction.

I pushed aside the irritating sting of the man's passion. He spoke like a prophet, whether he really was or not. I hadn't felt that sort of fervor rise up in my soul for a long time. Not wanting to stir up the previous conversation, the question left my lips anyhow. "What do you think about Nineveh?"

"As in, why does God allow the corrupted city of Nimrod to flourish? Why does he not squash it like a beetle under a rock?" His thumb flattened three olives against the dish before he scraped them out and dropped them in his mouth.

I nodded. From the corner of my eye I saw Amaziah lean back on the tree trunk, an expression of disinterest crossing his features.

"Perhaps-" Amos was clearly tempering his emotions as he responded. "Perhaps, they are a tool in God's right hand."

A tool. A weapon. A weapon that might be turned against Israel. I knew that's what he meant. Hearing the man say what had passed through my own mind was unsettling. I purposefully unclenched the fists I had made.

Amos continued. "Or perhaps there is compassion, even for those who stand against the chosen. Perhaps, God tends the goats outside his sheepfold."

His last statement was said in quiet tones. Amaziah's response was as well, but with his words came the searing heat of anger. "To love Nineveh is to hate Israel. There is no alternative. And God. Does. Not. Hate. Israel."

Amos ran fingers through his unkempt hair, releasing a shower of debris that landed on his shoulders. His face was tight, brows pinched. For a moment he closed his eyes, then opened them without the fierceness he had been revealing. Now his expression spoke of sorrow. "No, the Father doesn't hate his children. Our transgressions though, he hates every last one. And a good father disciplines the children he loves."

THE SAILOR

Joppa at last! I never tired of arriving at this particular port, one overtly hospitable to the seagoing ships that made her manner of living possible. She offered entertainments a man in any country enjoys, some legal, some not. I was one to taste and see what each port had to offer me, especially after a spell of weeks on a ship. Nothing was off limits to a sailor with a replenished stash of coins jingling in his belt.

There was always adventure to be found in the bustle of a city this size, eager to buy low and sell high, to spread fortunes among its patrons so they could lose them in a night of frivolity, only to win them back the following day, sometimes in an honest manner, sometimes not. That was the rhythm of living at the sea's edge, the tide of good luck and bad, of gain and loss. There was never the flat routine of inland towns.

It was usually only a matter of days before my fun grew wearisome however, the clamor overwhelming. Then I'd pine for the sea again. There was no monotony on board as one might think. The majesty of the open waters never dulled the senses, nor did the fear of dying there. Sailing was a profession I'd chosen perhaps because of the conflict. The thrill of life, the threat of death. A gamble.

Faith in the gods had proven itself in the twenty years I'd lived this life. The breath in my lungs was evidence enough. From an indentured boy to second in command, I'd weathered more storms, more shipwrecks, more foul infirmness that drained me of fluids in both directions, than I could count. And I survived. The gods had been good to me.

I had tried over the years to figure out which one was actually in control of the tempests and waves. If the voyage went well, noting what gods were represented by the men on board. If it went poorly, what gods were there and what ones left on shore? I hadn't been able to answer my own question on the matter, so openly encouraged a variety of beliefs when men were hired on. Some ships preferred only their own countrymen, but I liked sailors of all nations and colors to man a vessel beside me. It was best to be over-protected by many gods than to rely on one or two.

Gripping the halyard, I managed the mainsail for approach. The Amphitrite was well seasoned, a responsive vessel, needing little coaxing to do my bidding. The captain made the final adjustment to our position before ordering the men to row the remainder of the distance and dock the vessel.

It was hoped to be a short turnaround time and I intended to make the most of the land under my feet. Joppa was alive with interests for a man without the eyes of his wife or mother-in-law upon him. My first stop, once the ship was secured and unloaded, was always to the shrine of my own deity. It was a matter of principle to give homage to the being that had seen me to dry land once again.

PERSIS

A hand jostled my shoulder, waking me from a restless sleep.

"It's me, Ra'eesa." The whispered voice was strained.

I rose in the darkness of the sleeping quarters, careful not to disturb the other women. If any of them were awake, they kept both eyes and mouths closed. Every one of our husband Tariq's secondary wives understood why I was summoned in the deep of night at times.

The child in Ra'eesa's womb did not belong to Tariq. Records kept by the steward, listing dates and names of which concubine was chosen for the night, would prove it to be true. She had not been selected in four months. At least, not by the only man who had rights to her body.

I led the young woman to one of the baths, a room at the end of a hall, where the herbs that would fatally sicken the child were stashed. The concoction I mixed would threaten Ra'eesa's own health, but not end her life. In a few days of seclusion timed with her moon cycle, she would be back to her duties. The rest of us would assist with her tasks, covering any residual malaise from prying eyes.

We didn't speak, the threat of being found not the only reason for our silence. Neither of us wanted to be there in the dark cover of night, the unspeakable task and agonizing three days a choice handed to us by a society that placed no value on our lives.

Ra'eesa sat on cushions near the pool and waited for me to mix the ingredients. It was a familiar recipe to all Assyrian women, yet few would administer it to themselves. The oldest among the secondary wives, I no longer counted how many times I had been asked to make the blend, then hold the agonized mother in my arms. No one benefited from suffering alone. Physically or in her heart.

Juniper, bitter apple, and parsley herbs had been added to a pot of water four days ago, steeping beneath the sun's rays on a window ledge. Now I added hyssop leaves, dates and honey, then allowed it to rest until the tea was a deep russet brown. The tepid mix was poured through a sieve into a cup. I placed the brewed poison in Ra'eesa's trembling hands. Three cups tonight, and for the next several nights, until the life within her was stilled.

The young woman had sleek black hair and eyes the blue-gray of a storm cloud. Her beauty was a detriment. The same men who protected our husband abused the women of the estate. Everyone knew what happened when the Master was gone and a guard pulled a wife away from her duties.

Four women had been beheaded in as many years for the assumption of infidelity. The children they had already born were sold or given to one of the temple gods in exchange for a blessing.

No woman deserved to be in the position in which we found ourselves. Our children should have been our greatest blessings. Not even Tariq's children by a primary wife were guaranteed favor. Each had as much chance of a privileged upbringing as being a gift to the gods, sacrificed with the promise of favorable rains or victory in combat.

Only two of my eight children remained beneath Tariq's roof. Illness and the battlefield claimed the wealthy as well as the poor. The gods took another portion. Dagon's outstretched bronze hands had held three of my newborn children longer than I had been allowed to hold them to my heart.

I abhorred providing the killing herbs, but the futility of birthing a child only to have it snatched away and burned in the fires was a far deeper anguish. There were those who believed it was an honor to give up a child in that manner, but for me, the infant cries had been seared into my heart as wounds that would never heal.

Watching Ra'eesa sip the bitter liquid, I could empathize with the painful hours that lay ahead. I had sipped the same tea.

JONAH

I dunked my head beneath the cooling waters of the stream. Stopping the chariot beside the welcomed refreshment, I stood at the crossroads of Aphek, where the road from Bethel either led me home, or if the spur was taken, to the sea.

I'd been to the seaport city of Joppa, and disliked it immensely. There was the odor of too many fish, too many people, too much indulgence. While I could appreciate the beauty of the sea itself, I had no reason to venture out upon it. I had no desire to test God's ability to preserve me by such foolishness. He gave me lungs and legs, not gills and fins.

And yet, I wanted to run away, to turn from home and leave my current predicament behind. No resolution fell upon me in the city of Jacob's pillow. No miracle, or voice of the heavens. No guidance. Nothing but the words of Amos, and his thoughts about a father disciplining his children. My people hadn't heeded that message for years. Would the Ninevites?

I shook my head and sprayed water in all directions. The men who protected me as I traveled remained on horseback, watching my every move. There was no running away.

Plunging my head in the water one final time, I held my breath until my chest ached. Gasping for life giving air when I lifted my head, I knew my heart, and my feet, would never find themselves in Assyrian territory unless my sword was drawn.

MICHAL

"Wrap the bandage firmly enough that it stays on, but not so much that the blood flow is restricted. Try again. It takes practice to find the correct tension."

My husband shifted to a more comfortable position on the ground as Ethan spiraled the wrap up the ewe's leg again. The docile beast bleated a brief protest to the tether keeping her from skipping off with the others. Jonah responded with a rub to her head.

The shepherd knew how to manage his flock of real beasts. It was the human sort he struggled with, their selfish requests and stubborn ways irksome. With his children, the teaching came naturally and usually was without distraction.

"Better?" Ethan had his eyes locked onto Jonah's face.

His father's attention was elsewhere.

"Did I do it better?" The repeated question came with a tug on Jonah's arm.

"What? Oh, yes Ethan. Much better. If she had a real cut on that leg, what would do?"

"Come find you!"

Jonah smiled, removing the wrapping and rolling it back up. It was a distant smile, his mind heavy and dark since the return from Bethel. "Yes, true enough for now. When you oversee the animals yourself, what will you do?"

Ethan frowned. "Why by myself? Where would you be?"

In that speck of time between questions, I saw my husband wince.

"When you have your own flock. When you get older and get married."

"I'm not doing that!"

Jonah ran a hand over his son's cheek, a look of sadness flickering over his features. Then a ruffle of the boy's hair and a grin. "We'll see about that, I suppose. Anyhow, I want you to know how to care for all that God entrusts to you. How would help the ewe?"

"Salve, you mean. If there was a cut, I would rinse it with strong wine first, then put on an oily yarrow salve, then wrap it up like I just did."

"Good, Ethan. See if you can find me some yarrow. I'll show you how to make the ointment." He handed the boy a cloth pouch and pointed toward the brush. He'd already demonstrated how to mend breaches in the stone-walled enclosure, and reinforced lessons on identifying wild animals by the signs they left behind. I assumed he wanted to make up the time for not taking his son to Bethel.

My husband joined me on a stone bench. His men were among the sheep, inspecting them for injury after finding the remains of a ram that morning, and tracks of a lion. His eyes went from them to Ethan, then back again, keeping watch.

"How is Amaziah fairing?" Two days since Jonah returned, this was the first opportunity we'd had to talk. He'd filled his hours with chores and time with Ethan.

Jonah snorted. "Same as ever, with an inquisitive batch of students at his heels."

My husband's hands couldn't keep still. He picked up a stick and peeled at its bark.

"What did you discuss with them?"

He breathed in and out a few times before responding. "Nothing new."

We used to discuss the matters of God with one another. I tried again. "What old topic, then? What concerns the young prophets in training these days?"

Jonah tossed the stick into the wind and watched until it fell, then picked up another. "Judgment, as always. Why God doesn't destroy the enemies of our people."

"The Assyrians." I said without thinking.

Jonah jerked his face toward mine and clipped out his words. "We have more enemies than those savages. Why must everyone always bring them up in conversation?"

I forced myself not to push away from his anger, putting my hand on his arm and massaging the strong, taut muscles. "How could they not come to mind first?" Other than marauding fractions of Canaanites, only the Assyrian empire was a threat of any consequence.

His own hand covered mine and squeezed apologetically. I gripped it with both hands and held on, allowing that line of conversation to die.

"Do you think the others are truly welcome among us?"

I followed his gaze to the young Scythian in the pasture, hair a striking color of straw and eyes the blue of the heavens. Japheth, son of Noah, had tribes with that coloring who chose to settle where the land turned to snow and ice each year. This fair-haired slave Jonah purchased, and freed, was brown as I was now. He was also circumcised, by his own choosing, and claimed our God as his own.

"It's been done for generations. Our father Abraham allowed inclusion into the chosen. King David's own lineage included a Canaanite and a Moabite."

"But are they truly *of* us? Among us, yes, but of us?"

My eyes searched the fields for the son not of my own womb yet assuredly born of my heart. He was walking on top of the stone fence.

I caught my breath as he picked his way along, then released it. Ethan was sure on his feet. "Yes, I do believe they are welcome by the Most High if they follow our laws. Adopted as children of Abraham."

"How many? I have three Scythians, a handful of Midianites, and a Phoenician in my employment, all adhering to our rules. Is there a limit?"

Jonah pulled his hand from mine and pulled out his knife to start the peel of skin from another twig. I thought about his question, uncertain what he was struggling with. It was deeper than his words, I knew. "Why would there be a limit? Wouldn't God be pleased to have many acknowledge him as the only god? Wouldn't he want all the sons of Noah to return to their knowledge of him?"

Only the scrape of his knife filled the space between us for a few minutes. "For Sodom, it was ten righteous men," he said. "That was all. If there had been ten, God would not have sent his rain of fire to destroy them. It was a city of thousands and he only required ten."

"There weren't ten, though."

"No. God followed through with his plan."

He didn't elaborate. His prophet's mind was churning and I struggled to keep up with the flow of his thinking, connecting Sodom to a quota in the number of chosen approved by God. My mind went back to the history of the wicked city, then to Nineveh, a most wicked city of our generation. The conclusion I reached lifted my spirit.

"Nineveh has been spared because there *are* righteous men and women living there! There must be more than ten, and perhaps-"

"Michal! No! That's not what I meant."

"Oh," I said, with enough disappointment in my husband's rebuke to be noticed.

Jonah put an arm around my waist. "Nothing good lives there. You know that."

I bit my teeth on my lip to keep my thoughts locked inside. Surely the God of our people was somewhere in that vast city. "Then what are you trying to discern? What troubles you?" I said instead.

His eyes followed Ethan's movements. "If God did intend to destroy that place, would he change his mind if only one man repented? Or ten?"

"How many to spare the city? No one can answer that. If God intends to strike his hand, he will strike his hand."

"If ten had been found in Sodom, it would have been spared. He said he would destroy it, but he would have stopped himself if the conditions had been met. God's own words of destruction would be..."

I didn't fill in the destination of his thoughts out loud. Jonah was heading toward dangerous ground if he was questioning the reliability of the Lord.

I stood, eager to fetch Ethan away from danger of his own finding, the hornet's nest that held his attention. Jonah looked right at his son but wasn't seeing him. The teaching opportunity seemed to be over, sliding away as the boy's father turned toward issues in the heavenly realm.

"Righteous judgment trumped mercy for Sodom and Gomorrah," I said. "Mercy is trumping judgment for Nineveh, it seems, at least for now, and that is God's concern. Not ours."

I left my contemplative man alone to ponder without me. In the brief conversation, I wasn't sure I was really involved, merely putting words in the air for his rejection.

He was the prophet. Let him answer his own questions.

I could never believe there was a limit to the number of people God was willing to secure beneath his wings. And foolish or not, I believed he could make his presence known in the deepest pits of humanity, were a soul willing to let him in. For the mothers, and daughters, sisters, and wives who lived in the Assyrian lands, I would continue to pray for mercy to reign.

JONAH

The stone slipped from my grasp, pinching my little finger between it and the rock below. I stifled the curses exploding in my head, shaking off the pain silently. I didn't want anyone or anything to hear me, or come find out what I was doing. Above me, the night sky was a blanket of stars with a bright moon to light the work I intended to complete before sunrise.

Although the temperature was cool in the third watch of night, sweat beaded on my brow and dripped its saltiness into my eyes. I swiped it away with the back of my hand and chose another stone to tip and gather up in my arms. With a team, I could have completed the task in short order. I chose to do it alone. It meant more that way. It was my monument, my place to reach out to the God with whom I had entrusted my life.

Stone by stone, I dismantled the altar.

God hadn't rescinded his command, and I had no peace. The nature of the prophecy was drowning me with its implications. There was no reconciling what I wanted with the words I was given.

Righteous judgment didn't always prevail. If that was so, there would be no one on the earth except the Israelites, and even they were guilty of sin. God was the judge and he served only two sentences: mercy and justice. Never had there been injustice. A holy god was incapable of such a grievance. Give one man life and another death, one received mercy and one his just due. It was our God's prerogative which sentence was pronounced. That's what I always told the masses that clamored for answers.

Heaving the stone into my chest, I staggered to the edge of the hill and dropped it, shuffling my toes out of the way. Then I pushed, forcing it to roll off the edge and down, down the embankment where it would crash against the many others that I had banished. From the same grave, I had hauled the stones up the hill and built the altar, a young prophet whose expectations of the Almighty were dashed in one violent raid. I vowed then to never be weak, not of spirit or of body. Constructing the site had served to strengthen me in both dimensions.

What did it matter now?

Where had the daily prayers led me except to a mundane existence and a command so reprehensible, I was willing to turn from the face of my God?

Running my arm along the stones, the remaining ashes were swept to the earth. My ritual sacrifices had meant nothing. I wasn't a Levite and shouldn't have offered them, but since I was called by God, I thought he'd be pleased. Apparently not.

I had always clung to the pillar of mercy, believing my own level of righteousness earned me favor. Hadn't I proved my loyalty? Hadn't I demonstrated obedience? I clung to the laws more rigidly than Amaziah, and he was a priest! Now God was going to offer the opportunity for repentance and life to that malicious horde of Ninevites. At my expense.

It wasn't fair.

I marched from my sanctuary into the deep darkness of the early morning, leaving a ruin, the rubble strewn about where once I bowed my knees to the heavens. I would never return to the hilltop. I would never ask again, never listen for words that I knew weren't coming.

No, justice did not always prevail. The call of judgment was a call for repentance. A prophecy of doom was opportunity for its recipients to change their ways, opportunity for God to change his mind. Warning of impending destruction meant there was still time to plead forgiveness.

And if Nineveh sought repentance, God would grant it. Instead of the destruction they deserved, they would live.

And my own nation?

From the time of our arrival in the promised land, Moses had warned us, 'if you don't obey the Lord, you will be defeated before your enemies.' We were living in God's mercy, but for how long?

My people could find repentance. They could avoid discipline. But when? Israel had a poor history of maintaining even the first law of Moses, 'Thou shalt have no other gods before me.' Disregard for the one God rule was blatant. Even in Bethel's temple there was a forbidden golden image. It was meant to honor the Lord God, but it was compromise, and compromise wasn't obedience.

Long in the night I had come to a conclusion: If I went to Nineveh, enough men would seek forgiveness to prevent their destruction. I was sure of this now. I was being sent to warn them because at least ten would listen. God could have wiped the earth clean of their foul stench already. He hadn't, and was sending me there because he wanted to pour out mercy.

God's loyalty to his chosen was wavering.

Mine wasn't.

I wouldn't warn the Assyrians of judgment. I would not be the one to encourage repentance. The fire had to fall on Nineveh. To preserve the purity of Israel, the protection of my nation, Nineveh had to burn.

There would be no mercy triumphing over justice on my watch.

Finding my way back home, I crept inside and rolled some belongings into an old length of cloth, making a bundle I could carry on my shoulders. I had to leave this home, this land. I had to run from my calling before the living God and face the consequences somewhere far away so the wrath from on high that would surely follow me wouldn't land on my wife and children.

I had to get as far from Gath-hepher, as far from Nineveh, as possible.

I had no alternative.

MICHAL

My husband was gone.

In the night, when I realized he wasn't beside me, I felt his absence from more than the bed. I felt it in my heart. There's no way to explain it, really, just that the vacancy that waited for the fullness of his love had grown wider. Jonah, my husband and father of my children, had drifted further away. For the first time in years, I allowed myself to cry.

Miriam, I imagined. I was reasonable enough to know it wasn't only my sister he pined after. She summed it up, a blessing from God that was snatched away. My husband yearned for the life of his past. God had spoken to him as he had to Elisha, and Jonah was eager to make a difference in this land he so loved. Filled with expectation, revered at a young age, he was asked to sit with the elders before he could grow a respectable beard. With bounty from King Jeroboam rolling in, Jonah had it all.

Then Miriam was gone, and the voice of God didn't return. Continuous demands on his time had little to do with repentance or righteousness. Even gifts from the king lost their luster.

Still, no one's life is satisfied to the brim. There are longings that never get satiated, and it is by choice that we find contentment. I didn't know why Jonah couldn't find enough gratitude in his blessings. His land and home, flocks and herds. His status in the region and sound health. What of his sons and daughters and grandchildren? What about his wife?

The exhaustion that comes with sorrow led me into a deep and dreamless sleep. I didn't know if my husband came into the room at all, to see me once more and place a kiss on my forehead before he disappeared into the darkness. There was no note, no indication of his intentions, no reason to believe he was gone forever except that my heart said it was so.

Had he awakened me, I would have had a chance to speak reason, to speak of his family and of putting the past where it belonged. I could have reminded him of the good in his life, the good he was doing, whether or not it was of great importance. I would have reminded him of his calling before God. If nothing else, I could have clung to him and pleaded and made his leaving a struggle.

He didn't rouse me, however.

Then came morning. I went to the altar. His altar. In the rubble, I knew that my husband had left me in body as well as in soul. And not only me. He had clearly walked away from his God.

MICHAL

"Where's Father?" Ethan shot the question out as he ran to the well ahead of us. Both strong little legs propelled him over the rocks beside the path rather than around them.

"I don't know." I answered quietly, knowing the question would be raised again when he was close enough to hear. For now, the boy was distracted enough to not fully comprehend his father's absence. I chose to be honest with him, as was right. If I could soften the situation though, I would.

Tears threatened to escape but I wouldn't allow it. What was I supposed to say to this boy? What was I supposed to say to any of our children or friends or leaders of the city? It was past midday already. The men in our employment knew their responsibilities but Jonah's absence would be noticed if he didn't check in on them at all.

I suppose I hoped he would return before the day closed, and I wouldn't have to respond to the question of Jonah's whereabouts. Perhaps whatever he needed to run from or to, he had done already and would be eager to be home in his own bed by nightfall.

Timna noticed my subdued mood. "Not on the hill?"

I shook my head. "No." I had not told anyone about the state of the hilltop sanctuary, or that Jonah's cache of coins had been partially depleted. He took very little on his travels. The chariot flagged him as The Prophet of Gath-hepher, favored of both God and King. Because of it, he was given all he needed. No one dared bring offense to those my husband served. But the chariot was in the barn and all the horses and donkeys accounted for. Wherever Jonah went, he was on foot with resources to provide for his needs.

Timna stopped and confronted me openly. "What's happened, Michal?" Her tone was soft, as always. Older than me by two decades, she saw straight through my emotions.

"He's gone. I don't know where. In the night, he left."

"Back to Bethel, do you suppose? You said he was more troubled when he returned from there than before he left the last time. Perhaps he had unfinished business with the priest."

"Not so far, Ethan!" I changed the direction of my conversation to prevent my son from climbing over the edge of the well as he drew up the bucket. Back to Timna, I hesitated. I didn't know what lay in store for me. I didn't know where my husband had gone or when he would return. If he would return. Presuming out loud what my heart feared was too much at that point. "The chariot is still here." Facts would speak for themselves.

"The pasture, the city gates?"

I shook my head to each suggestion. I had checked those places already, and the market and anyplace he might have gone. "The children haven't seen him today. No one has. I've asked as if it were nothing of importance, but he appears to be gone."

Timna shifted the water pot to one hip and put a hand on my shoulder. "He isn't careless or irresponsible. He'll be back soon with a tale of some sort. Try not to worry too much. Let's wait to see what the day holds first."

I scanned the rolling hills, green with vegetation only in spots, the rest rocky and dry this time of year. Timna was right. I didn't know where Jonah was or what he was doing, and he had always been reliable. He had used coins from the coffers in the past, and he still traveled, gone for days when he went out to do his work as a prophet. Perhaps he simply forgot to tell me that he was leaving.

I stepped around a pile of rocks and felt the weight on my heart return. Jonah's altar was in disarray, most of the larger stones tossed down the hillside, and that was not by accident.

THE SAILOR

The sun's harsh beams prodded my eyelids until I forced myself to open them and ease into a sitting position. Morning came much too early in every port, no matter where I was, or what sort of natives I'd found myself among. Drinking companions in all my travels liked the same set of hours, the late ones. First swigs or last dregs draining down your throat had no prescribed time once the sun was gone, and there was no closing time along the docks until the last man passed out cold. Usually, that was me.

The motion of sitting up was enough to make my head swim. When the dizziness cleared, I wiped the grit from my eyes and looked around. I was in an alley, alone, and after a moment of concentration could recall which port this one happened to be. And what sort of evening I'd had.

I chuckled, seeing in my mind the shop I'd stumbled into, the one that sold grain during the day and everything else a man might want at night. Beside me, a blanket had been folded to cushion my head from the cobbled street. I picked it up and inhaled, wanting a waft of perfume to stir up the night's fuzzy memories, but smelled a lingering trace of vomit instead. Only my own, I hoped.

It was a cheerful bunch I found when my duties on the ship were complete for the day, a group of working men who laughed and told tales no one believed. I wagered on a game of dice, then another, upping the bids in direct proportion with my intake of spirits. Checking the money pouch attached to my belt, I was relieved to find a few remaining bits. Another reason to love Joppa. A man could thoroughly enjoy himself, pass out, and still not be robbed. This port understood hospitality.

Splashing my face with water from a puddle, I returned to my ship, working out stiff joints along the way. Sleeping on a paved alley was far better than the beach I'd found myself on a time or two. A blanket of fleas or crabs didn't make up for the more yielding surface. Renting quarters was always an option in a port city, but to me that was money wasted. I never seemed to make it back there once I paid and left for the evening's entertainment.

The Joppa harbor was smooth, colored the deep gray of morning as it slapped at the shore line. I paused to look out to the open sea, where sunlight was making golden waves, crested in brilliant white. Humid, salt-laden air blew across my face, as it would for weeks. In a day or two, the ship would set its bow toward Tarshish.

I had been to the remote port only three times and was eager to leave with each visit. Exotic enough to entertain me, it felt too far away, too close to the edge of nothingness for my liking. The waters of the sea stretched away from its ports to lands a great distance beyond, and I didn't want to adventure that far away from the security of land.

The Amphitrite's belly was nearly filled to capacity for the voyage, one that was certain to be profitable. Only a rare traveler wanted passage on this route, so little space was preserved for accommodations of that sort. Traveling to Tarshish wasn't a journey a man chose for adventure. Unless he had goods of his own to sell, it was the route of a criminal seeking escape.

I purchased a couple of oranges to wipe the staleness from my mouth, eager now to sail and return again to this port. It would be a long time before I saw my wife and children, and a longing for them rose in my heart. Instead of my normal four to six weeks away, it would be close to four months this time, a quarter of the year gone before I held them in my arms again.

If I did. A lengthy journey magnified all the dangers of the trade. I suppose that's why the port calls had to be full of living. I never knew when it would be my last. Sailors weren't known for their longevity.

Contemplating the voyage and my options, I once again reconciled with the fates that governed the winds. I wanted to return home, to firm ground. I knew I might not. Every voyage was a chance on death. Today, I opted to gamble. I'd be on the deck when the time came to sail.

THE FISH

"Swim!"

JONAH

I kept my head turned as I negotiated with the old man. The horse in question was beyond prime, and like her owner, had joints that creaked and groaned. She didn't protest to being ridden, the man said. It was all she knew, having been in the king's army at one time. The old girl would take me to Jerusalem without collapsing on the way if she wasn't pushed too hard.

Paying for her, and for a blanket and reins, I mounted and rode back to the main road. If I had been recognized, the man had said nothing, and if questioned, would say that the man who purchased his beast was heading to Judah's temple. Wearing a simple tunic and old cloak, I counted on no one suspecting that I was Jonah, the prophet.

I caught up to a small convoy of farmers near Megiddo, their carts laden with goods for the Joppa market. With permission and a small fee, they permitted me to ride nearby. The steady, mindless pace left time for my mind to churn. It had been only a day since I left home and returning was still an option.

Were they looking for me yet? Probably, locally, since I had not taken the chariot. Michal would have noticed my absence yesterday. She wouldn't have panicked. She would do what she always did and take care of the situation, checking the obvious locations. This morning she would have voiced alarm to the city officials. Family and friends would comb the region for a few days. There would be no answer.

Guilt made me rein the old mare in, and slow my pace. I didn't want my family to suffer in that manner. Was I making a mistake?

The ancient preacher of righteousness, Enoch, had been taken to the heavens without tasting death. The prophet Elijah was whisked off the earth in a chariot made of fire, seen then unseen. I wanted the city officials to believe this of me, that God was pleased to take his prophet away without leaving bones behind for burial.

No one would really believe that, of course. For all my efforts to be the voice and hands of the divine, I was no Elijah.

In time, my disappearance would fall to the side of other more urgent news. I hoped it would be the fall of Nineveh. This was the consolation I focused on, and returned to the convoy as it moved toward the sea.

Was there a middle ground somewhere that I was missing?

How many times could I ask myself the same question, only to arrive back on the same conclusion. I had asked no one else's opinion. How could I? If anyone knew what God had commanded of me, I'd have to act. I couldn't maintain my status as prophet and not respond.

Who would I consult, anyhow? The people came to me for council. King Jeroboam would chain me in a dungeon before allowing me to warn his enemy of impending destruction. Amaziah would say I was demon possessed. My own father would turn his back on me. Not one of my friends or city officials would support the endeavor, whether God said to do it or not. I had no reason to ask any of them what I should do, except to validate not going.

But then they would realize I was rejecting the voice of God. I would be shunned, mocked, either way.

I couldn't please God and the people of Israel.

The one person who might have helped me find a place where both God and man were pleased was the mother of my children. I took a long drink of water from a leather flask and pictured Michal in my mind. Never rash with her answers, she sought to understand issues from every conceivable viewpoint, with the Law out-weighing all others. Very little could persuade her to change her mind once she came to a conclusion.

I trusted those conclusions, and almost woke her up before I left. Wisdom and compassion seeped into her conversations and I needed some of both. I needed to share the great burden handed to me from the heavens.

Standing at the door after demolishing my place of prayer, I listened to the rhythm of her sleep, a ragged cadence as if dreams were warning her of the days ahead. She would have persuaded me to stay home, at least for that night. There would be logic as to why I should or shouldn't heed my calling, and I knew I'd probably never have made the decision to walk away.

Then where would I be? Stuck with the indecision of pleasing God, pleasing man, pleasing myself, and pleasing my wife. No, I couldn't tell her. This was my decision alone and the consequences would be mine alone.

Besides, it would be easier for her this way, not to know the details. She wouldn't have to explain it to anyone and feel the shame of her husband, the great prophet, abandoning his duties. And it would be shame that she'd feel. Her heart wasn't as hard as mine when it came to the Ninevites.

Disappearing this way, Michal and the children could grieve my absence without losing respect in the city.

I couldn't help the respect she'd lose for me, whether I stayed and she knew everything, or now, just leaving without a word. There was only one way to keep her from looking down on me, and that was to follow God's command.

And I couldn't do that, not even for her.

"The Lord will uproot and scatter Israel because of her sins."

Ahijah prophesied, yet my people had not shown repentance. The complacency had deepened, the outright disobedience finding soil and establishing tenacious roots.

Protecting the Ninevites was simply not an option. Their power was on the rise. They were a real and viable threat to my people.

I slid off the horse and led her to a stream, replenishing my supply for the remainder of the journey.

It would be a difficult time for a short while, then it would be better for Michal that I left as I did. God's wrath didn't need to fall on my family as he pursued me, nor did they deserve to live in the shameful wake of my actions.

My wife was competent and could manage the household as well as anyone. She wouldn't suffer long with me gone, and would make certain little Ethan was properly raised. My other children had families of their own and my opinions as a prophet held no great importance anymore. This action I was taking was justified. By leaving, I was actually preserving the lives of those I loved. Nineveh would fall without the warning of doom, and Israel would stand firm.

In the generations to come, perhaps I'd be remembered as a hero.

MICHAL

"I don't like this." Adin, my eldest son, spoke softly, the alarm in his tone not intended for my ears.

He stood on the hill among the fallen stones with his brothers, neighbors and men from town. His father had not returned, gone now for at least a full day and part of the night before. All were armed, prepared to search for Jonah. Seeing the destruction of a monument to our people's God led them to the same conclusion. I had to be the one to say it out loud for them, not needing protection from truth.

"You believe he was taken by bandits," I said.

A collective intake of air was the response, along with eyes that lifted from the earth to the surrounding landscape, as if they could see thieves with my husband in captivity among them.

"Ninevite raiders?" The conversation among them continued.

"It would explain this desecration." A neighbor kicked a small stone over the edge. "They enjoy insulting gods not their own. It shows whose deity is stronger."

"Not necessarily Assyrian men. Could be remnant Canaanite tribes."

"Could be. Taking only one man isn't the style of Assyria, especially-" The speaker paused and looked at me a moment before continuing his thought. "Alive. Jonah wasn't killed here. No evidence of that."

No, they all agreed, quite firmly for my benefit, that my husband hadn't been killed. Not there anyhow.

"Why take him, then? There's been no demand for ransom."

The thought reminded me of the secret cache of money Jonah kept beneath the floor near the hearth, under a stone cap that could be pried up to reveal the storage space inside. It was always obvious to me when he had opened it, the area of disturbed dust catching my eye. I knew he had been there recently. Had he taken money for a reasonable cause, then fallen into harm?

In my heart, I didn't believe it, yet I couldn't discount it either. "He may have had gold coins with him." As soon as the words left my lips, I realized how terrible the notion sounded.

"Why would Jonah be up here in the night with money? A payment of some sort?"

I straightened my slumped spine and lifted my chin. "My husband did *not* make illegal or immoral deals here before the altar to his God, or anywhere. He wasn't hiding something in the cover of night."

"No, no, Michal. We know that. No one is accusing Jonah of wrongdoing."

The murmurs all agreed, however I could see in their expressions that a new seed had been planted.

"Would he have done this himself?" Adin asked, kicking the rubble with his foot. He understood his father's frustration at God's silence.

It was Jonah who had taken the altar down, I felt this assuredly in my heart, in the dark places I wanted not to see. I had no proof however, and didn't want to express the thought out loud. Jonah was an elder in this community, their own prophet, and Adin's flesh and blood. I wasn't going to cast stones at my husband's reputation outright.

"I don't know what happened here," I said. "Someone tore this altar apart but I don't know if he was involved."

"We'll continue with a search. He might still be nearby, perhaps injured. Lion tracks have been seen near here again. If anyone finds anything, sound the alarm."

Teams of men left me, armed with weapons and small ram's horns. I would conduct my own search to see what was missing besides the coins and the knife that he carried, the one from my father years ago. Perhaps there was a clue to his whereabouts in the items he had taken with him.

Timna and Caleb met me at the front steps. "They might be gone awhile," Caleb stated, following men with his eyes as they dispersed. "I'll search your grounds again, in case we've missed him somehow."

With his weak leg, it wasn't reasonable for him to traipse in the back country for any length of time. I was glad my friend would be nearby, finding strength in his presence.

"And Ethan?"

"I sent him to Lydia's with bread and cheese. She'll keep him distracted." Timna checked my expression for approval. I nodded. I didn't want my son here in case they did find his father, injured or worse.

Caleb had his hands on his hips, looking toward the barn. "I could take a horse, look for him on the roads. I can't imagine it's much different than the back of a donkey. It would be faster though."

Even Jonah refused to sit on the black stallions. The pair were hard enough to control from the chariot. "They've not been trained for a rider," I said. "The chariot is safer, but you need armed men to go with you."

Timna shook her head. "If he was in plain sight along the road, someone would have found him and brought him to us by now."

"Unless he's been beaten badly, and they don't know who he is."

"Then we pray he's in the hands of a physician, and we'll hear of it. Once the region knows the prophet is missing, word will travel to us."

Timna made good sense. Caleb wasn't convinced. "I could go and ask in the nearby towns at least."

"No." I blurted the word out. He wouldn't have the stability in the chariot as a man with two strong legs, and I didn't want him to leave. "Please, not yet. Tomorrow, with Adin, if they aren't successful today. If my husband is close by and wants to return, he'll find a way."

Caleb's forehead creased with confusion. "Why would he not want to return?"

"Oh." I made my hands release the fabric of my tunic that I had been twisting and slapped one over my lips.

"Michal?"

"I meant, if he's able to return..."

Timna took my hand and waited until I looked at her squarely. The oven-baked bread aroma wafting from her clothing held comfort and safety. So did the tenderness in her expression. "Do you think he doesn't want to be found? Did Jonah run away?"

There, it was out. She put words to my fear. I swiped the unwelcomed tears off my cheek as I nodded and looked behind me, needing to be certain Ethan hadn't quietly arrived. My heart longed to say no, that I knew this man would never abandon his family, never abandon me. I wanted to deny the truth that had been born in my heart when I first stood on the hill and saw what Jonah had done.

Caleb put a gentle finger on my chin and lifted it, my weeping eyes to his. "Michal? What do you know? Where's your husband?"

"I don't know. He left, I think, of his own accord. Jonah left us. He left me."

MICHAL

I found nothing missing except perhaps some dried raisin cakes and salted meat strips. It didn't appear that any good clothing was missing, nothing from the king's offerings anyhow. I couldn't find his sturdy shoes, the ones he wore for manual tasks, and thought a few of his plain tunics were gone. That was all. He wasn't going to see the king then, or Amaziah. He would never disrespect them in that manner, dressed for labor.

In the barn, I plopped down on the chariot and leaned against the interior shell. Carved into the sycamore sides were massive oxen, symbol of the tribe of Ephraim. Their hooves pinned both lions and winged bulls to the earth. The imagery was an insult to the southern tribe of Judah, whose symbol was the lion, as well as the Assyrian empire and its favored imagery.

The chariot itself was a message as it traveled, a prideful stance that my husband overlooked as he rode within its splendor. The boasting of kings wasn't his concern, he'd said. This gift was one I'd return, if I had any say. The day of the raid on Gath-hepher, I'd seen those bulls on the shields of the warriors. I didn't want them in my home.

My thoughts lingered on that eventful day. The ferocity of the attack for so little plunder, it was sport rather than necessity. The men weren't hungry or in need of supplies. They stole the very heart of so many because they could, taking treasure that can't be traded in the marketplace.

I stood and went to the bin of cloth we kept, bits too worn for clothing but useful as patches, and bandaging when torn into strips, or other projects needing a remnant. Miriam's golden veil was still in there, where I had placed it years ago. I'd never been able to tear it up for another purpose. Jonah had never used the piece either, that I knew of, not willing to see it gone any more than I could.

Searching, my hands dug through faded remnants, dull stripes and natural hues, fine linen weaves and scratchy burlaps. I lifted out scraps of an old saddle blanket and shook it, and examined the sleek folds of a silk tunic stained in blackberry juice. One by one, I took the pieces out and laid them aside until the bin was empty.

There was no golden rectangle of cloth.

Jonah had taken Miriam's memory with him.

THE SAILOR

A warm wind blew along the coast, heralding good sailing conditions. It was the kind of weather I liked, the perfect temperature for ripping off my outer garments and allowing the sun to soak into my bronzed skin. I was a strong man, and proud of the muscles that rippled in the light. I hoped I might get to exercise them in more than loading crates. I didn't care for the man who had been loitering around the docks that morning. Something about him wasn't right.

Joppa was a busy seaport, dozens of vessels anchored in her harbor and along the docks. Every color of man walked the streets of town, and spoke languages I'd never grasp. Merchants and seamen, traders and craftsmen, sellers and buyers from far inland. Caravan masters brought wares and hauled others away. A camel came loaded with wine and went away with silks. The port moved continuously, the shuttle of humanity weaving through the warp and weft of goods and ships.

Every man, every beast, every last crate of oil, had one thing in common. Purpose. That's what the stranger lacked, why he stood out like an eel in a crab pot. He wasn't enjoying the view, trading goods, or examining merchandise. He spoke to no one, and retreated to shaded corners after pacing the docks.

For the fourth time, the man wandered close enough to speak to me, then didn't. He chose to lean against a nearby pier post instead, watching a fisherman deftly relieve his catch of their guts. The man stared at the murky water, as if the swirling churn had meaning, his future foretold in the scraps of lifeless fisheyes and broken spines.

The stranger's clothing was that of a working man, as were his hands. He carried no excessive weight like the rich and spoiled, and was strong, yet not as lean as a man who worked for his pay doing hard labor. He was no sailor, for certain. The bundle he carried was a simple fabric roll tied with leather strapping. His headpiece wasn't the style of the locals, and if I had to wager on a guess, I'd say the man was one of those Israelites, who claimed this land for the time being.

His appearance said little of his occupation, or more to my concern, his intentions. It was his eyes that drew out the suspicion in me mostly, either looking over his shoulder or at the ground, never eye to eye with anyone. That was never good.

Purposefully, I walked behind the man and bumped into him.

The stranger tipped toward the watery churn, limbs flailing to prevent the unexpected bath. I grabbed his arm and pulled him back. "Excuse me," I said with no effort to keep the dripping sarcasm from my voice. This man needed to know who had the upper hand, who had the right to be there and who was the intruder. I was hoping he would spew an insult and our fists would be given a chance to fly.

The stranger calmed himself quickly once he found his balance, not a bit of anger breaking through. Another emotion had been stronger, as clear to me as the waters of Cyprus. He had been frightened. Beyond startled, there was deeper fear in his features for a moment. Any smart thinking man would be more scared of me than a dunk in the sea, but it wasn't me that made his eyes go wide. It was the threat of falling into the water.

"I was in your way, I apologize." The stranger spoke Aramaic with ease and offered a polite smile and a flicker of eye contact as he stepped away from the edge of the walk. "I enjoy a good swim, but perhaps not in that." He tipped his head toward the stew of sea and guts, where gulls where squabbling and scrambling for choice bits.

No good fight then. I dropped disappointed fists from my hips and crossed my arms over my chest. I knew I was an intimidating presence, a head taller than most men and certainly more chiseled. Adding a direct gaze made the stranger look away from me and take a few more steps toward the safety of the solid ground.

"What's your business here?"

The man turned toward the harbor. He let out a tired breath and shook his head. "I'm not certain."

"Move on, then."

"Yes, I will. Sorry I disturbed you." He gave another nod and walked back toward the shops, the bundle held tightly to his chest.

I watched until he disappeared in the crowd. I wasn't satisfied. The man had been spying on the Amphitrite. Were there weapons in his bundle? Did he intend to rob my vessel or steal her merchandise? He had yet to look at me squarely like a man with a clean conscience. He was hiding something.

Or himself. That made more sense. The man was running from something or someone, shifting with the guilt of an inexperienced law breaker of some sort.

I spotted the stranger hours later, once again nearby but obviously avoiding the zones of loading and unloading, of sailors and merchants. And the edges of piers.

By then I'd had enough wondering.

THE SAILOR

With muscled experience, I pulled the man from his shady hiding spot under an eave, hauling him into the alley and behind a stack of barrels where we could converse without witnesses. I pinned my prey to the brick wall with one meaty hand clenched over his throat. The other hand located the knife he carried. I positioned it near his ear, liking the feel of the old carved ivory in my hand.

"I don't like you," I said. "I don't trust you."

The man's limbs were rigid in fear but he didn't squirm or attempt to fight once his throat was caged. Now, finally, he fixed his eyes on mine as he forced himself to breathe and to keep balance on the tips of his toes.

"Who are you? What do you want?" Each question came with a satisfying squeeze of flesh on flesh. My palm could feel the man's throat tighten and relax as it tried to swallow down fear and bring up resolve. I liked that sensation, the man's life in my complete control with the flexing of only my fingers.

"No one. I'm no one." The words were choked out, eyes still on mine.

"What's your business here?"

He hesitated, so I gave him incentive to answer me with a dig of my thumb into his neck.

"I, I need to find a ship, need to travel."

"Where? Why?"

He didn't look away from me, his expression one of indecision, as if he didn't know himself why he was leaving dry land. I could tell when he stopped fretting, and the decision rocking to and fro in his head had finally found firm footing. His body relaxed slightly, enough that I had to loosen my grip so I wouldn't actually choke the man, allowing him to stand flat-footed.

"Where," he said, "doesn't matter."

He offered no more explanation. I released his throat and held the knife in front of his heart.

The man glanced at it, and rather than any sort of plea for his life or lies or bribes or falling on flattery, he seemed to calm a bit more and had the mettle to negotiate. "The why, doesn't matter."

He was challenging me, the fool, telling me not to pry into his bag of worms, his business remaining his business. Calm and thoughtful with a weapon threatening his life blood, he was asking me to let him be on his way without answers to my questions. If he wanted death, he'd lift a fist or hurl an insult. Apparently, he didn't want his life to end, but didn't seem too afraid of losing it either.

I couldn't remember the last time a man hadn't cowered before me when confronted, a sober one, anyhow. As much as I loved the satisfying crack of ribs, I didn't like to kill, or even permanently maim. Fighting was sport. But he didn't know this.

I didn't trust this stranger any more than I had before, but I decided I liked him.

Flipping the knife around, I handed it back then crossed my arms over my chest, a door preventing escape from the alley.

He exhaled audibly. "Your ship, where is it headed?"

I ignored his question. "What are your intentions?"

He rolled his head back and rubbed the back of his neck. "I need to leave Joppa. I'm not a thief or a criminal. I have no intentions other than to find passage. Soon, preferably."

"You're running away and not from the law? Would that be your opinion only or would the city officials agree with you?"

Another hesitation. "I've not broken any laws, not harmed anyone or stolen anything. I'm an honest man."

"Not smuggling?" I kicked at his pathetic roll of belongings.

He didn't flinch as if there was something of value within. "No."

"Haven't left a dead man in your wake?"

"No."

"Wife nag you that much then, have to escape?" I meant to bring humor to the situation. The man shook his head without smiling.

"No, she...No, not that."

I hadn't expected to find a passenger for this voyage, and knew it would please the captain to get the fare. "Tarshish," I said.

His eyes opened wide. He was educated, then, knew that we would sail many weeks to reach the point of earth that peered over the seemingly endless expanse of waters. He didn't bother to ask about other vessels, where they were going. "Tarshish," he repeated. Not to me though. To himself. He was asking himself, or affirming or something that no longer interested or concerned me.

I left the stranger there to solve his own issues, striding from the shadowed alley into the bright sun, back to my labors. The fool didn't even ask the cost as he considered, which broadened my grin. I decided I'd give it a twenty-eighty. Twenty percent chance I'd see the likes of him again.

Heaving the first crate onto my shoulder, I turned and was glad I had no real wager placed on the stranger. He came up behind me, his voice leaving no doubt as to his resolution. "When do we leave?"

PERSIS

"Oh, thou great and fearless one who swims beneath the sea, who soars in clouds of rain and hail and grants good will to me."

The lines of homage to Dagon were chanted by his priests in an unending litany, hundreds of memorized lines repeating as the sun rose and set, set and rose again. Every man and beast would perish without Dagon's blessings on the fields, so he was praised without interruption. He filled the rivers and streams with the waters from the sky and made the soil fertile and bountiful in harvest. An angry Dagon withheld the storm clouds or turned the water into hail stones of destruction.

Oiled from head to foot and wearing only loincloth, the young priests' shaved skin shimmered in the lamp light as they circled the massive bronze altar. From the center of the platform, the fish-god reached out from the waves, his hands eager to accept whatever sacrifice was offered to gain his favor. His belly glowed with the coals of the last offering.

I nodded at the five girls with me, indicating a place to kneel and practice the sacred words. The tiled sea-life images beneath our knees were swimming in the azure and turquoise and gleaming white waters of the Great Sea.

I had never seen the sea, far to the west. It was tainted with salt, the same salt that Dagon used to form man, it was said. A man's blood and sweat were proof of his origins. At the work of his hands or the shedding of his blood, he was to remember, and praise the god of the waters.

It had been foretold that a man would be formed again from there, son of Dagon, come to protect the city. Two plagues in the last few years had not drawn him out despite the deaths, nor had the ominous day when the sun was blotted out and darkness filled the midday heavens. Watchmen sent to the coastal towns under the king's orders waited for his arrival. I believed they watched in vain.

Man came from the earth, according to my father, not the sea. Knowing he was dead didn't wipe away his words. Truth and lies alike find fertile soil in a child's mind when her father sows the thoughts, so I had never truly embraced the teachings of Dagon. The sea was too far removed. The land, I could feel. My father's body, arising from dust and returning to dust, meant he soared with the blowing winds, and was with me, wherever I went.

I knelt with the girls in the back of the circular room, mindlessly repeating the chants that I had said so many times before. I wanted to believe they mattered, that the fish-man image rising from a barley field had ears that heard our words. Deep in my heart, I knew it couldn't hear or see or help me.

Practicing the words of homage wasn't the reason I had come, just the excuse I offered to be allowed to go into the city. Ra'eesa was in the hands of the physician. Tariq's wine taster found her asleep in her room after the others had gone to dine, and forced his way again. She had not stopped bleeding since the attack.

The wine taster's head was now on a pole in the palace garden, his body dragged out of the city and left to the wild dogs. None of us knew who told Tariq what had happened, or what else may have been shared.

The trauma came too soon for Ra'eesa's body, her womb still recovering from its insult. The herbs I'd administered left her tissues in a fragile state and she'd bled profusely. If she lived another day I would be surprised. My medicines were to blame as much as the man's actions. The beautiful woman's blood was on me.

Unwrapping an alabaster jar I'd hidden in my pocket, I rose to my feet and motioned the girls to follow. At the foot of the god, I broke the container of nard and poured it onto the ashes, pleading silently for the blood stains to be scrubbed from my soul. It wasn't Dagon I pleaded with, despite my presence in his most sacred temple. There was another god from whom I wanted forgiveness, a god from the land to the south whose name I'd never spoken.

JONAH

Tarshish.

Could I really go there? I had no plan as to where to flee, but Tarshish? It felt so permanent.

Isn't that what I wanted?

I stood near the Amphitrite in the early dawn, going straight there from the room I rented. Sleep had been fleeting. Part of me wanted to sleep soundly and not awaken in time to get on board, and part of me knew I had to be on time. The latter portion won, and I woke repeatedly to gauge the hours before sunrise.

What good would it do me to be closer to my homeland? I'd always be hiding from eyes that might remember the prophet of Israel. Tarshish was good, the more I thought about it. I could dissolve and become even more of a no one.

If I lived. God's eyes would follow me, even there. I could make my bed in hell and not be hidden from the one who formed the heavens and carved out the seas. His hand could still my heartbeat at any hour of judgment, anywhere I went. There was no place I could go without his knowledge, no place beyond his wrath.

But the voice wouldn't follow me. God wouldn't speak to his fallen prophet ever again.

Despite the darkness still covering Joppa, I kept my head down. The sea front was already in motion as the tide rolled in, and more men filtered around me the longer I stood. Had anyone decided to look for me in this city, I wouldn't be difficult to recognize once it was light. I was clearly not a sailor or a local.

The anxious tumult in my gut was unrelenting as I looked at the ship and the nothingness beyond. The Amphitrite wasn't new, its belly barnacled, sides a patchwork of repairs. It wouldn't have surprised me to see holes in the sail when I first looked at it. Observing the diligence of its three dozen sailors, I changed my mind. They scrubbed decks and checked every length of rope for fraying, every oar for cracking, every detail of matters I knew nothing about. It was a seasoned ship, but a well-tended one. I supposed it was as sound as any other vessel in the Joppa harbor. It was also the largest, and that's what drew me to it.

Other than fishing once on the Sea of Chinnerath, I had never been on a boat and didn't relish the thought of being on this one, regardless of its size and sea worthiness. It was too vulnerable. I had no ultimate control of my safety and hated that feeling. I could swim if needed but not long enough to make it to shore once past the harbor, I feared. It was not a challenge I wanted to face.

From the streets of Joppa and the bowels of vessels, sailors emerged a handful at a time. My new nameless acquaintance finished lashing a stack of crates together and waved me over. I felt myself bristle at the site of him, still perturbed that another man could get the better of me. I kept myself strong intentionally, never wanting to be soft and therefore useless in a fight. This sailor had been stronger and for that I wanted to dislike him.

"That there's the captain," he said, pointing at a stout man on board whose barking orders to the working hands were followed immediately. "You don't bother him. Ever. You do what he says. Always. Understand?" His breath was tinged in garlic and spirits.

I nodded.

"He's glad to have you join us if you mind yourself. If he doesn't like you and wants to part ways, you're looking at a long swim. We don't turn around. Understand me? You aren't hired on, so stay out of everyone's way unless told to do something."

"I understand." No one had asked my name and I would not ask theirs. Other than the captain, they used a variety of insults and foreign terms to refer to one another. The nicknames were earned, I assumed, and I hoped I would merely be the Passenger and left alone.

"First port is Tyre, and we'll be there yet today if the winds remain favorable. You can get off, or anywhere along the way, but no refunds. You pay today for the whole distance. If you dawdle at port and we leave, your problem. We sail when we sail and wait for no one."

"I understand," I said again, shifting my roll of belongings from my right hip to my shoulder, facing the planks of wood that led me up to the ship. I would turn and run if we didn't sail away soon.

"What's your god, then?"

I spun around and faced the sailor. "What did you say?"

"Just asking what god goes with you. Any of 'em is fine. All are welcome. Just asking."

I turned away, feeling the drain of color from my cheeks. My God was he who created the heavens and the earth and breathed life into dust to form man. He was the one who spared Noah from wrath, walked with Abraham, and called Moses from exile to lead my people to a plentiful land of our own. He who dwelled in the winds of Israel and promised a Redeemer was my God. It was the Lord Almighty whom I had served, and who now asked of me the one thing I could not do.

"I'm not certain any god goes with me."

"No one leaves their deities behind for good reason. Is your chosen god limited, or do you choose to impose limits upon him?"

I did not want this discussion. "Neither," I said in a tone that obviously revealed irritation. I tried to pass him but he blocked my path, his strong weathered hand clenching my shoulder.

"It's from him you flee, then."

A statement, not a question. The sailor's eyes narrowed and his muscled arms tightened. "Don't bring troubles on my ship. Appease your god before we leave."

I met the intense gaze with one of my own, shrugged off the hand and boarded the ship without responding.

There was no appeasing my God now.

MICHAL

I was thirteen when Jonah arrived with the mohar, the gift to my father in exchange for Miriam. It had been a long stretch of weeks, waiting for the payment that would seal the betrothal, one that I dreaded. That payment marked the beginning of the end of my sister's companionship, one I'd had since the day I first breathed.

I didn't know the particulars, how much value my father placed on Miriam's contribution to his home, or how much Jonah and his father were willing to pay in compensation for my father's loss. It was the topic of the moment, one I dodged when the old women tried to corner me in the market. All I knew was that no one offered me any compensation even though my loss would be the greatest. My sister was my best friend.

"You're more anxious than Miriam," Mother said when she found me, once again on the roof looking along the road where Jonah would come over the rise.

"Maybe he changed his mind." The betrothal agreement had been discussed two months ago, and while I didn't want Jonah to ever take my sister away from me, I didn't want him to crush her heart either.

Mother ran her hand over my exposed hair, combing the messy tresses with her fingers. "He'll come when he's ready."

"He's a prophet. What if God tells him not to marry Miriam?"

"He needs a good woman to tend his home so he can go about the work of being a spokesman of the Lord. A bride is a blessing for his faithfulness."

"But-"

The scent of mint engulfed me as she pulled me close, squeezing her love into my heart. "Stop worrying, Michal. He'll bring the mohar. Then you'll have to start all over with the waiting. Jonah has to finish the home he's building before he comes back to collect your sister as his bride. He can't do that overnight."

Miriam would move to the far side of Gath-hepher, and we'd see one another regularly. It would just never be the same. The bond would remain, but other threads would be woven in. I didn't want to share Miriam, and I didn't want the sort of changes that came with becoming a woman and securing a husband and leaving mother and father behind. I wasn't about to say that to anyone, however. I didn't want to sound like a baby.

Watching for Jonah was all I could control. Every time I looked down the road and saw no one meant my sister was still at home.

Miriam crawled under the covers beside me one night, squeezing onto the pallet we had shared until she crossed into womanhood and received her own. "Why does it bother you so much? Are you so eager to get rid of me?" Her elbow jabbed me playfully in the ribs.

I stifled a giggle and whispered back. "No. I just like things the way they are. All your chores will fall on me once you leave."

Her smile found me in the darkness. "It won't be for long. You'll be waiting for you own groom in the next year, I imagine. Has Father said anything yet? Have you chosen a favorite?"

I groaned. I was of an age when every woman asked me that question. In truth, I'd been considering several of the boys I knew, just hadn't decided which one I liked the best, or which one annoyed me the least. I dug my pointy elbow into her side and jimmied it until she squealed for me to stop. We laughed until Mother shushed us.

I snuggled into her, and whispered truth from the pit of my heart. "I want your life to be perfect."

Miriam fluffed the blanket that covered us, tucking it under my feet before settling down to sleep. "God doesn't promise a path without stones," she said.

My mother's mother had always said those words. I knew my sister's life wouldn't be without pain, nor mine. God provided the way for his chosen and we took careful steps to maintain the course. Some parts were meant to be rougher than others, but some were through meadows of wildflowers. That moment with Miriam was saturated in sweetness.

Two days later, I was the one who saw Jonah first, and for once, I wasn't even looking. Laying out flax fibers to dry beneath a warming midday sun, the time had come.

Actually, it was the sheep I heard first, then saw, long before the man himself came over the rise. I abandoned my chore and leaned on the roof ledge to gape wide-eyed at the number of animals trotting toward the house, bleating opinions and bumping off one another in a controlled swarm. The wooly mass might have entered the front door had my father not bolted out and waved them to the side, towards the pastures beyond. I couldn't hear his laughter over the din, but I could read it on his face.

"Get your brothers!" Father's word finally made it to my ears so I ran down the steps to find them. Jonah didn't need more help, having brought his own men to manage the flock. It was for the celebration my father wanted his sons.

By the time the gift had been sequestered in its new fold, the trail of refuse shoveled aside, and everyone collected beneath the shaded awning wearing dust and sweat and exhilaration, it was evening.

"Well, then," Father said. "The betrothal is sealed." He couldn't keep the grin off his face. Jonah had pleased him immensely, delivering twice the animals than had been agreed upon. It was a costly gift that spoke of Miriam's value.

Jonah ran a hand over his forehead to swipe the hair back from his damp skin. He, too, had lips that couldn't stop smiling, and eyes that tried not to stare at Miriam yet couldn't seem to restrain themselves. My sister sat at Mother's side and watched his every move from behind the edge of her veil. Her hands caressed the intricate hand mirror he had given to her. It came wrapped in expensive silky linen, dyed the golden hue of late season wheat.

Miriam and Jonah would have gone off together right then if it had been proper. Even I knew what would happen if they did, and it made heat rise up my cheeks.

"I plan to add another window. The evening light is nice on the west side." Jonah had changed the subject to the home he was building for Miriam. As a prophet in King Jeroboam's favor, he had resources of his own. Adding a room onto his father's home for his bride had only been considered briefly, my sister in full favor of the new construction.

I relaxed against a tree stump, aware of sheep dung drying a second time between my toes. A thorough bath would have taken me from the festivities and I didn't want to miss a moment, not with that chore, one I could do later.

My heart was full of happiness. Miriam expressed adoration for Jonah in her expressions and simple gestures. In the presence of such joy, I couldn't help but feel light inside, an untethering of all concerns. And for the first time, I thought about my own marriage in a positive light. I could see in my sister what I wanted, that bounty of love, of value worth more to a man than his own wealth.

I couldn't know at that moment, on that glorious day, that soon there would be more than stones on my path. There were boulders, insurmountable and crushing.

MICHAL

"Let's go to the market, just the two of us," Miriam said. She knew I craved her attention.

The flurry of activity to prepare my sister for Jonah's return had deflated the happiness I'd held when the mohar was presented. Jonah's home was nearly finished and she would be gone before the next new moon. Managing a home of her own would fill her time, as would their babies, and the grand feasts she was eager to host. Time with her alone would be rare in the years ahead.

Tucking the sewing basket away, I handed Miriam her golden head veil with its new hems. I'd taken extra care to make my stitches even and tight. My sister draped it over her long, black hair, securing it in a knot behind her head then coiling the ends over the top. Teasing out a few curly tendrils, she admired the image in the hand mirror. "Your work is perfect."

I soaked up her praise as I donned my own head covering, wrapping it as she did, but not pulling out locks along the edge because my mother said that was a vain and shameful act. Officially a woman, I had to cover my hair in public now. The young men of Gath-hepher had already taken notice of my status change, and were no longer allowed to romp in the fields with me, or even speak to me in public. Overnight it seemed, I became a different person in the eyes of the Law. The days in my father's home were indeed numbered, though no one had been selected for me as of yet.

It was a clear day, a gentle breeze and wisps of clouds not hinting at the darkness that awaited the town.

Afterward, no one blamed me for what happened to Miriam. Accidents, injury, illness, all are part of being alive, I was reassured. Calamities fall from the sky unforeseen, unpredicted. On that day, it rode in on horseback wielding a sword.

Had I stuffed my selfishness aside, been content to sew binding on a blanket or form a few more clay bowls, the day would have ended far differently. The raiders had not gone door to door in a death march. Only men who rose up to defend their property were slain. It wasn't until the market they killed for pleasure. My sister and I would have been safe inside the walls of our home.

My fault, not my fault. I had to reconcile with both sides. Carrying the guilt and unloading it over and over and over was as familiar as rising with the sun.

Decades later, I could see why I needed Jonah to be happy again. If he would let go of the pain, maybe I could forgive myself. Blame could be lifted from my shoulders if my husband took it and buried it, then refused to let me dig it back up. A mended spirit in him would be the balm that healed me.

That couldn't happen now. Jonah was gone. It had been four days since I discovered him missing.

I stood in the window and breathed in the night air. The men had searched and found nothing other than fresh lion tracks, which they followed and still came away without any sign of my husband. They had looked in all the obvious places, and the not as likely, covering the terrain while watching and listening for any indication of his presence. His disappearance was still a mystery.

For my children and their children's sake, I almost wished they had found his blood in the lion's den. How does a mother explain a father's decision to walk away?

Yanking the shutters closed, I took the lantern and headed

toward Ethan, who slept fitfully and dreamed the dreams of an abandoned heart. Tomorrow I would meet with the city leaders. And speak truth, that my husband turned away from us of his own will? Or another truth, that I didn't know for certain where he was, what had happened.

I wasn't sure any of it mattered. Jonah the prophet was gone. I didn't believe he planned to return.

JONAH

The minimal contents of my gut were hurled into the blue waters of the sea. I gripped the wooden rail and planted my feet against the hull so I wouldn't fall over the side as the ship tipped one way, then the other. Lifting my chin to stare at the horizon as I had been told, the wind caught the fabric of my head covering and peeled it from my head. I watched it soar for a moment, then rest on the waves, a downed sail left in the ship's wake. To have saved it, I would have had to unclench a hand and reach out, and I wasn't willing to do that.

I didn't know how God intended to kill me. Or when. For now, I knew the agony of punishment.

On the dock, when the sailor intentionally bumped into me, I'd had the first taste of fear. It was irrational because I would never have drowned in that depth, yet I'd felt an overwhelming helplessness. Firm footed one moment, falling the next. There was vulnerability I didn't want to acknowledge, and the realization that I might not even leave the shores of Joppa. Truly, my life was in the hands of the God I was disobeying.

No prophet was guaranteed long life and yet I'd always felt protected. King David compared the Lord to a shepherd, and that was a good analogy. A good shepherd defends his flock and ensures their safety. He rewards faithfulness with abundance, always seeking the greenest pastures and clearest of streams for his beloved ones. Trust in the God of the heavens was like that, a shepherd and his chosen, a shield to the Israelites. And I always believed there was an extra measure for his favorites, the prophets he called to be his mouthpiece.

No longer did this apply to me. I revoked that status.

There was no reason for my life to be spared. God had killed his disobedient spokesmen before, and I had no doubt my life would be cut short. Amaziah's most repeated lesson was of the young prophet told by God not to enjoy the hospitality of Bethel after being sent there, and yet he did, sharing a meal with an old man. He was in the jaws of a lion before nightfall. It was meant to be a powerful lesson but made little impact. At that age, we were too full of our own importance to believe we would ever disobey the Lord.

And yet, here I was, on a ship bound for the ends of the earth.

A quick death by wild beast was more humane than one of agonizing length. At that moment, I felt as if my entire insides would be cast out into the waters, until even my heart was discharged. The turmoil in my belly refused to be quieted and there was no escape from the ship's incessant motion, the horizon rising, falling, tilting, without rhythm.

I slid to the deck and rested my head on my knees. As much as I wanted to live, I knew I deserved to die. I hoped it would be swift, and no trace of me would remain, no questions raised. Just a man here, then gone, as if I had never lived at all. I didn't want to be one of Amaziah's lessons.

THE SAILOR

The gray-faced passenger was pitiful. He was too absorbed in his misery to acknowledge that our laughter was aimed at him, trying in vain to stand stiffly erect rather than absorbing the three-axis heaving through his thighs and ankles. The leather soled sandals he wore didn't help him grip the wet deck. Bare feet were superior I told him, as was a linen loincloth rather than a restrictive tunic. He'd been told to wear a turban if he wanted his head covered. He hadn't listened.

By my estimate, we'd been gone from shore three quarters of an hour. The Amphitrite's passenger had a long and unpleasant journey ahead of him.

"Sip on this," I said, handing the wobbly man a mug of beer. "It'll quell the sickness."

The ship lurched as the passenger lifted the wooden cup to his lips, the froth and half the liquid soaking his beard.

"Been on a ship before?" I asked, knowing the answer, and feeling no guilt in the delight I took in his distress.

The man shook his head, then closed his eyes and pinched his lips together as that motion made him dizzy.

"Thank the gods for favorable winds and a smooth sea. This is as nice as it gets out here, a merchant ship's paradise. We'll make good time today."

"We're going north," the man said.

I allowed a jab of irritation to pass by me. There was no patience on this vessel for passengers who thought they understood navigation better than the sailors. The more learned, the more mouthy it seemed. An inlander's knowledge of currents and winds didn't keep the ship on course, despite the hot air they spewed, and I wouldn't hesitate to banish this man to the hold. The last man to question one of my knots found out just how well they held after twenty-four hours lashed to a beam.

This passenger didn't actually ask if my captain knew the route to Tarshish and offer to draw up a map. He simply stated a fact. "North, yes," I said. "To Tyre, remember? For another load of goods. Purple and crimson dyes mostly. You'll survive until then."

"How long will we stay?" He tried again to drink and managed a swallow with only a small belch.

"As long as you want."

The passenger's expression showed his confusion. "Why is that up to me?"

"By the looks of you, I assumed you intended to get off this ship and not look back. We'll dock and load and be gone by afternoon." I steadied the man as he swayed against a pitch, catching the mug that dropped as he grasped for the rails again.

"No," the man said.

"No?"

He shook his head, eyes to the blue on blue expanse of the favorable sky blending into the open waters that stretched before us. "No, I won't be staying there. I'm going with you. I'm going to Tarshish."

Resolve was overriding the man's fear and discomfort. From whomever or whatever he fled, those consequences were worse than his present state. I had to respect that sort of perseverance, though it raised my suspicions another notch or two. Just what in the name of Nanshe had he done?

Turning my attention to a net basket nearby, I drew out an oyster gleaned from the waters before we left the shores of the port city. The saltiness would ease his sickness. Its shells popped apart with a twist of my blade, then I offered the meaty morsel to him. He took one wide-eyed glance, turned to the sea and heaved again.

"I can't eat that," he said when he was able. "It's unclean."

I shrugged and swallowed the fare myself. A little sea water rinse had already washed the sandy grit away. Looked clean to me. "She'll smooth out somewhat beyond Tyre," I said, patting the oak rail. "When we can move off shore a bit further. Then we're off to Cyprus. Now that's a port to enjoy. Island women welcome visitors in a most hospitable fashion, you'll see."

The man showed no interest. "How long to Tarshish?" he asked.

"Depends on the winds. A month or so. Numerous ports along the way first. Know someone there?"

"No." He didn't elaborate. "Following the coastline then?"

"Of course. Whales don't carry a purse."

He gave me a confused look again.

"No profit where there's no port."

The man nodded. "I see. Good. It feels, uh, safer." His knuckles were white, matching his face.

"A direct line across the sea is risky in this type hull. We're meant for cargo and that creates an instability in stormy seas. With the shore in view, we can move inland if a squall arises, reach a protected harbor."

The man nodded again. Resigned. His shoulders relaxed a tiny bit. "Never been shipwrecked, then?"

My burst of laughter made him grip the rail with ferocity, as if the noise alone would push him over the side. "I never said that. Of course I have. Goes with the job, and it's a long swim, whether you can see the shore or not."

I turned away, leaving the man sicker than when I found him. It was a good laugh at his expense, and a good beginning to a voyage that promised adventure and riches along the way. Nothing could sink my mood except losing all my money to a game of dice. And even that came with enough spirits to keep me smiling.

JONAH

"Get off."

The captain pointed his stubby thumb at the gangplank without bothering to make eye contact as he brushed past me. I collected myself and stumbled to shore so I wouldn't be in the way while the newest stock of merchandise was secured inside.

Following the orders of the sailor, I forced myself to eat dried bread and drink weak wine so there was something inside my stomach. He answered to Squid, a name originating with a woman in some remote port in reference to arms that came from everywhere and never stopped groping. He was proud to tell me this bit of unsolicited information, yet still didn't ask my name.

There is a profound loneliness in anonymity. I found myself wanting him to ask for details, who I was and how many sons, what was my profession, or native country. It was a foolish desire of course, and I'd have to lie rather than reveal myself. It wasn't the time for establishing friendships. I was a no one for a reason.

Even on land my head swam as if still on a moving vessel. I sat after one lap of the docks, seeking the shadows of the great Phoenician port where I could see but not be seen. My people traded wheat and olive oil for colorful fabrics and fruits in this city. I couldn't be certain I wouldn't be recognized.

The moment I was told I could return to the Amphitrite, I made my way back inside. It was no easier the second time. My heart was making the same choice as it had the night I tore down my altar. Every step led me further from home. Further from God.

The quarters below deck were cramped and creaky. It was

primarily a cargo hold, wooden crates and clay amphorae nestled with precision to maximize the storage capacity. Pathways between the cargo led to short benches jutting from the side walls, near portals that were utilized for oars. They were the only place to sit, as I was told not to touch any form of cargo in any manner, not even to rest on a sturdy box. There were no actual sleeping quarters, just ropes suspended from beams.

My guest accommodations included one loosely woven sling-bed in the far end of the vessel, and one pot for whatever fluids I needed, or was forced, to expel from my body. Meals were on my own at the ports or with the crew if we were at sea. As if I could eat. I planned to sleep as much of the voyage away as possible, if I could make my mind drain out as my body had.

Once I figured how to not fall out of the sling, I plumped my bundled belongings into a pillow, weary from travel that had only begun. For the first time, I noticed what old cloth I'd grabbed in the darkness. Ethan dug it out the day I was teaching him about doctoring the sheep. I saved it from being ripped into bandaging, tossing it back in the bin because Michal held a deep attachment to her sister through the yellowed remnant. Not able to keep it close or toss it away for good, it lived in the barn.

Miriam's presence wasn't welcome in my home. The mere mention of her name drew up emotion from Michal that I'd never fully understood, like anger and hurt and disappointment all rolled into one pained expression. I supposed she pushed discussion of her beloved sister aside to avoid stirring the ache in her heart. And, while she didn't say it, the angry portion wasn't only for the Assyrians. It was directed at me, and I could only assume it was for not saving Miriam that fateful day.

Over the years, trying to talk about the good memories I had of

Miriam had been received coldly. I didn't want her to be forgotten or trivialized, but my wife refused to share her thoughts on the matter. It was easier to avoid speaking of her sister all together.

My life hadn't turned out as I'd envisioned in those days of betrothal. I had done little to sway my people back to the righteous ways of God, as I believed was my calling. One prophecy, then nothing. It was a disappointing course I'd chosen to follow.

Securing Michal as a wife over her sister was one aspect I never regretted. We were more suited in temperament, something I couldn't see in her then. She was a child in her sister's shadow when I was seeking a bride. In her own light, Michal found herself, a woman with practical expectations and deep-rooted convictions to the ways of our ancestors.

Would she miss me? I rubbed fingertips into my temples to ease the ache. Envisioning her raising Ethan alone, in the same house, the same routine, only without me there, stabbed my conscience. There was nothing she couldn't handle on her own, except being a father. Our older sons would step in, I knew, and see that their youngest brother became a man. If I went back, no matter how long I was gone, my home and family would be in order. Michal didn't need me there.

If I went back? How could I allow the notion to gain any purchase in my mind? Walking away from a position before God was not an act I could revoke. I had renounced my decision to be a voice for the heavens by leaving my homeland. Even if God didn't chase me down and end my life, I could never go home. I couldn't allow the rebellious man I had become to infect Israel. I was precisely what I preached against.

MICHAL

Gath-hepher held its forums at the city gate, which was more a patch of land near the main road rather than a structure since there were no surrounding walls of protection. A tent provided shielding from the sun, woven mats protection from the hard soil. I had no reason to be anxious around these men, I wasn't on trial. Still, my heart thumped inside my chest.

Ethan sat contentedly on his grandfather's lap. Beside him was Caleb. My old friend wasn't an official elder, and neither were many of the others gathered there. It was a strong showing of support for the beloved prophet, and for me. The curious nature of Jonah's disappearance pulled in merchants and mere acquaintances, too. With all of my sons present, we were overflowing the confines of the tent, spilling into the shade of nearby buildings and trees. Word of the proceedings traveled the breadth of the city like a spark in desiccated brush.

Hiram, the chief elder, led the discussion. "Do you want Ethan to stay, Michal?"

I nodded. My son wouldn't hear anything that I hadn't already discussed with him already.

"Tell us again, if you would, how this began."

I interlaced my fingers to keep from fidgeting and told them about my husband not coming to bed, and being gone in the morning, the altar destroyed. I told them his chariot was still in the barn, as were the horses, donkeys and all wagons. I thought he had taken money and food, but not good clothing. I said nothing about my sister's veil. I had told no one I thought Jonah left me to find the life taken from him.

"There was no evidence of a fight, nothing to suggest he was abducted." Hiram said. "The altar couldn't have been taken apart quickly. I don't believe that was the result of a struggle."

"A spiritual one, perhaps?" My father spoke the words gently. He was trying to hide his fears from me, but the past week had brought an evident weariness to his face.

Hiram acknowledged the suggestion by looking at me.

"Did my husband tear his holy place apart himself? I don't know. It's possible. I don't know why he would have done so, unless..."

"Go on, Michal. Speak freely."

I controlled my breathing before I could speak. "Unless my father is correct, and Jonah did it in anger."

"At God?" Hiram's voice held disbelief.

Nodding was all I could do to respond.

"Zeb?" Hiram turned back to my father.

"He was frustrated sometimes, wanting more of the Most High's attention."

"But Father prayed there daily," Adin said. "I can't believe he would destroy it."

"Maybe God told him to." Ethan's timid voice carried through the crowd. Warm smiles filtered back, acknowledging his innocent faith in their silent God. If anyone else believed that their prophet had actually heard the voice from on high after all these years, no one offered the opinion for discussion.

Hiram continued. "Amaziah, the priest in Bethel, said he didn't know any reason for Jonah to simply abandon us. Nothing was said the last time they spoke, nothing to indicate any particular concern. They spoke of Israel and her condition, nothing they hadn't debated previously."

The discussion continued, covering and retracing the same ground. Nothing would be resolved, it was evident. There was nothing new to add to the mystery, no bit of conversation overheard by a merchant, no one who saw my husband in a nearby town, no remembered link to give us a clue to his disappearance.

My father cleared his throat as the comments dwindled, speaking what no one wanted to say in my presence. "It appears he left on his own accord, on foot with at least some provisions. The question of why can't be answered, nor the real concern. Is he intending to return?"

I bit down on my lip to stifle a cry. Was I not enough reason?

Caleb's head snapped my direction, then just as quickly turned away.

"Michal, how do you intend to proceed?" Hiram's question was one I anticipated. It was a simple one to answer, yet the words clogged in my throat, admitting this was real, that Jonah might not ever come back.

I composed myself, choking down the lumps of torment rising from my soul. "I'll see to my home as before. The children will help me. We'll expect nothing from the king at this point, but we have more than enough. We'll manage."

The elders nodded solemnly. I wasn't directly under a husband's protection and yet I wasn't a widow. They would assume I'd want to remarry had Jonah been found dead. But he hadn't been. No one knew if he would arrive home today, or next month, or if he would ever, making it impossible to consider any change in my life other than managing without my husband's presence.

"Yes. We wait for now, wait and see."

"Will God bring Father home, if I ask him to?" Ethan questioned the wise leaders around him, his eyes moist and nose dripping until he swiped his sleeve against his face.

There was a time when all of my people would have believed that the creator of the heavens would hear such a plea. Our kings and prophets, judges and priests, the children of Abraham from generation to generation had pleaded and cried out with the understanding that God's ear was always turned in our direction. I said my own prayers dutifully, clinging to the faith that they were heard.

But would God act? Would he restore my family? I didn't know how to answer my son.

"We don't know. The Almighty's ways are not our ways," Hiram said. "But you should ask, son of Jonah. He might answer the cry of an innocent child."

The solemn faces beneath the tent, those of friends and family, elders and priests, all nodded in agreement. Many of them prayed to gods made of wood and stone along with the Lord, who had no carved image. Some, like Caleb and my father, walked steadfastly in the ways of Moses, having only the One God. Despite our differences, my people wanted Ethan's prayers to reach the ears of heaven and hoped someone there would respond. Gath-hepher wanted its prophet to come home.

I thought I did as well.

In that moment, I realized my cache of emotions wasn't entirely made up of grief. I found anger there, smoldering, the embers ignited long ago fanned by Jonah's disappearance. If my husband left me of his own accord, if the resentment stirring in my heart was justified, I wasn't absolutely certain I wanted him back.

THE FISH

"Wait."

JONAH

What was death? I gripped the rail and stared out across the water, Tyre to my back and the isle of Cyprus somewhere ahead. In every direction, water had swallowed the land, and no reasoning with myself could bring a sense of security. I rode a large vessel by the standards of men, but out here, it was nothing more than a toy, a speck on a vast expanse. I couldn't help but think of my vulnerability, my mortality.

"Won't see land 'til tomorrow." Squid stopped beside me, perfect balance without holding anything. He squinted against the glare of late day sun, a vibrant stream of gold that coated the water and side of the ship.

"We sail at night, then."

"Yes, with the Phoenician Star in the North sky to guide us. We'll anchor outside the port and go to shore at first light. These winds are in our favor now but they'll die out by nightfall and the sea will be more hospitable to your gut. You'll be able to sleep, I imagine, if we don't make too much ruckus."

"You won't sleep?"

"I'll take a turn. Later." The sailor smiled broadly, exposing numerous gaps where teeth had been knocked free. "Have to earn some refreshment first."

I turned and watched the sailor as he joined his companions, a dozen or so men gathered in a circle on the deck. A rowdy game of some sort was underway and every free hand joined the revelry. On schedule, if not ahead, the mood on the Amphitrite was light. Even the captain allowed himself a few rounds of tossing sticks and counting points according to how they landed. It was a game of chance, losing earning more spirits than winning, so no one grumbled with the outcome.

I had not been asked to join and was grateful. My mind and body were weary from the tumult of my present circumstances. I wanted nothing more than to sleep in the hold below, and for at least a few hours, to forget where I was.

And why.

JONAH

The grip that shook me awake was anything but gentle. "Get up!"

My eyes snapped open in the semi-darkness, a man's face in front of my own.

"Get, up!"

I gripped the edge of my swing bed, trying to make sense of what was happening, then was slammed into the hull. Not by the fierce man, but from the rocking of his ship.

"How can you sleep? Get up and pray to your god!" The captain yanked me from the netting and pushed my shoulders against a beam. He spun around in the heaving vessel, staggering toward the ladder. I immediately tipped sideways, and had to brace against a stack of crates to prevent myself from falling. Around the hold, murmured prayers rose above an insistent howling of the winds outside the ship.

"Dagon, save us!"

"Baal, protect me!"

"Nanshe, have mercy!"

The favorable seas were gone.

The Amphitrite was alive, frantic with activity. Sailors fought to keep upright as they hauled ropes from a storage bin, passing the coils rapidly along a line of men. Others took the rope and secured it to brass rings on the hull, then ran it along the front of the cargo. The stacks of goods were already tethered and bound to the walls, yet even I could see the wisdom in the extra measure of security. Crates squeaked and shifted with each rise and fall of the sea.

The churning content of my gut refused to stay put. I gagged and let it out, then reeled into line with the others, taking the rope thrust at me and handing it to the man next in line. The overwhelming grogginess I'd had was replaced by the keen alertness that comes with fear.

"What's happening?!" I raised my voice to be heard. I'd collapsed into an exhausted sleep while the others ate supper and gambled topside, awakening only once in the darkness. The snoring of sailors and gentle sway of the ship on peaceful nighttime waters had lulled me back to oblivion in minutes.

"The winds! Too strong! Keeping us at sea!"

I knew in that moment that I would never place my feet on the sands of Cyprus.

With a jerk, the floor in front of me tilted sharply upward. Men fell back and toppled against me, and I found myself on the floor. It was wet, slick with the oil of broken storage pots.

"Look out! It's coming!"

I heard a new sound among the warnings, that of ripping as ropes securing cargo in the stern ruptured. Heavy loads shifted, sliding easily on the saturated floor. As the ship rose on the next wave, they slid in my direction. I scrambled sideways to avoid being crushed, then rolled onto my side, dodging more cargo as the ship lurched. Crates crashed and splintered against the hull.

Sailors found their footing and grouped together in the storage space where the cargo had just been, counterbalancing the added weight in the bow. The crash of waves and prayers of desperation competed for dominance.

"Horus!"

"Molech!"

"Amun!"

Squid's voice called out, a tone that made me jump to my feet.

"Move it out! Now! All of it!"

Men reacted without hesitation, chasing merchandise that had broken free, slashing the binding ropes that remained, and filling their arms with crates. A new chain of men formed, retrieving cargo and passing it forward, thrusting the heavy loads into hands that continued up the ladder and out onto the deck.

The shifting ballast rocked the ship with each roll of the waves. There was no way to secure it again, to find balance. The loosened cargo created momentum as it slid and given the chance, would tip the vessel on its side.

Part of an amphora was thrust into my arms, the shattered clay container slicing my fingers as I jammed it into the hands of the next man. Dozens more followed, the wine and oil flowing freely on the floor, running all directions at once and mixing with the sea water that ran through the oar portals when the vessel leaned to one side. Yanking off my sandals, my bare feet had little purchase on the heaving floorboards.

Crates traveled from man to man, up the ladder to the deck. Rhythmic splashing confirmed what I knew, that they were being tossed over the side. Piece by piece, all merchandise once held firmly in the ship was freed. From every storage space, a fortune of goods was sent to the sea. Costly purple dye, thick Persian rugs, linens intricately embroidered, gold jewelry, wine, oil, and dried grains. All the cargo would be lost.

And all the men.

The sailors were frightened, and that's how I knew this was no ordinary occurrence. God was blowing his breath against us.

Against me.

I heaved again. Around the hull, the prayers were screeched into the howling winds. Ishtar. Ashtoreth. Shamash. The sailors cried out to all of them. Surely one would listen and intervene. Surely one would show mercy and save them from drowning.

A prolonged creak, like a scream of agony, broke through the cries. The ship itself was desperate for salvation.

One god had not been called upon in the frantic chorus of the doomed. With no right to cry out, I couldn't help but scream my own plea into the din. "God of mercy! Save us!"

But there was no calm in the winds.

MICHAL

Caleb tipped a sheep onto her back and nestled her shoulders against his knees. "She won't fight you much if she's comfortable, and if you keep her feet off the ground." With the hand shears, he cut the first length of wool along the animal's belly. "That's a good girl. Let's get this coat off."

I smiled at his cooing. Jonah talked to them in the same fashion, putting a heavy beast at ease like a baby in its mother's arms.

For all the times I watched my husband do this task, I had never had the notion to do it myself. Caleb instructed me now a step at a time, at my request.

"You won't have to do this. Your boys will take care of it. Or I will."

"I know, Caleb. I want to understand and do all I can on my own. It's my responsibility to see to the business. In case…"

He gave a quick nod of his head without looking up. "Stretch the wrinkled skin so you don't nick it, like this." The wool detached under his hands, the smooth cutting motions having a calming effect on the sheep. He turned her to one side and continued, then to the other, talking to her and to me so we both understood that he was a kind and good shepherd. When the beast was sheared, he allowed her to jump up and run free with a pat on the rump.

The sheet of wool was thin, having only grown for a few months. In my restlessness, I didn't want to wait until it was a dense mat, and therefore, a profitable skin. I needed to know now, so I could sort my new responsibilities out, and merge them with my old ones. My life had changed and I had to have a structure in my head to keep it all in order. To keep myself in order.

Caleb shook the fleece and spread it out, picking bits of debris that remained. Once he was satisfied, he rolled it up and tied it with a leather cord. Rising from the ground, he ran his hands over his clothing, brushing away dirt and wooly bits. He sat beside me on the stone fence, taking a long drink of water from a jug. His right leg had never been as strong as the left, and the work was more trying for him than he allowed anyone to see. He'd never allowed the weakness to stop him, that I knew of.

"In case," he said, returning to my previous words. "In case he doesn't return."

I exhaled loudly. "Yes."

Beside me, I was conscious of Caleb's breathing, of the light sweat speckling his skin, and the grime beneath his nails. Dark eyes that always seemed to smile, he was genuinely kind, and wise, in his own quiet way. Never one to fight over his own rights, his opinions were often over-looked. Generally, they proved to be accurate if anyone paid attention.

Jonah and Caleb, along with only a few dozen men in Gath-hepher, chose to serve the Lord God as their only deity. Preserving the strict ways of his own father, Caleb took his family to Jerusalem for Passover, refusing to place one foot in Dan or Bethel, where the golden calves held reign in his God's name. He wasn't one to compromise. I wished my own family held to the Laws with such tenacity, but of course, Jonah wouldn't anger the king by doing so.

Caleb had been with me at least a part of every day since he learned of Jonah's disappearance. There was unity among those of us adhering to the ways of Moses, and my friend's loyalty brought a balm to the places on my heart that ached. I reached over and squeezed his hand, grateful for his words, his ear, and the easy silence we were sharing. Above us, puffs of clouds, like sleepy lambs dotting the pasture on a warm afternoon, were content to remain still. I was too.

I couldn't help but turn my thoughts to my husband. Where was Jonah at that moment? Was he looking at the same calm sky, thinking about me? Was he at peace with the decisions he had made?

Caleb gripped my hand more firmly but didn't look at me. He was trying to form the words to say something, but all he got out was my name, spoken with tenderness and, and what?

The opportunity to find out was gone with the sound of footsteps on the path. "Mother!" Ethan's little body was running toward us, Timna following at a slower pace.

My old friend wrenched his hand from mine and picked up the water jug. My little son ran to him even though he was calling to me.

"I want to shear a sheep. I'm old enough." His wide eyes looked at Caleb with expectation. He had cried more than laughed lately, lost without his father, and unable to grasp why the man he adored was simply gone without explanation. 'When will he return' and 'what if he doesn't come back' competed throughout the day and nighttime hours, when we both were awake and lonely together. I had nothing more than the consolation I received from others, that I didn't know, but God did.

"It would take ten of you to weigh as much as one of them, and your father hasn't taught you how yet," I said. "I'm only learning it myself."

"I'm big enough." He poked out his chest and stood tall, hands on his hips. "And father..."

The man tickled Ethan's ribs before the tears could fall. "Soon enough, young man."

"But I want-"

Caleb interrupted. "It isn't about what you want. Until you're stronger, both you and the animal could be injured."

Ethan picked up a stone and heaved it over his head. "I know how to do it. This is what Father does sometimes."

"You'll be a good shepherd, just like him. Strong but gentle."

Ethan dropped the weight. "Will he come back?"

Caleb ran a hand over the boy's head and spoke sincerely. "I don't know. If not, your brothers will teach you all you need to know. Or, I will."

He looked at me intentionally as he said the last three words, and I saw what he was trying to say when we were alone. There was an intensity in his expression, a reaching for my heart. He was willing to step in for Jonah, and not just as a father to my son.

I turned away from him and caught a sharp breath.

"Michal?" Timna put a pail of berries on the path and came to my side, placing a hand to my forehead. "You're pale."

I shook my head to clear the dizzy sensation. "Too warm, I think."

Ethan put the water jug into my hands. I avoided Caleb's eyes as I drank, knowing he was watching me as the color warmed up my cheeks again. "I'm all right," I said, with more bounce than I felt in my soul. "Let's collect berries by the river."

Satisfied, Ethan skipped toward the far end of the pasture. Caleb gathered the fleece roll and tucked it under his arm. "I'll put this in the barn and be on my way."

His tone had stiffened, putting the fence between our hearts back in position. "Thank you," I said. "You're a good teacher."

Caleb nodded at Timna with a polite smile, then me, catching my eyes briefly. "Yes, next time. Shalom."

I intentionally turned so I didn't stare after him as he walked away.

My heart was thumping. The image of Caleb teaching Ethan was too much. It should be Jonah teaching his son the skills of living. But he had left the duties for someone else to complete.

Caleb?

Caleb and me?

I shook it away. I didn't believe that my husband was dead. I wasn't a widow, my son not fatherless. At any moment, Jonah could arrive with a plausible explanation for his disappearance. I couldn't entertain thoughts of life with another man. Not even Caleb.

JONAH

"Don't go up there!"

The sailor screamed in my ear to be heard over the din outside the hull as he thrust me to the side. I maintained a grip on the stair rail with one hand, jerking the man's hand off of me with the other. I had to go up, had to see what was happening to the waters.

Men pushed past me as the cargo dwindled to nothing more than solitary items floating in the sloshing water and wine about our feet. They clambered for the steps, slipping back as the ship lurched, then disappearing out the hole above my head. I followed the last one onto the deck, choking back the bile of fear as my feet threatened to slide out from under me, and having no walls to stop a fall.

It was daytime, mid-morning when sunlight should have been streaming from its place above the eastern horizon, yet the sky was gray-green, thick with heavy whorls of cloud. Sporadically, a jagged shaft of lighting ripped through the denseness, revealing a churning sea in all directions.

There was no land to be seen.

I wrapped my arms around a post, gripping my wrists so I wouldn't slide off the deck as the vessel pitched and rolled. Around me, the sailors tossed lines and tied them or loosened them, securing some things and setting others free. Cries to their gods were lost in the roar. Fear permeated everything.

The tempest had not surrounded this ship by some whimsical fate. God's angry hand stirred the sea. He followed me with his wrath.

PERSIS

The blows came from an iron rod, smacking across my bare shoulder.

Only an hour ago, I had soaked in the deep baths, where I had been sent. The pools had been filled with fresh water and the slave had scrubbed me clean with a soft cloth, then applied scented oils, rubbing them into my skin. Afterward, my curls were coiled elaborately on my head, golden chains draped over my forehead and jeweled bands fastened on my upper arms and wrists. A long silky garment was pulled over my head, crimson fabric draped over one shoulder so the other was bare. Perfume was dabbed on my wrists, and embroidered slippers placed on my feet.

I sat on the marble bench in the soft glow of lanterns when the process was complete. Alone, and afraid.

I hadn't been selected to be with Tariq in months. My husband's recently acquired slaves kept him occupied at night. His men secured their own secret access to the newcomers and had been of minimal nuisance in the women's quarters. It had been a calm time, a welcome time that required no use of the killing herbs.

The call for me to go to the baths to prepare for him had been a surprise, as had the extent of pampering I received. It was the sort reserved for the youngest wives, not to one who had aged many years beneath the roof of the man who called himself husband and master.

Anxiety flitted in my stomach. Tariq had a light-hearted nature that was opposed by a darker one, a need to control and inflict pain, be it verbal or with his hand, or with the trading of one of us to another man. The wives never knew what to expect. Lately, his screams could be heard echoing about the stone walls and more poles had been added to the garden for the poor souls found wanting.

Footsteps on the pavement drew my attention to Tariq. Realizing I held my breath, I dispelled it into the warm night air. He wore a deep blue and gold robe over his white tunic, a crown of jasmine on his head. It was celebratory attire, what he wore for a feast or a wedding. He smiled and sat beside me, gently caressing my hand.

"My wife of many years, dressed as a goddess tonight. A goddess worthy of sacrifice."

I tipped my chin and said nothing. He was a handsome man, older than me by only a handful of years. He emanated the nobility of his heritage. In his presence, I had to intentionally subdue the trepidation that came with my own humble origins.

Tariq took my chin between his thumb and forefinger and lifted it, holding on until my eyes met his. His thumb rubbed at my skin. "Too bad you've wrinkled."

He dropped his hand and snapped his fingers. A slave emerged with a tray containing a pitcher of wine and two golden cups. My husband took one and gave the other to me.

"Tell me, Persis, how it is among all my wives. Are they happy?"

I nodded. "Yes, my lord. We are treated well and have no time for disharmony."

"And they respect me? Follow my rules?"

"Yes."

"All of them, including you, my dear Persis?" His inquiring tone was tinged with malice.

I glanced at his face. His mouth was smiling, not his eyes. "Yes, my lord."

He exhaled, disappointed like a father knowing the child was caught in a lie. I sipped the wine, trying not to allow the tremor in my hand to show.

"Why do you suppose my new slaves are beginning to bulge with my offspring and yet my own wives are flat and empty?"

I choked on the liquid. Tariq said nothing as he took the cup from my grasp. I coughed and fought to regain a measure of composure. "He has not favored us lately," I said.

"Hmm. Is that the reason?"

Sweat trickled down my back. I squashed my hands together to still the fidgeting. "And some of us are beyond those years."

The Master turned sharply and studied my face with intensity. "You are past being an asset, aren't you? Many of you are, and yet I keep you. Trust you."

"Lariya and Shey are with child again, and Mara gave you a son a month back. Your wives continue to bring you honor." I tried to sound unconcerned with the nature of the inquiry.

Tariq said nothing. I turned away from the probing eyes.

Abruptly he stood and poured himself another measure of wine. He didn't sit down again, pacing in front of me and staring into the cup that he swirled in his hands. His strong physique wasn't hidden beneath his clothing, his intensity of emotion not masked by an appearance of serenity.

"I was fond of Ra'eesa," he said. "I hated to hear of her death."

I made myself breathe in deeply and evenly. "We were all saddened. She is missed."

"She said something interesting to the physician as she grew weaker and the bleeding wouldn't abate. What was it? Ah yes, she said, 'Get Persis to help me.'"

Licking my lips didn't take away the dryness.

"That request was interesting, don't you agree? Why would she say that about you? You're no physician. Perhaps you have trained yourself, all the time spent in the library deciphering the tablets? Is that what you do there?"

I shook my head. My knowledge of medicine had only one purpose, and that had been taught to me by a wife sold off long ago. "I'm not trained. I could not have stopped her bleeding."

Tariq stopped behind me and rested his hand on my neck, his thumb kneading uncomfortably into my throat. I didn't flinch. He bent down and whispered in my ear. "Perhaps you started the bleeding. No woman ever died simply because a man took her for pleasure."

"She was abused," came out in a hoarse breath. "Raped."

"Not so, according to the physician. There were no bruises, no injuries to indicate such an atrocity under my roof. She was a willing whore." His hand left my throat and found the top of my head, stroking the braided and coiled strands mindlessly, as if he were petting an animal.

I stiffened my spine, looking at the empty courtyard. There was no one here to witness the interaction. No one to witness what I believed was my impending death.

"The gods, then. They punished her for her unfaithfulness. They made her bleed her lifeblood away." It was something he might believe. There were many gods in the home.

"Perhaps. But why did she ask for you in particular, I wonder. What medicines might you have?"

"I, I don't. She was confused, frightened, asking for a friend."

My head snapped back as Tariq dug his fingers into my hair and yanked it toward him. With his other hand, he tipped the wine so it dribbled down onto my face and ran off my cheeks. I squeezed my eyes closed.

"Liar."

"No. Please."

"The physician told me why the woman died. I didn't believe him, didn't believe you would betray me. Shey confirmed his words, confirmed what you did."

The young woman's face had been purple with bruising soon after Re'eesa's death. Afterwards, she'd been granted many favors in the home, a reward for speaking the truth despite the method by which it was obtained. Shey had avoided all interactions with me since then.

"How dare you interfere with my property." The low voice was seeped in malice now. "You killed Ra'eesa. You killed her child. And how many others?"

I pulled against the hand that held me, my fingers clutching his arm to move it away. His other hand hurled the cup toward the fountain where it shattered, then gripped my shoulder. No hint of compassion remained as he screamed in my face. "How many!?"

"No!" I wanted to defend my actions. I couldn't. I had been disobedient to my husband, no matter my intentions.

Tariq yanked me backwards by both hair and shoulder, dropping me onto the stone patio.

I pulled my hands over my head in protection, tucking my legs, waiting for the anger to be released.

His sandals clicked on the stones as he circled me, then stopped again, merely prodding my knee with his foot.

"Get up." My husband's words were smooth, controlled.

I rose to my feet and stood before him, quivering inside and out. Fear like this wasn't new to me, I had tasted it before and lived. I hadn't always wanted to, and wasn't certain I did now. Death removed the dread of man, the pain of this life. But that decision wasn't in my control.

The Master snapped his fingers to slaves waiting in the shadows. To me, he pointed at the bench.

The courtyard began to fill. The two primary wives came first, followed by the concubines, eyes opening wide when they saw me, faces full of questions that were whispered back and forth. Shey alone stared at the earth.

Filing in last were our children, those still under twelve years of age. Not at all concerned about the lateness of the hour or the reason they were forbidden to go to bed, they giggled and squirmed once told to sit. I searched among them for my own eleven year-old girl. Raised by others, her allegiance was to her father alone. For the first time, I was grateful.

Tariq smiled warmly at his family. "If any of you is unhappy with your place under my roof, speak up."

The silence grew thick. The children felt the rising tension and had no need to be hushed as they stopped talking on their own. Every woman looked at the Master, so as not to appear inattentive.

"Are my rules unfair?" He walked slowly among the group, running a gentle hand on cheeks and patting heads of little ones.

Nothing.

"Do any of you not like me? Do you want to part with my generosity? Speak up now. You can take your leave." He swept his arm through the air as if to usher anyone who dared towards the city beyond his estate.

No one moved. They wouldn't. Even the newest slaves and youngest children understood the meaningless words of the man who owned them. No one simply walked away.

Tariq rubbed his chin with one hand. "Good. Good," he said. "I have a grateful family. Except for this one." It was a casual flick of his hand in my direction. "This wife believes she knows better than her husband. She has broken my rules."

Every eye turned to me. The wives of my own station understood what was happening. I could read their trepidation. None of them knew what I had revealed. None of them knew where this gathering might lead. It wouldn't be the first household in Nineveh to be wiped cleaned by its lord. New wives were plentiful to nations that thrived on conquering others.

"She has stolen from me, stolen from the gods. By her own crafty devices, she has deprived me of heirs and gifts to Dagon. Her shame reflects on my household. It falls on each of you." He picked up a girl in his arms, a tiny one with dimples and endless smiles. He tickled her belly until she squealed in delight. "I could punish everyone here for what Persis has done. Or, I will allow you to punish her instead."

The courtyard was full of statues. Neighboring kingdoms feared the Assyrians because of their might, and their cruelty. Every man under Assyrian rule learned weaponry and combat, none too young to wield a knife and creativity in execution applauded. No one in Tariq's presence dared to breathe.

The Master carried the child as he walked among the women. "No vote?" No opinion?"

Silence.

"Well, I shall have you decide then." He spoke to the girl as he set her feet on a ledge then put a protective arm around her. "Do I punish you, or does this betrayer of my household get punished?"

The little child poked out her bottom lip. "I no want punish."

"It is decided." He lifted her gently to the ground, then clapped once. A slave approached from his position in the shadows, and handed Tariq an iron rod. He put it in the girl's hands and led her to me.

"Hit her," he said.

The child looked up with confusion. Her father repeated the command.

"Is she bad?"

"Very bad."

I held my breath as the girl and I looked at one another. "Go ahead," I whispered. The child would be disciplined herself if she hesitated.

Barely able to lift the rod, she smacked it into my shin, then dropped it and stepped back. Her bottom lip trembled.

"Well done," Tariq said, patting her silky hair, then retrieving the rod and putting it back into her hands. "Who's next? You get to choose who goes next."

The youngest girls and boys struck their blows, followed by the older ones. If one didn't give good effort, he was made to do it again. The oldest children understood the necessity of pleasing their father and swung hard. They were rewarded with praise that trumped any doubt in their hearts. My own daughter hit me without hesitation.

The rod fell on me, again and again.

Thwack!

Thwack!

Thwack!

The women were next. They too had to give a full blow or repeat the action until the Master approved. No apologies or sympathies were permitted, even tears were grounds for additional blows. The women masked their horror, and one by one, left a welt on my flesh.

The one exception was Shey, barely able to walk toward me in her shame. Tariq took the rod from her hand and kissed her cheek before allowing her to return to the others. If no one knew who had betrayed me, they did now. My pain would be no greater than hers, the loneliness of a shunned existence lasting longer and penetrating deeper than any physical wounds.

I wanted blackness to take me under, to be hit so hard as to never awaken. My husband had permitted no blows to my head, however, allowing nothing to take me away from feeling the full sting of punishment.

Crumpled on the ground, the beating finally ended. The women and children left in a solemn mass.

"Disobedience can't be tolerated," Tariq said, tenderly brushing hair off my brow. "You must repay me."

I could not respond.

"The sacrifices you've taken from me with your poisons will be repaid to Dagon. Your life for theirs."

THE SAILOR

Angry skies opened their storehouses and allowed the winds to drive rain at the ship. It pelted my skin, like a barrage of tiny stones released from a slingshot, only the supply was unending. I was forced to keep my head down so I wasn't blinded.

Rain shouldn't hurt, and storms shouldn't arrive unannounced in the midst of fair weather. There was always a breeze too strong, a gathering of certain clouds, or a sudden lack of seabirds to make me alert to foul weather on its way. Sometimes it was simply the smell of the air and sea that changed, or the red hue of dawn that said to be wary.

There had been no warning that morning. The fierceness simply descended from the heavens.

It was no ordinary storm.

Without guidance from sun or stars and no landmarks, without the familiar currents or the sighting of other vessels, I had no idea where we were in relation to Cyprus. Had we been tossed closer to her shores, or further away? For all I could determine, we were in the same location as when the storm fell, pushed and pulled and churned about, without headway in any one direction.

I wrapped a rope around my forearm twice, a secure hold as we managed to remove the mainsail completely. It was a tattered rag of a thing, laden with water. Heaving it over the side in an effort to free the vessel from anything adding to instability, my gut lurched. Never had I had so little hope, so great a desperation, that the sails were tossed away. Even when ship wrecked, they'd gone to the depths still bonded to their masts.

Beyond the deck the sea rose in a wall of water, the horizon line above my head and ominously coming toward the ship. I prepared myself for the swell to lift us, above the sea for a moment on the back of the wave, then drop us back down. Up and down. Up and down. Striking at the right angle, the ship would topple onto her side. And that would be the end. There was no swimming ashore in this torrent. I had no idea where land was located. No man would survive.

The captain clawed his way over to my side and yelled in my ear. "Take the men below. Cast lots. See who is to blame!"

Yes, I nodded and proceeded to send men into the belly of the groaning vessel. A god was angry. Identifying the source and making retribution might save our lives. I couldn't help but allow myself to identify the man already. He couldn't out run whatever god he feared.

We spread ourselves out in the hold to distribute the weight, each sailor and the passenger finding something to grasp for balance. Water slapped against my shins, and we needed to bail before it became the ballast of our death. First, the lots.

I found the thin polished sticks in the hollow of a beam where they were stored, and counted out one for each man present. All were a hand's breadth in length and white as a gull, but one. It had a black band around the middle. The man who chose it was the cause of this calamity. It was him the gods despised.

Wedging my hips against the hull and bracing my feet on the legs of a rowing bench, I freed my hands so I could hold all the sticks between them, all level and with the black-banded one mixed among them. My palms concealed the mark that declared a man's guilt. I held them up.

No one moved to take a turn. My men were terrified. None seemed to know whether or not he was the one who had angered his god.

I purposefully turned to the passenger, knowing we could end the lots quickly if he chose first. There I found fear side by side with resignation. His face told me everything the sticks would confirm. The fool brought about the destruction we were facing, perhaps my own death, and yet I didn't want it to be him who was condemned. I liked this man with the impudence to flee his deity.

The passenger raised his hand to draw a stick, then grasped only air as the floor swayed, losing his balance and falling. I altered the timing of the inevitable, thrusting my hand to the man on my right. He drew a white stick and exhaled loud enough to be heard. The next man did the same, and the next. All thirty-four men of the sea drew white sticks.

There were but two chances remaining in my grasp. Mine and the passenger's. Three men helped him stand and gain footing with one hand free to draw.

For a moment, I wasn't absolutely certain the lots wouldn't fall on me and I felt an anchor settling in my gut. Quickly, I pushed the lots in front of the passenger. His choice established both of our fates.

The man drew a white stick from my hand, a stick with the mark of death encircling the middle.

MICHAL

"He looks at you differently now, Michal." Timna plucked the green olive from a branch and dropped it in the bag draped across her chest.

I picked several firm fruits for my own bag before I responded, not certain I was ready to discuss Caleb with anyone. "I realized it yesterday, when he was talking to Ethan about the sheep. It surprised me. He adored his Beckah. Has he said something to you?"

"No, not with words. He's always been fond of you as a friend, of course. These past few days I believe he's been searching for solutions along with the rest of us. Thinking ahead of what will be. Or might be. Seeking bandages for open wounds."

"And what are his intentions, do you think?"

Timna stopped working to look at me. "Good ones. Only good ones. He's willing to marry you."

"I'm not a widow."

"I know. He does too."

"Then I don't want him to think of me that way. I'm not free to marry."

"Yet."

I leaned against the tree and pulled off my veil so I could run my hands through my thick, long hair, pulling strands back from my face. "Yet? We don't know if he's alive or dead. We don't know anything."

Timna pulled off her own veil and stopped to rest her arms. "No one but God knows if Jonah is alive. If he doesn't return soon, you could ask the elders to declare him dead. Ask if you could be permitted to marry Caleb."

"Or not Caleb. Marry someone else."

My aunt's laugh made me smile as well. "But it would be him, wouldn't it? Any of your sons could teach you the sheep business. You chose Caleb."

I had to keep the defensiveness from my voice intentionally. "He was here anyhow, and-"

Timna shook a finger in my face with a glimmer in her eye. "You like the man. Don't pretend with me."

"Of course I like him, but I already married a man who wanted my sister before me, and I'd rather not be in that position again. I don't want to be Caleb's second choice, or third more accurately, since he was married to Beckah. Caleb is an honorable man, and his being willing to be my husband isn't the same as him wanting to marry me."

Timna folded her veil and used it as a pillow as she eased herself to the ground, reclining in the shade, hands tucked behind her head. "At your age, you won't find a man who hasn't been married already."

It was cool in the shade, and I followed my aunt's leading. "I don't want to remarry."

"Not yet. It's too soon. But you're young, and in time Ethan will have his own family and you might find the loneliness to be too much."

"What if I never know? If Jonah is alive, it's adultery."

"The leaders will grant you the status of a widow at some point. Don't fret over it now. Put Caleb in a safe place in your heart and deal with his intentions later. He offers you the gift of security."

Sparrows bounced in the branches above us, a happy twitter among the silver leaves. Unconcerned. Unburdened. They stirred the rich, earthy fragrance of the olives, the scent of life in Israel. Offering fruit for sustenance, oils for cooking and healing, it was the aroma of worship and blessing. I found comfort beneath the wings of the ancient tree.

Timna tossed a twig at me. "Jonah chose to marry you, Michal. He didn't have to."

No, he hadn't been forced to marry me. He'd paid the mohar to my father for Miriam though, double the agreed amount. He never had the opportunity to take his bride home. It wasn't my father's fault the raiders came. Legally he owed Jonah nothing, but Father wanted to do right by the young prophet of God, and offered me in my sister's place.

I had not been consulted. The arrangements were discussed, the new agreement signed, and I was officially bound to Jonah. Still grieving, it meant little to me, the loss of Miriam a far greater concern.

There was no waiting in anticipation for the mohar once it was my turn to be betrothed, as it had been paid. I had only to wait until the agreed upon age, fifteen, before I left my father's home. For me, there were no overt preparations in those two years. I was given all the gifts my sister would have provided for the new household.

When I was of the proper age, Jonah came for me. As I was stirring a pot of stew one afternoon, he came over the hill in a chariot, his first one from the king. It was a boisterous approach, and he made a show of spinning his ride around the house and raising the dust.

His groomsmen came along, and my bridesmaids were quickly fetched. Mother and Timna presided over my ceremonial washing with great enthusiasm, and tears that I knew weren't only for me. Cousins packed my belongings, and sounds of preparation filled the air ahead of the anticipated walk to Jonah's home.

I did my best to smile and appear happy. Miriam's absence was bitter, yet there was another thorn that day, a disappointment that pricked what should have been a joyful occasion. The mohar for my sister had been extravagant. I hoped when my wedding day arrived, Jonah would offer my father a token that validated my own worth. He had not. I believed he would bring me a gift, a simple item to cherish and commemorate the day like Miriam's hand mirror, something to show to my children's children and bury in my hands. He had not done this either.

It was a silly notion, the mohar was paid and nothing more expected. Jonah had no reason to even consider offering another gift. I knew this, and tried to pull the thorn from my heart. I couldn't. I covered it up so no one would know what sort of disenchantment festered there.

The chaotic delivery of sheep was replaced by my father and brothers examining the chariot and its fine stallion, needing to test it out for themselves. I waited inside with the women, trying not to be covered completely in dust on my wedding day.

Jonah finally looked around for me, took my hand, and led me away, maneuvering the chariot to his home. We went slowly so the wedding party could keep up, and caused quite the commotion going through the city. In this region, only royalty and nobility rode chariots in times of peace.

The only time I rode in that contraption was on that day, and had never ridden in the newer ones. I didn't want public displays of status. I wanted a lamb placed in my father's arms. One small animal didn't seem like such a burden.

Wasn't I worth just one?

In times of sorrow, people need celebration, and that's what Jonah offered. We consummated our union, then the feast began. Two years after the raid that took Miriam, it was as if Gath-hepher unofficially wiped that time out with the marriage of their beloved prophet. It was an abundant celebration, lavish, and was talked about for months afterward.

No, Jonah didn't have to marry me. He did so out of respect for my father, and because he had paid a handsome price for a woman already. I had done my best to make sure he didn't regret the decision, stepping into the role my sister should have carried. I was sorry that I had failed.

Timna suddenly sat up and looked among the trees of the olive grove. "Where has Ethan gone off to?"

I stood and called his name. He had been climbing the trees while we harvested olives, always within sight. There was no sign of him now, and no response to my call.

MICHAL

"Ethan!" I called my son's name again as I made my way through the grove, searching the branches for a mischievous little boy. Timna paralleled my path with the same search, eyes combing the branches above and the scrubby grass below, behind rocks and among tall weeds.

"He isn't here, Michal. He can't be far. Do you want me to go for more help?" Her voice was coming out with a calm that I knew she didn't feel. Her face said otherwise.

In the handful of days that Jonah had been gone, my son had struggled for answers, and part of the battle was the shutting out of my voice. A growing sense of abandonment was casting dark shadows on his trusting heart. Last night, rather than hugging himself into my side after supper, he had remained as far from me as possible. We both cried ourselves to sleep.

"If anyone sees him, they'll know he isn't where he's supposed to be," I said, looking in all directions. Ethan found entertainment everywhere, and danger. He had no idea he wasn't invincible.

"I'll check the house, then. You go to the stream."

I nodded, appreciating her taking control. We had just done this for Jonah, a search that ended in nothing. I could hardly grasp that I was now doing it again for my son.

"He's not gone, Michal," Timna said, reading my thoughts. "He'll be found."

Nodding again, I turned toward the stream that coursed through our land, a favorite place, and not running swiftly or deeply enough this time of year for much concern over drowning. Behind me, Timna's footsteps were rapidly retreating, and I knew she'd gather others to help.

The water was cool, a gently gurgling brook with no child stirring it up and altering its course with dams of stone and mud. I followed it downstream until I reached the cliff, a rocky ledge no more than three times my height. Although Ethan could scamper down it easily, it wasn't permitted by his father, the cliff a boundary he wasn't to cross alone. My son wouldn't have done so last week. I wasn't certain now. All of my sons tested their independent spirits on me at some point. I knew it would come from Ethan, too. With the others, there was a turning in responsibility at that stage, when Jonah stepped in as the primary authoritarian. We had never agreed to raise them that way, it just happened naturally. Content to obey their mother, they were mine to manage. Old enough to make choices of rebellion, their father put them to regular work outside the house and more constructive tutoring in the ways of Moses. All of our children brought honor to their father by raising them this way.

I needed Ethan to remain my baby for now. I needed him to need me and not bring fear to my heart.

Dropping to my knees, I lifted my hands to the heavens. "God of all creation. Protect the child you gave me." Ethan hadn't come from my womb, and while I claimed every fiber of his being as my own offspring, the woman who had given him life did as well. Her baby was placed in my arms, but that didn't take him from her heart. There was a bond that connected the two of us through him. I owed her his safety. She trusted me with this treasure that, for whatever reason, she couldn't keep. I didn't want to let her down. I needed Ethan safe in my arms for myself and for her.

And for Jonah.

I didn't want to fail at protecting our home and family while he was gone. He left it to me, and I didn't know for how long. Forever, perhaps. For any duration, it was my responsibility to keep the order, keep us fed and dutiful to the Lord. And keep us alive.

Thoughts of my husband and duty unto God led my eyes to the hilltop, to the sanctuary shared by the two of them. I stood and directed my feet there, running as fast as I could.

My son was on his knees, pushing his entire body against a stone block. It slid a bit, then a bit more. Three others had been moved in a similar manner, the drag marks evident in their wake.

"Ethan." I was breathless and angry and grateful and emotionally exhausted all rolled together.

He didn't answer me. I said his name again, louder, and with that tone of mothers that best not be ignored.

My littlest boy fell onto his rump, pivoting my direction. Tear tracks lined his cheeks, trails through the dust and grime. "What?" he said. Not a question spoken in belligerence, but a sincere one of a boy whose insides have been churning with too many unanswered questions. A man-boy having to think of his world in different terms and not knowing how. Security, gone. Value, questioned. Future, unknown. One parent left, would the other leave too?

I sat beside him, pulling him into my lap despite his protests. "What are you doing?" I asked.

He leaned his back against me and gripped the thumbs of each of my hands. "Getting it ready for Father. For when he comes back, the altar will be ready."

I admired his optimism, and wanted it for myself. He informed me he intended to manage the sheep and fix the broken place in the fence line and find a new rope for the bucket on the well. He was going to do exactly what I had been planning, keeping our lives in proper order until Jonah returned to his duties.

If Jonah returned.

How was I going to raise this boy? He needed his father. Or, a father.

"What would he speak from the scriptures if he was here with us right now? What words from King David, do you think?"

Ethan scrambled from my lap to the single line of four stones and took the position of prayer as he had seen Jonah do many times. His chin pointed towards the blue canopy above, hands open to catch the blessings. "The Lord is my shepherd. I shall not be in need of anything," he began.

I joined him. "He makes me lie down in the green pastures, and leads me to the still waters. He restores my soul."

Yes, Lord of all, restore my soul, I said to no one but God as my son thought about the next words. *I can't handle this alone.*

Ethan continued. "Even though I walk through the valley of the shadow of death, I will fear no evil. For you are with me."

You are with me. With us. I hugged my precious boy as he spoke the remainder in a loose translation of the words he heard from his father. Peace was something I had to seek and grasp and I chose to do so for that moment. We weren't alone, Ethan and I, and somewhere in the land of Israel, our same God was also with my husband.

JONAH

Within the hull of a ship repelling thrashing waves, torqued about without guidance in winds that reeled and pummeled her sides, there fell an eerie calm.

I held the incriminating stick. The lot had fallen on me, and I knew it would, yet still I stared at the tiny rod as if it would somehow transform itself to one of pure white.

Guilty, the stick said. Guilty.

And lives were in danger because of it. Not just my own.

The sailor pulled the stick from my hand and we locked eyes for a moment before the others began throwing questions at me. He had told me not to bring trouble on board.

"Who are you?"

"Where are you from?

"Who are your people?"

They spoke over the top of each other, desperate for answers that might still save them from sinking beneath the waves.

"Jonah," I said. "I'm Jonah ben Amattai of Gath-hepher, in Israel. I'm a Hebrew." I paused, knowing the next part was no longer true. By disobeying, I had left my post, abandoned that which I had been chosen to do. "I'm a prophet for my God."

The men groaned and spat into the water that sloshed higher and higher, nearing knee level. Everyone knew of the blessings and curses that followed the prophets and priests of any given deity.

"A god from whom you are running." The sailor didn't say the fact with malice but the condemnation was there. "Your trouble came with you."

I nodded, falling to my hands and knees as the vessel lurched, remaining there as the men cursed me openly. Justifiably.

"What god do you worship? To whom shall we pray?" one asked.

"I worship the Lord Almighty, the God of heaven, he who made the sea and the land."

I wouldn't have thought my answer meant anything to these people of lands not my own, nations with many gods. My assumption was wrong. The men gasped as one and stared at me with unconcealed dread. They could see, hear and feel the power of the one from who I fled.

Two fists gripped my tunic and pulled me to my feet. Anger spewed from the burly man. "What have you done?"

He pushed me away from him, screaming into the air. He wasn't alone in the distress, the others expressing their fury, with words and gestures only. No one lifted a hand against me.

The sailor steadied me against a post.

I looked at each man, their faces registering what my own chosen people had forgotten. These pagans, men who worshipped carvings made of ivory and stone, acknowledged the might of the Hebrew God, the One God of creation who held control over the elements. I doubted they knew my nation's history, the names of Adam and Noah, Moses and Abraham, of David and Samson. But they found reverence for this deity greater than their own, the God of infinite power.

They had a holy fear far more profound than my own.

For the first time since walking away from all the Lord had given to me, I felt shame. Profound shame. Who was I to question him? Who was I to believe I could control his plans?

"I've angered my God. He has sent this storm."

The men watched me with an uncomfortable intensity.

"What can you do? How can you appease him?" the sailor asked. "You're running from him, but we can't take you back to Joppa. We have no control. The ship is in your God's hands."

I swallowed hard against the lump constricting my throat. I wasn't a man of the sea. It wasn't supposed to be me making decisions. Especially the one that needed to be made. I knew God would kill me eventually for refusing to do what I was told. I deserved wrath, but I wasn't ready. I didn't want to die.

The ship shuddered and groaned.

I shook my head and spoke honestly. "There's nothing I can do."

"What about us, then? What can we do to appease your God?" The sailor gripped my shoulder. "What will make the sea calm again? What sacrifice?"

The hand on my shoulder was wrenched away as the floor tilted. The vessel screeched and righted, then fell hard to stern. We all fell into the water that sloshed and churned around our legs.

If I wanted to save the men, I had to speak what I knew in my soul. The angry hand of God wanted me as payment for the wrongs I'd committed.

"Pick me up." I said. "Throw me into the sea. Only then will it become calm. It's my fault the storm was sent. It's the only way to save the ship, the only way to save yourselves."

The men looked at one another and made no move to do what I commanded. These strong sailors could heft crates above their heads that others could scarcely slide across the floor. They brawled in the alleyways and fought off pirates to protect their cargo. Loud, rude, and intimidating, yes. But they weren't killers. And they had no desire to cross this God of the Hebrews by harming his prophet.

"It's the only way." I made the plea again, knowing if they didn't throw me over, I would have to do it myself.

The sailor shook his head. "No," he said. Then louder. "To the oars, men! And pray to Jonah's God!"

I was pushed aside as they scrambled for the plank benches and unlocked the oars. The poles were stabbed into the churn through ports, now open and permitting the sea to enter as it crashed into the hull. Even I knew it was a futile attempt. No vessel could row against the waves. Rowing was for harbors and calm seas that caught no wind in the sails. The men, determined as they were, could not row out from beneath God's wrath.

The sailor gave the call, the beat to which the rest of them pulled in vain. "Row. Row. Row."

The first oar snapped within minutes, strong cured oak splintering like a twig. Curses filled the hold again, then prayers. As the next oar gave way, the captain descended the stairs, abandoning the deck.

"What are you doing! Pull in! Pull in!"

The oars were drawn from the waves. The men stayed on the benches. No one knew what to do. They were facing the end of their lives and nothing in their power could save them. The great vessel groaned in her own agony. It would disintegrate into thousands of splinters. The ship and her men would all be lost.

I stepped toward the captain, then fell onto him as the floor shifted. "I'm to blame. The lot fell on me. Throw me over the side. You have to. It's the only way to appease my God."

The captain grabbed my arms to hold me up. His eyes went to the sailor, seeking confirmation.

"Now," I said. "Before we are all lost. I'm but one man."

The sailor paused.

The wind screeched.

The ship shuddered.

The sailor nodded just one time, resolved.

"Do it. Quickly!" The captain thrust me into the sailor's hands before returning to the torrent above.

The sailor spun me around to the stairs and pushed against my hips to keep me from slipping down again. The rain fell like pellets, hard and cutting. I closed my eyes and tipped my head down, gripping the rails as I climbed, heart pounding in desperation of what was about to come.

"God of Jonah! Don't kill us for taking this man's life. Don't hold us accountable for taking an innocent man's breath from him! You have determined this course!" The sailor cried out his prayer into the storm. Praying to the Hebrew God. To my God.

The men staggered to the listing deck, all capable of slipping into the sea themselves. One end of a thick rope was tied around the waist of the captain, then uncoiled. Another was tied to the sailor. The rest of the men formed two lines and held the tethers, keeping the men on the ends from falling off the ship as they made their way to the edge.

I slid my feet on the wet wood, between the rows, my hands clinging to men on both sides. Prayers surrounded me. Peering into the storm, I saw nothing but death. The sky, the sea, all shrouded in the black fury of my sin.

At the side rail, I stopped. The sailor stepped behind me and slipped his arms under my shoulders, pulling me into his chest as the captain lifted my feet.

Suspended above the deck, I fought the urge to resist the men who held me. I squeezed my eyes to the pelting rain and tried to inhale, able only to pant against the fear.

The sailor allowed his hold to slip until his hands found my wrists. He gripped them tightly.

"Heave!"

I swung away from the waves. "My God!" I had no right to cry to the one I abandoned.

"Ho!"

My body swung towards the sea, and for a moment, had no tether to it, nor to the ship, nor to any other man. No link to my past, no connection to my future. I was in the midst of nothing, hovering between life and death, all that I knew and all that I feared. "Forgive me!"

I smacked onto the sea, face engulfed in water, the cold salty fluid filling my mouth. Arms and legs flailed against the doom, self-preservation prevailing over all reason at the moment of a terrifying end. There was no sinking gently into the deep. I couldn't survive, wouldn't, but had no ability to stop myself from trying.

Beneath the waves, my lungs burned and screamed for air. I thrashed as the surface fell away, pulling at the water to move it aside, pulling, pulling to climb back up, until my limbs had no more purchase.

Exhausted. Sinking, as the last of my air bubbled out, I stopped trying to save myself. I surrendered to the blackness of death.

THE FISH

"Swallow!"

THE SAILOR

Tears poured out of me before I could stop them. Mortified, I kept my back to the deck and stared into the water below as I got myself under control. Never had I done that in my years sailing the seas, not even when storms made the vessel beneath me shiver in fear. Of course, I'd never been in a tempest like the one that overtook us, and never had I killed a man.

Gentle blue waves lapped against the Amphitrite. Swiping my arm across my face, I looked up again at a sky that had simply rolled up its clouds and whisked them away.

Or at a God that had done so.

We didn't want to kill that prophet. Most of us were simple family men, choosing the sailing life on a merchant ship because it was a sound profession, and paid well if you were smart. We enjoyed the sort of life that others feared, enjoyed the hard labor that kept us strong. None of us were sluggards or slobbering drunks, not once the ship left her dock. The captain used no slaves, either. He wanted men who wanted to sail by their own choosing, and who had pride in a voyage run without incident.

Not losing a life on board was something to take pride in, and although we bullied unruly passengers, and tormented the whining ones, we had never permanently harmed one. Locked a few in the hold with a chain on his leg, perhaps. And gags were useful at times. Tossing one into the sea was a threat meant for our tongues only, not one we actually intended to perform.

Once we threw the prophet Jonah into the raging torrent and the waves swallowed him, the sea heaved like a belch, then settled into a peaceful puddle. All of us left on board had tongues tied in knots, no ability to speak of what we had done to that man, or to what happened afterward. One thing I knew we all were shifting around inside our heads, and that was wondering about the nature of that Hebrew God.

No god I worshipped could raise a storm and dismiss it just as readily.

We were bound for death, all of us, and by killing that one man, saved our own lives. How could I ignore that God? How could I not fear him?

The azure of the waters connected on the horizon to the cerulean sky. Blue on blue in all directions, a sun overhead, bright, proclaiming mid-day. Only hours had passed since the storm arose.

We had no sail, no cargo, and only a general sense of direction. As the sun dropped and the stars emerged, we'd get our bearings back, and row toward the nearest shores. Our clothing would make a sail of sorts, and somehow I knew it would be enough. The strain on my ship was tremendous yet she wasn't going to break apart now. I would feel the solid earth beneath my feet once more.

My eyes skimmed the surface of the waters again, although I knew the man was gone. Jonah disappeared beneath them without a chance of swimming free, even as the sea calmed into the serenity it now enjoyed. He drowned, as his God demanded, buried alone at the roots of the mountains in a shroud of seaweed.

I hated to be the one to toss that man to his death. I'd never forget the horror of it, and might not have let go of him at the last second, but he was wet, and my hold slipped. I'd be dead if I'd pulled him back on board, the ship would have gone down by now. His life for mine. The thought rattled me.

I rather liked him, despite the calamity that he brought to the

Amphitrite. In another situation, Jonah might have been a friend. 'Retch' would be a good nickname for the man with no sea legs.

Why was he running from his God, I wondered, and who had he left behind in the land of the Israelites. A wife? Sons? Was anyone in that desert land of sheep and cattle and olive groves who would miss him?

"Should we catch it?"

I turned to the young man at my side, pointing at a gull that had perched on the remnants of the mast. It was the first any of us had spoken, all on the deck together and alone at the same time.

"You can't eat that thing," I said. "Search below for food, if any survived."

"Not to eat. For sacrifice."

The man's voice carried to the others. "Yes, that's good." The captain affirmed the plan and was already dragging up a soggy bit of net while eyeing the bird.

"How do we sacrifice to the Hebrew God? Anyone know? What is he called?"

Only shrugs. "Creator of the sea," I suggested. "And they burn offerings in their temples."

We had neither the ability to burn something nor carved images to see our efforts. Yet, I felt in my soul this was something we needed to do, to thank the God we didn't know yesterday, and now knew in a most profound manner. Would this sacrifice please him? I didn't know. If the darkness returned, we would have that question answered.

The gull was captured, its neck swiftly twisted and now lay dead at our feet. "Say some words," the captain said to me.

My prayers to other deities were memorized. Not knowing this one's preference, I decided to say words that at least sounded like ones in the holy scrolls of Israel, like priests I'd heard a time or two at port. "Umm, God of the prophet Jonah, you who created the waters and the dry land, you who sent the storm and took it away, we magnify your greatness. Don't hold us to blame for your servant's death. He who ran from your presence was punished as you saw fitting." I looked at the others, not certain how to continue. They looked back at me, seemingly satisfied. "Guide us with your breath, steer us to safety," I concluded.

The captain knelt over the bird and pulled out a knife, cutting it into thirty-six parts. Each of us took his portion and cast it into the waters where the prophet had drowned. From the depths, brightly hued fishes surfaced and stole the bits away.

"Look there!"

I turned the direction the man was pointing. As the ship crested a wave, I could see what caught his attention, a smudge of green rising above the watery horizon. Land. Our lives, saved.

PERSIS

The purples had faded to yellow, the last of the beating to remain evident on my skin. No internal organs were damaged, no bones broken. Tariq didn't allow any blows to result in damage that might threaten my life or give lasting injury. The strikes were for pain and humiliation alone.

Shey helped me to dress. Guilt rode her conscience, and she had apologized profusely for her part in my punishment. To her dismay, our husband now used her as his messenger to the secondary wives, an honor she abhorred.

"He says you are to resume the training of the girls. You have to take them out today."

I hadn't left home since the beating, left alone as ordered. Food was delivered, but that was all. None of the wives had been permitted to apply cool compresses or even give a consoling word. No doctor had been sent for, no herbs for medicine. Slowly the swelling and ache in my body diminished. The ache in my soul had not.

Hate wanted to take hold of my heart. Yet, Tariq hadn't killed me. There was gratitude in that, I supposed. Death might have been preferable, but he had shown mercy. I didn't know if he truly intended to have me sacrificed or if it was a threat made in anger. In either case, I intended to be fully obedient.

"I'll have to drape a shawl over these arms. I don't want my bruises to show."

Shey rubbed her bulging belly. "The girls will ask you about the punishment. They'll want to know why it happened. What will you tell them?"

"They don't know?"

Shey shook her head, golden coins jingling across her forehead. "We were forbidden to discuss it and no one dared disobey. I don't know what the children believe. They are mindful of all the rules, though. Our husband has made certain he's made everyone afraid."

"Fear of the Lord is the beginning of wisdom." The old words slipped out without thought. I smacked a hand over my lips. In the last few weeks of solitude, I'd had much time to think about the mountains and valleys of my life.

"What is that saying from?"

The wives could worship any of the gods as long as Dagon was chief among them, though I doubted the Hebrew deity was included. Those people were despised. "A phrase my father used to say." The words were part of a song that a king in Israel had written many years ago, back when the nations were afraid of the god who ruled that region.

"Do you remember more? The words are poetic."

I coiled a beaded band over my arm, covering a splotch of fading bruises. "Some, but only in pieces."

"Who is your father's god?"

"Was. My father's dead." I pretended to focus on fastening a bracelet to my wrist, not certain how far my trust in Shey should run. She had our husband's favor, and his ear.

"Does that god remember you, do you think?"

"No."

"He didn't help you when you were beaten."

I ran a hand over the residual welts on my forearm. "He doesn't remember me."

The woman put a gentle hand on my arm. "You weren't killed.

One of the gods was merciful."

Shrugging off the hand, I draped a linen wrap over my shoulders and went outside to the courtyard. Three wives stood near the fountain, where we often stood to talk and not be overheard. The splashing water masked conversation and no one could approach unseen. A hushed discussion stopped immediately.

"The ban is lifted. You may speak to me."

The women glanced at one another for approval, then Ketahni spoke softly. "What about the herbs? Will you still help us? Most of us know how, but..."

I shook my head. "No. Don't ask me. You witnessed what happened. You hit me along with the others."

Ketahni kneaded her hands together. Not yet twenty years old, she was a timid girl, with small bones and a smaller spirit. She had been crying by the look of her red rimmed eyes. "The field hand with flame colored hair? I think I carry his child." Her voice was filled with shame, and fear.

"You think?"

"It might be the Master's. I don't know."

I ran a hand over the girl's hair, a deep rich brown. Her skin and hair tones were the same as the Tariq's. The child might have her coloring and no one would be the wiser. A fair, copper headed child would be her death.

"Ra'eesa died," I said.

"What choice do I have?"

None, they all knew. The young wife was won in a drunken bet and favor would not likely be granted if there was any question regarding the parentage of the baby. Not to her, the infant or the servant. All three would perish.

I felt my own tears burning. There was a time I felt my life had meaning, when I was too young to know anything but what I was told by the adults around me. I would be a good wife, a good mother, a good example, a good something. There was no doubt then, no reason to think my existence had no purpose at all.

Later, I chose to believe my life had value, even here, even in Nineveh. In a marriage beyond my control, in a land not my own, helping women in the same situation was all I had to offer. My life wasn't worth trying to preserve, anyhow.

Despite the risks, I nodded. "I'll get the supplies."

JONAH

Death wasn't what I expected.

Closing my eyes to the descending darkness, my breath gone, limbs no longer able to fight, I thought my soul would takes its leave and that I would simply be no more. At least, in the flesh. I believed that my essence would live on without bones to give it structure and blood to give it life. David, our great king, believed he would dwell in the house of the Lord when he died, and Job was eager to see God. Even Enoch, grandfather of Noah, spoke of returning to earth from the sky one day.

Me? I wasn't certain how to explain any of it, other than to give the mystery to God and go about the process of living. Aiming for righteousness for any given day, and the next, when the death knell sounded, I'd address its concerns then. Where was the pit of Sheol and would I go there? Where was God, would I see him? I didn't have solid answers to those questions, choosing not to speculate at any great length on what my soul would know or feel or want after my heart was stilled in my chest.

What I felt in the seaweed shroud was not rebirth into another life, more the opposite. My drifting body was suddenly sucked into a canal, headfirst, squeezed and pressed and passed back inside a womb. With no breath to give, my lungs compressed to nothing, and new pain burned from the effort to fill them with something, as they were made to do. Instead, the force on my body in the narrow passage forced the sea water inside me to gush out.

Violently emptying myself, I rose to my knees and lifted my

head, so I wouldn't choke on my own vomit. As my skull hit a solid surface, my gasping mouth swallowed something other than more waters of the deep.

Air.

It was then I realized I was still alive.

At least, I believed I was. My hands ran quickly up and down my torso, finding the body I expected, and the wet garment that had clung to my skin when I had last been on the ship. I detected no broken bones or injuries. My mind and flesh were still united.

Gulping the life-giving air, choking, painfully spewing more water, I marveled at the simple state of my existence.

Then came the fear.

Alive or dead, my senses struggled to interpret my whereabouts, but swiping the darkness from my face was a useless effort. Burning eyes, wide open, searched in every direction, and found not one speck of light or motion. I waited for them to adjust to the darkness as they do in a cave or a cellar, adapting and at least giving a sense of position and immediate surroundings. The adaptation didn't come. What I could see was absolutely nothing.

A sharp motion threw me off balance. I splashed as I fell sideways into the water, or whatever it was, puddling beneath me. The liquid sloshed over my legs, and it stank, the putrid smell of rot and damp coating me, and drawing up the nausea I had been familiar with since leaving the dry land. Running my hand in it, there were solid bits, and mushy bits, and nothing that felt familiar until I pulled a piece out and felt it squirm in my grasp. A fish. I flung it away and heard the wet smack nearby, then a splash as it returned to our watery bath.

I vomited again, heaving acrid fluid into the mix.

The surface beneath me was slippery and firm, smooth and undulating in tiny hills and valleys. In a sitting position, I stretched my arms out. The container was perhaps a cubit higher than my head. The walls were further than my reach so I got on my hands and knees, intending to crawl through the liquid. I slipped as I moved, the rounded floor pulling me back to the center as I tried to climb. I dug my hands and knees into the surface, gaining purchase as best I could. Then the surface heaved, and sent me back to the slosh where I started.

"My God!" I cried out. The sound bounced back to me without echo or response. The lapping waters, splashes of living things around me, and my own heart pounding weren't the only sounds. There was another beat, a steady, relentless rhythm. The boom, boom, boom reverberated in my chamber, along with the whooshing of water through a reed pipe.

Or blood through a vessel.

Boom. Whoosh. Boom. Whoosh.

It didn't take much effort to realize that although this felt and smelled like death, it wasn't.

I was fully alive and inside the belly of another living creature.

JONAH

"Where can I go from your Spirit? Where can I flee from your presence? If I go up to the heavens, you are there; if I make my bed in the depths, you are there. If I rise on the wings of the dawn, if I settle on the far side of the sea, even there your hand will guide me, even there my God will be."

My voice was loud in my ears even though I spoke the ancient words softly. How often had I said them over my lifetime and taught them to my children, and yet not understood them until I had been tossed into a raging sea and swallowed whole?

Who was I to run from the One who ruled the earth and sky, who poured out fire on Sodom and filled barren wombs with sons? He who was and forever would be, who had no equal?

Did I really think he couldn't follow me? No, I knew he could. I thought he wouldn't. I hoped he would simply be done with me, at least for a time. I wanted God to go about the business of protecting Israel and forget the man who walked away.

That opinion was long gone. In the fetid belly of some great fish, I desperately wanted my God's sustaining presence.

Boom. Whoosh. Boom. Whoosh.

I was overwhelmed with my situation. There was nothing I could do to change it, no wise thinking or planned course of action. No amount of strength, no amount of reasoning. I had only prayers as I sat alone in my womb-prison. Waiting. For what, I didn't know.

By tossing fish towards the walls and listening to the sounds, I estimated the belly to be twice as wide as I was tall, and perhaps three or four times the length. It was roughly cylindrical, and tapered away. Knowing where it went from there, I kept myself as close to the front as possible.

Somewhere beyond the cavern, there was a mouth. I had come through it and survived. Not relishing the thought of being in the sea again with nothing to breathe, I didn't attempt to force my way back through the canal.

Were the seas still churning beyond the jaw that swallowed me up? I doubted it. The beautiful weather surely returned once the sailors had thrown me to my death. What a miracle! I hoped they understood fully what had happened, that it was my God who made the storm and took it away. They lost a fortune in cargo because of me, but had a tale to beat all others. If anyone would believe them.

There was no way to determine time in the dark confines and I found myself counting to the beat of the fish's heart before my thoughts took me away again. I slept after a while, extending my legs out fully so I could plant my feet beneath the stomach fluids and keep my head and torso above them, resting against the sides.

In the awake moments, memories surfaced, and led to other ones. My life had so much more good than bad. The prophesy of my youth, the respect, then prosperity. I'd never gone hungry for long or been in want of any necessity. All my sons were strong, my daughters, pure and industrious like their mother. I lost Miriam, yet gained Michal because of that loss. And Michal was a good wife.

My sigh filled the chamber. Perhaps I should have told her about the call to go to Nineveh.

Had my choice to leave been so wrong? I didn't want to give Nineveh an opportunity to live. I wanted them all to die under God's hand. I still did, if I had to be honest.

But I didn't want to die. I wanted another chance to live in peace with my God.

In my tomb beneath the great sea, I saw no way for that to happen.

MICHAL

My father drove the axe into the stump, wrenched it free to arc through the air, and repeated the motion. When the slice separated and fell to the ground, he planted the tool on the earth and leaned on it. "See how I kept moving, Ethan? Train your body to follow a pattern and the work becomes easier."

My son lifted his own smaller sized tool with both hands as he had seen his grandfather do. The head fell against a log and glanced off, talking the boy to the ground with it.

"I can't do it!"

"You will. Your muscles need to get some strength to them yet. It will come. You've only just started learning how."

"Ethan, come fishing!" His older cousins waited by the fence.

"Go ahead," I said. "And stay with the others. No going off alone."

My father dropped the axe and plunked down on the stump, wiping his forehead from the exertion. Despite the wrinkles, he enjoyed the labor as much as any younger man. Ethan could learn much from him, how to be strong in heart and mind and body.

"No word, then?"

"No, Father. I don't know where my husband is."

"It's only been a week."

"It feels much longer. I've aged more than a week."

He pulled a knife from his belt and ran the tip beneath a thumbnail, cleaning out the crud that had lodged there. "What does your heart say, Michal? What's happened to him?"

My father adored Jonah. I spoke truthfully without casting stones. "I don't think he's dead. I think I would feel it somehow if that part of me was gone."

He waited for me to continue, then spoke when I didn't. "Then he was taken by force, of which there is no evidence. Or, he left of his own accord. Where would he go, and why? He seemed content to me. He isn't the sort to abandon his family and his responsibilities. Why destroy the altar? I can't make any sense of this situation."

The children's laughter carried on the evening breeze. It was a good sound. Ethan wouldn't be alone if his father never returned. I couldn't protect him from that possibility. I couldn't protect my father either. I stared at the distant hills. "Jonah was tired of God's silence. Maybe he did rage against his calling, maybe he left his family to find happiness elsewhere."

The lack of response made me turn to look at Father. He was watching me thoughtfully, knife still under a fingernail. "Was he unhappy, Michal?"

"Not entirely. At least, I didn't think so. He loved his children and his land, and the animals he tended. There were some aspects that frustrated him. God. The people and their lack of discipline. And, I think he missed..." I couldn't say her name without hesitation. "He missed Miriam."

Father looked surprised. "That was a lifetime ago." He shook his head. "He loved your sister, but that pain isn't fresh any longer."

"He missed those days. A young prophet, favored by God and king, and his people. Miriam was tied into that dream, and the expectations of what his life should have been, then was never realized. Not completely. I may be a part of that, part of the failure."

"Hmph. All men want their stallion days back. All men. He's no different, and he knows it. Jonah wouldn't leave because he thought there was a better life for him outside this place. He understands his blessings are because of his faithfulness to the responsibilities given him already." He patted my arm roughly. "And you're not a failure in his life. He's pleased with you, always has been."

"I've never been certain."

"He treats you fairly."

"Yes, he does."

Father flipped the debris from the last nail into to air. "You worry because he was betrothed to your sister first?"

"How could I not?"

"He barely knew her."

"He could have had any girl in the nation. King Jeroboam would have given him a harem. He chose Miriam."

My father smiled, looking at the clouds and remembering. "He wanted a mate who would remain true to the Laws of Moses. And I wanted the same for her, and for you. She was older, and that's why Jonah's father and I made the arrangements for Miriam's betrothal. There was nothing about your sister that made her better for him than you."

"There was no mohar." I had never before said this to anyone, that my heart had been crushed the day Jonah came for me.

"He paid handsomely. You don't remember?"

"For Miriam, Father. It was for Miriam."

His brows pinched together as he tried to understand. "It was. Then that daughter was no longer available. I offered the flock back to him and he refused. Later we agreed for the two of you to marry instead. I could never have taken more from him. What kind of man would that make me?"

I breathed in through my nose, then out. I didn't know how to explain that it wasn't about him. It was about me, and about being chosen, and valued. It sounded petty in my mind so I left it there.

"Had you considered a husband for me, before Jonah?"

"Of course. The obvious one." He turned to the sound of boys being boys, yelling, laughing, challenging all rolled together. It was the sound of my brothers and the neighbor boys, the same games and mischievousness in another generation.

"Caleb?" I said.

He nodded. "That friendship was a foundation for a fine marriage."

"Miriam wasn't interested, so you thought he might settle for me."

Father looked puzzled again. "No. No, I never considered your sister. Caleb had no interest in Miriam. I thought you and he would be good together. You already were, as children."

"But, he followed her. He'd sneak away from the boys sometimes, looking for her just to say something silly or pester us."

"It was you he wanted to spend time with, Michal. She looked after you, so you girls were always together."

"Oh." I had been his choice?

"Jonah's father asked about you, and it was a means to putting a bad situation right again. Caleb's father would have as well, but I'm happy it worked as it did. You were betrothed to a fine man, one who is missing, but not because he regrets taking you as his own. I can't believe that about him. He's an honorable man."

"Thank you, Father." I needed to be alone, to think. "I'll check on the boys."

I stood out of sight, where I could see the children playing and be to myself. I was wrong about Caleb. Had I been wrong about my husband? My father seemed so certain that my instincts were off, and that Jonah had put Miriam away in his heart.

Was it me who tied them together, me who wouldn't let them separate?

The defensive wall that rose between us at the mention of her name had been in our marriage for so long, it was part of who we were. Had I been the one to build it? It was obvious as the memories washed over me, that if nothing else, I hadn't tried to tear that barrier down. I'd protected myself and my own sense of unfairness, blaming Jonah. I'd used Miriam as an excuse to keep my anger close by, within my reach when it suited me.

Had my husband tired of me and left? Or was my father right, that he would never have done such an act of dishonor?

But if my husband hadn't gone in search of the life he wanted, then where was he?

JONAH

There was air for me to breathe in the fish belly, but I had no idea how long it would last, or if there would be more. It was all I had to sustain me, as I couldn't drink the putrid fluid or eat any of its contents. My body would be depleted of its own water in a matter of days. Remaining in the creature, I would become its food, in one end and out the other. Any pride I'd held as God's spokesman was buried in the sands of the great sea with that awareness.

Along with my thirst, there was a persistent tingling to my skin. The mild burning was worse on my legs, the part of me that rested in the fluids puddling there. The water that gushed in had diminished, the remaining level concentrated in salt, turning the broth into a thickening stew of dead creatures. A constant oozing from the walls created the slipperiness of my surroundings. Digestive juices, inescapable, and caustic.

I realized I wouldn't become food. I was food already.

Trying to climb the sides for relief only resulted in me sliding back into the bath. There was nowhere to go.

Boom. Whoosh. Boom. Whoosh.

I wanted to die. I wanted to live.

As I waited for one or the other, I recited to the fish every Psalm of David I could remember, the Laws of Moses and rules for purification, the genealogies of Adam to Abraham to my father, Amittai. The judges of Israel were enumerated along with their triumphs and defeats, and then the same for the kings. I told it stories from my own life, periodically shifting in the space to transfer the burning from one side to the other.

In the midst of my ramblings, there came a sudden change in my captor's movements. I slid away from the front and slammed into the far end as it surged upward. The great jaw opened, the chamber flooded with the chilled waters of the sea.

I held my breath, once again submerged. Once again, certain my life was ending. But in only a moment, I was gasping air at the top of the chamber again, as most of the ingested water filtered out of the belly. Dozens of fish flopped around me in the aftermath, slapping at their prison walls with fury.

The chamber leveled out, and I sloshed to the front end. Nothing had outwardly changed except the replenishing of my air. I was still contained in a hostile environment, hungry, weary, lonely and terrified. But inside, hope had seeded itself in my soul. I had seen beyond the canal, through the open jaw as the fish skimmed the surface for food. As fresh air flowed in along with the prey, I caught a glimpse of dawn.

The sun, a sliver of brilliance in a pale sky, peered above the watery horizon into my dark tomb, like the eye of God. I felt his presence in that brief glimpse of light. No man on the earth knew where I was hidden, but one above the earth and seas knew, and had choreographed my life with that of some great fish.

I knew then, in the way that defies logical explanation, that this was not my grave. I wasn't in a cell awaiting judgment. The Almighty had not condemned his prophet to death within the belly of the gilled creature. The fish wasn't my destruction, it was my salvation.

The God who I abandoned had not abandoned me.

Overwhelmed, I sank into the fluids and wept. The prayer I wrote to my Lord is forever engraved on my soul:

In my distress, I called to the Lord, and he answered me.

From the depths of the grave I called for help, and you listened to my cry.

You hurled me into the deep, into the very heart of the seas, and the currents swirled about me. Your waves and breakers swept over me. I said, 'I have been banished from your sight, yet I will look again toward your holy temple.'

The engulfing waters threatened me, the deep surrounded me. Seaweed wrapped around my head. To the roots of the mountains I sank down, the earth beneath barred me in forever.

But you brought my life up from the pit, O Lord my God.

When my life was ebbing away, I remembered you, Lord, and my prayer rose to you, to your holy temple. Those who cling to worthless idols forfeit the grace that could be theirs. But I, with a song of thanksgiving will sacrifice to you.

What I have vowed I will make good.

Salvation comes from the Lord.

THE SAILOR

Unshifting land beneath my feet had never felt so wonderful. I wouldn't say it to the captain, but I was glad there were repairs to be made before we sailed again. The passenger's coins we'd found in the sloshing hold as we bailed would pay for the work, even after the men were given wages for the unprofitable journey. It was a small amount compared to what we would have received in Tarshish, but no one cared. There had been no grumbling over the sum distributed when we anchored in the safety of the Sidon harbor. The unforeseen events and certain doom gave even the crustiest one of us a sense of gratitude.

"You're leaving, aren't you?"

The captain threw me a line from the small boat we had taken from the ship into the docks. I caught it and secured the boat. "For a season. There are plenty of men to see to the repairs without me. I'll return before the Feast of Nanshe."

"Going home?"

I turned to the south. "No. To the prophet's land. To meet these Hebrews he came from. There must be family there."

"It isn't your duty."

"No. But if it was me that died, I'd want my wife to know."

The captain raised a bushy eyebrow. "Gonna' tell them everything?"

I nodded.

He snorted and spit a wad of mint leaves into the water. "They'll call you crazy."

"Been called that before," I said.

He reached inside a bag and pulled out a knife, handing it to me. "Take this to his woman, then. Found it below. Can't give you his money. He owes us that for the loss."

"I'll return as soon as I can. If I'm delayed, I'll meet up with you next round through here or Joppa."

"Good enough." He pointed toward Israel with his chin, then reached back in his pack. "Find the temple to that man's God and thank him again. Do it properly." He pressed several coins into my hand then left me alone on the dock.

I tied up my belongings and threw them over my shoulder. Very little about the land I set my feet toward was familiar. They were a prideful bunch living there, with a history richly tied to their deity. That I knew, and that they had a magnificent temple in Jerusalem. It seemed reasonable that its priests would know of Jonah the Prophet.

My captain had been right, it wasn't anyone's duty to report the death of a man who chose to board the ship he sailed. If it hadn't been for the storm, I might have let it pass. The brief but eventful encounter refused to clear from my mind, and if nothing else, I wanted to learn more about the God the man both worshipped and ran away from, the God who asked so much that Jonah forfeited his life in refusal. What kind of deity was that?

THE SAILOR

"Stop!"

I turned to see who yelled at me, my muscles tensing. The pinched-faced man striding my direction wore an elaborate blue robe over a spotless white tunic, gold trimmed and tasseled at the corners. The turban on his head was made of the same expensive fabric, and he carried scrolls beneath his arm. A handful of younger men followed in his wake.

Finally nearing Jerusalem, I had been surprised to find a temple to the prophet's god in nearby Bethel. I figured this one would suffice. I'd lost count of the days it took me to get this far and was already eager to complete my mission and return to the sea. Why these people didn't worship their deity in every town was a question I'd have to ask. Couldn't they see the advantage?

"What's the problem?" I said, quickly scanning the group for drawn weapons and calculating my odds if a fight was on the brink. The fancy dressed man was no challenge. His followers wouldn't be a threat either, even if they attacked me at the same time. They were a scrawny bunch for the most part, men who spent their time learning rather than doing. Fat heads didn't make up for weak muscles.

I hoped at least one of them had studied how to handle himself in a fist fight. That sort was fun to toy with, like a cat and the mouse it held by the tail.

One man held back from the others, older and stronger, and without the disdain I saw on the face of the fancy robed man. I kept that man in my line of sight as I addressed the one in command. "Is this not the public temple?"

"Yes, but you can't go in there."

We stood at the steps leading up to the impressive and well-maintained structure. I had already passed through a gate into the courtyard that housed it, passed men of all sorts, and none seemed to care about my presence. Certainly none had tried to stop me.

"And why not? Is your god not home today?"

The man drew in a sharp breath, then exhaled with unconcealed exasperation. "Who are you? I've never seen you here before."

"And for that reason, you don't want me to enter the temple?"

The students looked from me to the teacher, amused it seemed, but keeping it suppressed. No one was going to swing a fist from that bunch.

"You can't enter because you haven't prepared yourself. It's a holy God we serve, and you can't go in there like, like that." He pointed a single jeweled finger at my dusty clothing, wrinkling his nose at the rank smell coming off my hot skin. My face had the growth of a shaggy beard and one sandal was fastened on with rope after the leather strapping had cracked on the way.

I lifted my arm in his direction and whiffed at the exposed pit, as if I was surprised that I stank. "I'm a traveling man to these parts. Had I known your god was so fussy, I would have rented a room and groomed properly." I made no attempt to keep the sarcasm from being evident.

The students were wide-eyed, amusement and shock fighting for dominance. All but the strong one. He laughed out loud.

The teacher gave a curt glance at strong-man. To me, he put on a smile and said, "I'm Amaziah, a priest of this temple. Strangers are welcome if they follow my rules."

"And what rules might those be?"

"You have to cleanse yourself. There are basins outside the courtyard. You passed them."

"Ahh, yes. The basins. I thought they were meant to water one's camels."

"And you must present a sacrifice. They can be purchased from any of these merchants." His arm swept the perimeter of the courtyard, where tents were set up, cages of birds and pens of small animals there to be sold. "If you desire a larger animal, it can be arranged."

"At a fair price, no doubt?"

Amaziah smiled. "Of course."

"Fair to whom?" The strong man was ignored.

I watched a man purchase a caged pigeon, then walk over to a priest and hand it off before he entered through the columned structure. "That's it then? That's how I honor this God of the Hebrews? I take a bath and give him a bird?"

The priest grimaced. "There's much more, naturally. This is what's required of you right now."

Strong-man spoke up. "And do you also demand that a man be circumcised before he may enter the house of the Lord, Amaziah?"

I snorted. "Be what?" I would have nothing to do with that barbaric custom.

The man's thin lips pressed together. If there was a fight, I sensed it was between him and the strong one, someone with the audacity to raise questions of a religious nature.

"What does the law say, Amos? You tell me. Your shepherd's mind seems bent on knowing the words of Moses."

I held up my hands. "I've heard enough. I intended to honor this God but I won't be mutilated in order to do so." Digging out the coins from my captain, I put them in the priest's palm. "You do it for me."

"Will you tell us why you wish to honor a god not your own? What brings you to Bethel?" Amos smiled easily, genuinely.

With closer inspection, I could see that he wasn't that much older than the other young men. He was work hardened, a man who used his hands to earn his keep. He was dressed simply, wearing a clean, poor man's tunic. A curly short beard sprouted from his chin and fell unevenly, as if he chopped it himself with a dull blade. His companions were dressed in a finer weave, with the hands of those who believe thinking hard is the same as working.

I snatched the coins back from the priest and put them in Amos' rough hand. This was a man like me.

"Your god sent a mighty storm upon my ship, then took it away."

"How did you know it was the Lord God? You are Phoenician, correct? Why wasn't it Dagon who spared you?"

"A prophet of your deity was on board. He told us who controlled the tempest."

"He spoke truth. There is but One God, one far above all others in power and might." The strong man said the words simply, a fact I felt in my heart since the seas had calmed. It was this Lord God I wanted to serve.

"What prophet?" Amaziah asked. "Who was on that ship with you?"

I wanted to tell the man to shove off, not at all liking his tone, or anything else about him. Amos and the others had genuine interest written on their faces, so I relented and gave them the name. "Jonah. Jonah ben Amattai."

The reaction surprised me. All the men gasped. It was obviously a name they knew, a prophet well known in Bethel.

Color drained from the priest's face. "Jonah? Jonah was on a ship? Where is he now? Where did he go?"

"I don't know." I lied. I didn't want to be the one carrying news of death all of a sudden. I hadn't expected a whole crowd to know the man, or to care whether he lived or not.

"He got off the ship with you? Where is it docked? How long ago?"

I held my tongue.

Amos put the silence into words. "He didn't, did he? He's not with you."

"No."

"Where is he, then?" The priest's tone had softened but continued to ring with irritation.

I turned away from him, focusing on Amos. The man's eyes revealed the depth of his intuition.

"Is he dead? Is Jonah dead?" Amos asked what he already knew with intensity, sorrow woven into his question before I answered with an affirmative nod.

Amaziah's eyes glistened, his throat thick with emotion. "Dead. Dead at your hands? What did you do to him?"

Amos reached out and touched my arm, stopping me from raising it against the priest. "Why was Jonah on your ship? Where was he going?" he asked.

To say it meant they would all know. This prophet they loved had been fleeing his home, running from his God. I looked at the temple, bright white stones shining in the sunlight, Jonah's God inside its ornate walls. The prophet had not gone to the sea to find his deity. He wanted to find a place as far from here, and him, as possible.

I swallowed my own sadness. "Tarshish," I said.

The cluster of men lowered their heads, understanding. It was the end of the earth for these inland dwellers. No one from here went there for any reputable purpose.

Amaziah led us to a shaded portico and asked me to tell them everything. I did, save one fact. I didn't tell them that I held the arms of their prophet and threw him to his death. I found out in turn that no one knew where Jonah had gone, or why.

The priest led his students away as the awe, the grief, and the unanswered questions sifted in their minds. Amos led me to an inn, his arm wrapping around my shoulders for one vigorous squeeze as we stood together by the door. "His sons are in Gath-hepher. You're going there?"

"I am."

He nodded. "Good. Thank you. I'm glad you'll deliver the news yourself, a witness to the power of our Lord. But, it will be a painful revelation to those who know him best. I'm heading back to Tekoa tomorrow, heading south, or I'd go with you."

"You aren't a student here?"

Amos laughed. "No. I'm no prophet. I speak when the Lord stirs my heart, go where he sends me, and I torment Amaziah as I pass though." He grinned. "Sometimes I make a point of passing by this town, no matter where I've been." He started to leave then turned back, pulling out the coins I'd given him and dropping them back into my pack. "God isn't in that temple, not where a golden calf is worshipped. It's an abomination, a black stain on my people to allow its existence. Our Lord has no graven image. You've missed nothing by not being allowed entrance."

"Then where is your God?"

"He walks among us, unseen, yet seen in the works of his hand."

"Like the storm."

"Yes. Like a storm that rises and passes away. Our God is a torrential wind and gentle breeze. He's the consuming wrath of judgment and the tender kiss of mercy."

It was hard to reconcile this rough-hewn man with his poetic words. His eyes were moist, and I sensed a lasting connection to the deity he worshipped. "How do I find him?" I asked.

"Wherever you search, he's already there."

"And if you don't want to find him, or him to find you?"

The strong-man swiped his sleeve against a dripping nose. "There's no place to hide. Not even Tarshish. He sees. He knows."

"He knows that I killed a man, then?"

Amos looked at me with full understanding. "Our prophet's death isn't on you, my friend."

The man wished me well and walked away. I secured a room and remained there through the night, awake, thinking of the mysterious Lord of the Hebrews. Why had Jonah not appeased his God with a bath and a pigeon? Because it was more than that, I knew. It was the man's rebellious heart that had angered his great deity.

MICHAL

Caleb lived on the land of his father's father, many generations back. It bordered the land where I grew up, a path between the two still evident from the days when we ran to his home and he and his brothers and sisters tromped over to ours. I shouldn't have been following it with any sort of trepidation, yet I was anxious, and not because I feared what I might find, but because I knew the truth of the man who lived there.

Off the main trail were many spurs, leading to secret caves and stands of trees, places we knew we could hide from the world and not be seen. Many hours of my childhood had been spent in the private world with no adult supervision. Miriam and my brothers protected me there, although I couldn't recall one serious threat.

I picked my way through the low brush, relying on memory to guide me. The spacious caves where we held private meetings and made secret pacts were mere hollows on the face of hillsides. Our parents had never been fooled, I realized. Between the two homes, we could be seen, or at least heard, from any of the secret dens.

The trail emptied into a pasture. Caleb was stacking stones on the perimeter, mending a section that had fallen. Two of his sons were there, and a grandson. I hesitated, then chided myself. He was my friend and there was no reason to feel any sort of nervousness around him. It was years ago that he considered me as a wife, and we had both changed in the decades since then.

"Greetings," I said. "Father sends this honey to you. Says he has more than enough for now."

Caleb accepted the basket with its clay pots, stretching his spine and wiping his brow. "Thank him, and you for the delivery. How long's it been since you walked that trail?"

"Years. When did it get so short? And didn't we all fit inside those caves at one time?"

"I still fit." The boy was Ethan's age, and just as rambunctious.

"I imagine you do. I'll have to bring my Ethan over so you can show him the best hiding spots."

Caleb handed the basket to the boy. "Take these on home. We'll let your father and uncle finish here. He grinned at the men, and shooed the boy towards the simple home nearby.

"Come," he said to me, leading the way to a makeshift tent, a shelter from the sun. He rubbed his leg after he sat on the rug mat, kneading the soreness. "Have you heard anything about Jonah?"

"No." I dug my big toe into a root that protruded from the ground, leaning onto a post while struggling to find the right words.

"What's on your mind, Michal? I can sit for a while. My boys are doing fine without me."

I bit down on my lip, then opted to speak freely. "I had a talk with Father. About the past, when we were children."

Caleb nodded, his eyes crinkling in the corners as he smiled. "Good days."

"He said that you, you favored me." The heat burned my cheeks, saying it so bluntly sounding inappropriate.

My friend didn't answer right away, looking at the men hefting the stones into place. "He remembers right."

"I never knew. I thought you wanted to marry my sister."

He smiled again. "Second choice, perhaps."

"Why didn't you ask for me? It's been years, I just wondered…"

Caleb plucked a weed and chewed on the end. "With my leg the way it was, the physicians couldn't explain why it was so weak when I was born. They didn't know if it would get worse."

"You doubted your strength? Your ability to provide for me?"

He shrugged. "Partly. I started building on to my father's home so I could secure a bride, but I didn't speak soon enough. I thought I had time. I intended to ask my father about making the arrangements. Jonah was betrothed to you before I had the chance."

I turned my face to the man who had chosen me first. "You didn't speak up afterward. You never told me how you felt."

Caleb looked at me squarely. "Why? Jonah was a fine man with far more to offer. Your father did well in the arrangement, as did you. My Beckah made me very happy. It worked out well for all of us."

The air in the tent grew still. "Michal." He said my name softly. "Are you thinking about your options, if Jonah doesn't return?"

I couldn't look at him, watching the breeze whip up funnels in the dirt instead. "I may never know what's become of him. I may never have options."

Caleb stood and rested a hand on my shoulder. I covered it with my own, not caring who saw and who might think it inappropriate. His voice was controlled, matter of fact. "You never have to be alone as long as I'm alive. My home will always be open for you. As my friend, or as my wife."

He pulled away and left me there alone. I tried not to think about what might have been had Miriam and I not gone to the market that day, had my sister married Jonah and I married Caleb. There was no going back and finding out.

There was no turning to him now, either. Jonah wasn't dead, I felt certain. I might be alone in the house he built, might never see his shadow cross the threshold again, but I wasn't a widow.

THE FISH

"Spit!"

JONAH

Boom. Whoosh. Boom. Whoosh.

Time had no relevance to me as I waited for deliverance. It seemed as if I'd been away from my home for months, that many days of experiences had come and gone rather than the week that I thought had actually passed. I slept and sat awake for intervals of unknown duration. Hours at a time? Minutes?

With a change in trajectory and pressure on my ears, I knew that both air and sea water would soon flood in, and I'd need to hold my breath in the far end of the fish's gut only briefly. Sometimes the sky was dark when I peered out of the fish's mouth, sometimes light streamed in and hurt my eyes.

My belly grumbled in its emptiness, but I wouldn't eat anything that was swallowed and flopped about in the murky contents alongside me. We were in a similar predicament, these fishes and I, comrades in a battle to survive. Nothing I ate would stay down anyhow, not even bits of seaweed.

The juices in my holding cell continued to degrade my flesh. My legs were raw, wrinkled, and fragile, as if I could scrape the skin off like the peel of an overripe avocado. My clothing was disintegrating, and my toenails. Mostly, I was dreadfully thirsty. My lips cracked, burning constantly. The salty water that flushed over me only made me thirst and burn all the more.

Naked, hungry and dehydrated, skin dissolving, I intentionally thanked my Lord for his goodness. I knew his mercy saved me. He called the fish to preserve me. For what? That I had yet to see. If it was to preach the message of destruction in Nineveh, to give them time to repent and be spared, I would go. Yet deep in my unquenched soul, I hoped he would not ask that of me again.

I recited as many of King Solomon's wise proverbs as I could recall, dozed, told the fish of Noah, and slept again. The words of history were harder to remember each time I awakened, and my mouth became too sore to speak.

Sleep, long for home. Pray, change position. Recite, remember. Boom. Whoosh. Boom. Whoosh.

I estimated I'd been swallowed and living inside the creature of the sea for three or four days when a tremor inside the belly jolted me from fitful sleep. The motion pitched me forward, tossing me against the pinched orifice that led to the jaw, and the sea beyond. My parched lips screamed in fright. As odd as my circumstances were, there was comfort in the routine.

The slick surface relaxed. I scooted away from the door.

Boom, boom, whoosh. Boom, boom, whoosh.

The floor heaved again, rippling from back to front so that I was carried in the momentum. My head smacked the creature's belly wall with the putrid fish parts sloshing around me. I swiped the foulness from my face before the next wave hit.

The gut tremored, then again, each one violently constricting the chamber before relaxing. I locked my elbows and pressed into the walls to keep from being crushed. Jamming my legs into the flesh and tensing all my muscles, I strained to keep the space around me open.

My host didn't care for my efforts, or was tired of trying to digest something God wanted to keep alive. One last contraction pinched the belly chamber at the same instant the throat gaped wide. I was squeezed from the gut and spewed from the mouth in a wash of debris and fluids.

I held my breath. The sea would have me once again and I hoped the strength needed to swim would arise from within.

Then came the force of landing on a bed of stones. I gasped with the unexpected pain. It took a minute of panic for me to realize I had air to breathe, and was face down on a spit of land.

Land. The fish had thrown me up onto the earth.

My hands clawed at the rocks beneath me, trying to grasp firmly as if the ground would buckle and toss me back to where I had been. Sucking air into my burning lungs and unable to fully open my eyes to the harshness of light, the blackness of unconsciousness rapidly consumed me.

JONAH

Faces swam in the air above my face. I closed my eyes, then opened and tried to focus. A hand lifted my head and a cup was at my lips. I slurped cool water, then grabbed at the cup for more, gulping down the contents before falling back into the hands that held me up.

When I awakened again, I found myself on a reed mat beneath a palm tree.

"Rest. Don't try to move."

I turned to the woman's voice. "Michal?" I didn't recognize the raspy voice that came from my mouth, or the woman who leaned over me, dabbing ointment onto my lips.

She smiled. "Son of Dagon. You've come."

Surrounded by a dozen men and women, none looked familiar. The row of simple huts, the dense green hillside, the rocky beach and small harbor, nothing I'd seen before.

With a rush of clarity, I recalled where I had spent the last several days and nights, and how I ended up on the land. I struggled to get my elbows beneath me, rising just enough to see the great sea beyond the quiet harbor. Fishing boats were tied to wooden posts, nets were drying in the sun. "Where am I?"

"Nimmeron, a fishing village. I am Yamah, your servant." The woman pressed her palms together and bowed slightly. She spoke Hebrew with an accent I didn't recognize.

What had she called me? Son of Dagon?

"We saw it spit you out. Blessed are we to witnesses your coming forth." The old woman's eyes were bright as she gestured to the others with her arm. They nodded to confirm her words. "We welcome you, child of Dagon."

With help, I sat up. She was speaking Ugaritic, a tongue kin to my own, but which meant I was on pagan soil. Fortunately, it seemed friendly.

It hurt my lips to move them but I spoke so they would know the truth. "Not god. Man. Jonah. Of Gath-hepher, of Israel."

There was no response to my garbled sounds. I tried again, slowly, forcing my swollen tongue to form words. They understood that time, but didn't comprehend.

"Jonah, born from the belly of a great fish! We are witnesses to your arrival. The spirit of Dagon spewed you out from the deep cove and we were there to see it happen! We are blessed to be chosen." The lively old man indicated the small group surrounding me.

I shook my head, eager to explain what they had really seen but couldn't seem to find any more words, the bright colors of my surroundings blending and whirling. I squeezed my eyes closed against the dizziness and felt myself being stretched out on my back again.

The sky was awash in the colors of sunset when I woke up.

Yamah helped me prop onto one elbow and offered a chunk of bread dipped in honey. I lifted my hand to take it from hers, then stopped. My hand was white as a leper's. My arms were too. Raising the soft cloth covering my torso and legs, I saw the same bleached color, the skin ragged and peeling in thick flakes.

"Eat," the woman insisted as she placed the morsel in my mouth. I ran a hand over my jaw to wipe the drips of honey, surprised to find my chin clean-shaven and slick as a river stone. I'd had a beard since the first hairs grew in. Running my hand to my head I found smoothness there as well, not even stubble to indicate what had recently been full of curls. My chest, torso, arms and legs, not a hair remained.

"You're a miracle."

I nodded, amazed that she didn't fear me. My appearance had to be disturbing. No hair. The white skin of a leper on my entire body. Legs bathed in acrid stomach fluids that were now drying and peeling, like thick scales and-

Scales. Hairless. Expelled from a fish. What had she called me? Son of Dagon, son of the fish god. I groaned, finally understanding. I was a miracle, but not of the sort they imagined.

A man put soft cushions behind my back as I forced myself to sit. Yamah tore off another bite of bread and put it to my lips, feeding me slowly. When I could take no more food or fruity beverage, she tried to make me lie down, but I couldn't yet. I wanted to tell them who I really was. Or, more importantly, who I wasn't.

The villagers gathered around me in a semi-circle. Forty or fifty of them in all, watching me with expectation.

"I am a miracle, yes. A miracle of the Lord God. Not Dagon." It was like my days as a young prophet, speaking earnestly to the crowds. I had the attention of every last person as I told them what had happened to me. They seemed reluctant to accept that I was only a man. Part fish, part human, they believed I was the incarnation of an ancient prophesy.

The village allowed me to sleep endless hours at a time, someone always there when I awakened to see to my needs. Tiny carved idols surrounded my bedside at first. I tossed the lifeless figures into the cooking fires. There would be replacements the next time I awakened, out of my reach. The only one I spared was new, meant to look like me — made of whalebone, white and slick, with scales etched into my limbs.

To regain my vigor, I tried to eat heartily, especially the produce

of the land. The many fishes and shelled creatures the kind women offered, no matter how prepared or how well disguised in a stew, made my gut churn.

The weeks passed quickly as I slept and ate then slept some more. Four, then five, then six. I stayed in the shade as my skin sloughed and regenerated, relieved to see a faint return of brown pigment. Still pale and hairless, I was slightly less fishy looking than when I arrived. Covered in clothing to protect my fragile skin from the sun, my strength returning, I could have left the village. I didn't, not certain what to do next.

Did God still expect me to go to Nineveh or had that command been given to someone else? Go back to Gath-hepher? Remain in the village? I didn't want to make a mistake, yet was unable to initiate prayers to seek direction. I was afraid to hear the Lord's reprimand, afraid of punishment yet to be delivered.

Looking for stubbled sprouts of hair on my forearm one evening, the restless stirring returned to my soul. I recognized it this time, the awakening of my senses as the Lord approached. I went to the spit where the fish vomited me up, and waited, listening fearfully for God's penetrating voice above waves crashing against the rocky shore. I anticipated, and dreaded, the condemnation for my rebellion.

Fresh skin tingling, kneeling on the stones, it came as it had twice before, as a sound and thought and feeling all in one. "Jonah, Jonah, son of Amattai." My God's voice found me on the foreign soil.

"Yes. Your servant is here."

"Go to the great city of Nineveh. Tell them the message I gave to you."

I waited for more. There were only the squawks of gulls and shorebirds, and the rumblings of the tide as it surged over cobbles and filtered back out to sea.

The stillness prevailed as God waited for my response. There would be no harsh consequences to push me into obedience. The battle was my own.

I sucked in a deep breath and let it release slowly. Then again. Against a heart that begged for another calling, I whispered, "Yes, Lord. I'll go."

MICHAL

The man's rough exterior would have been frightening had I not seen him up close, and read compassion, gentleness in his eyes. His nose had been broken more than once and there were gaps where teeth had been. Muscular and scarred with only a knapsack slung over his shoulder, I assumed he wanted council with the prophet.

At the gate, he looked at me, then at his feet, fidgeting as he spoke. "Are you the wife of the prophet Jonah?" His clothing indicated Phoenician origin.

"I am. I'm called Michal."

"My name is-, well, I'm called Squid. I'm a sailor."

I smiled at the apologetic manner. "I won't ask why you're called that."

"No, best not."

He didn't continue. "My husband isn't here," I said. "I can offer you food and a place to rest. Otherwise, there are men in the city who can help you."

The man shook his head just perceptibly. "I know he's not here. It's you I was looking for." He looked at me to gauge the reaction. My heart thumped at the pain I saw clouding his expression.

"Please, come sit." I welcomed the sailor into the open courtyard and fed him while chattering about nothing more than his children and the places he'd traveled. He ate all that I gave him, then more. Hungry, or he wanted to be doing something other than telling me what was on his mind. I suspected some of both.

I replenished his drink for the third time then sat across from him in the shade of an awning. "Tell me of Jonah. Tell me the truth."

He hesitated, sucking in a deep breath and looking toward the horizon. "Your husband is dead." Reaching into his bundle, he retrieved Jonah's knife and gave it to me with a few foreign coins. "I'm sorry," he said. "Thought you should know."

I clenched the knife over my heart, the shock forming a dam against my tears. It would break, and once it did, I wasn't certain it could ever be stopped.

"Tell me. Everything."

He did, describing in detail their first encounter in Joppa, their conversations and Jonah's sickness, and the way he couldn't find his balance. About the storm, the lots, the decision the men had to make in order to save the ship. About tossing my husband into an angry sea that grew still as his body fell beneath the waves.

"I didn't want to. We had no choice, see? His God wanted him to be thrown in, and Jonah told us we had to in order to save ourselves. We didn't want to do what he said. We didn't want to kill him."

It was hard to take it all in. So many questions now answered but raising up so many more. "You did right," I said. "God was appeased."

Squid exhaled loudly and stared at me. "I thought you'd be mad."

"No. Not at you."

The sailor lowered his eyes. "He didn't mean to bring the ship any trouble."

"Why was he running from his God? Did he say?"

"He didn't."

"Where was he going?"

"The ship was headed for Tarshish. Other stops on the way, but he wanted to go the distance. Never said why. I'm not sure it mattered where he went, as long as it was away from..."

"Here. He was getting as far from home as he could."

The sailor dug a nail at a healing scratch, picking bits of scab from his forearm.

"Did he speak of his children? Of me?" I didn't want to ask, yet I had to know. My husband left his family, his land, his calling and his God. He traded his life for whatever he thought Tarshish had to offer. Had he remembered us? Regretted any of it?

The sailor looked away, watching cattle meandering in a pasture. "He did. He missed you. Felt bad about what he was doing."

I couldn't hold the man's lies against him. He cared enough about me, a woman he'd never met, to seek me out and tell me what had happened so I could stop watching for my husband's return. The sailor put my interests ahead of his own, which was far more than Jonah had done when he walked away in the night.

MICHAL

My husband was dead.

I collapsed on the remains of his altar and buried my face in my hands, again. I had no reason to doubt the words of the sailor, yet my heart couldn't reconcile the truth of what he told me.

Jonah would never come home.

I wanted to put all the pieces together. It would ease the pain to have an explanation. Starting from the end I could make a logical sequence, to a point. Jonah drowned off the coast of Cyprus. He drowned because the sailors tossed him into the sea, and they had to, to appease God and calm the violent storm. The storm was sent because Jonah was on board. He was on a ship because he ran from his home to Joppa, ran away from the Lord. Then I was stuck. I didn't know what preceded his flight.

I thought he was tired of me, of his work as a prophet and the life he had built. I thought my husband left all he knew, intending to start over somewhere else. Now I wasn't certain. The sailor said Jonah was running from God. After all these long, quiet years with no voice in his ear, had God spoken?

What would the Lord ask of my husband that would cause him to renounce his calling? I could only imagine it was something dreadful for my people. With the relative peace and prosperity since his last word from above, reliance on God had faltered. There was no justification for the inclusion of foreign gods, the laxity in following our laws for worship and for living. God could not be pleased with us.

Was punishment imminent? Had Jonah fled such a prophecy

rather than deliver it? Would he choose God's wrath over that of his own people?

I had no way to know. Jonah loved this land, the people and our history and yet I couldn't see him shying away from such a message. Drawing us back to the ways of Moses was a message he already preached. He understood the nature of righteousness and rebellion, of punishment and reward.

So why did he tear down his altar to God and leave? And if a profound task was required of him, or a grievous message given, why could he not tell me?

He ran in disobedience, whether or not his Lord had spoken. Jonah left his calling. He left me in shame. He left his family with questions we could never answer.

I stood and blew my nose into a piece of saturated cloth. Before they heard it from someone else, I needed to tell my children that their father was never coming home. Word would reach Gath-hepher soon enough since the sailor had been in Bethel.

Had I known if God was involved, I might have been angry. It would come later, I supposed, me feeling that he could have spared his prophet. Right then I just wanted to appease the one who made the land and the sea. I needed a refuge in the shelter of his wings as I processed how life had taken this turn.

No prophet was guaranteed a long and prosperous life. Still, it felt as if my husband chose death when he didn't have to. He had chosen to run from God and home, and all that he had. I didn't want to believe that no good thing would come of it. Somehow, I hoped there was purpose to it all.

One thing I knew. If Jonah had hoped to find Miriam as he ran, then sank into the depths, he had been disappointed. He would not find my sister in whatever shameful pit God reserved for the damned.

MICHAL

Ethan scrambled from my arms and ran to his sister. He fell at Lydia's feet and wrapped his arms around her legs, pushing his face into the folds of her clothing, refusing to look at anyone. She slid from the bench and pulled him onto her lap, rocking as he cried.

My son rejected me for saying what had to be said. I swallowed against the knot in my throat, having to restrain myself from taking him back into my own arms. I needed someone to hold, and someone to hold onto me. My children, my father, and siblings, Timna and so many others would comfort me now, but who would wrap me up in protective arms as the darkness fell night after night? In the midst of those who loved me, I felt an overwhelming wave of loneliness.

My family sat around the stone hearth, silent as I repeated the words of the sailor, waiting for a different ending to the tale of the ship and the prophet. There was no better ending to provide. I waited for the shock, the questions, the tears.

"How do we know that man was telling the truth?" Adin, my oldest asked.

"I don't know why he would come here and tell me something not true. He had nothing to gain by doing so."

"Perhaps Father paid that man to tell such a story." He looked at his hands as he made the suggestion.

"I can't know for certain, Adin. The sailor didn't bring the news with any joy. His story can be confirmed by the others on his ship, if anyone had reason to doubt."

"How far from shore were they? Father can swim." Lydia, of all my children, would grasp onto hope, no matter how small the fragment or how slippery the hold.

My thoughts and questions had followed similar courses to the ones I now answered. I shook my head. "The storm was violent, and they saw your father go under, and watched for him to surface."

I could see in their faces the lack of reasoning behind the sequence of events. Jonah was a strong father, expecting obedience and following the line of righteousness. He was kind and fair, and none had quarreled any more than growing sons tend to do with authority. They realized their father had faults, yet fleeing as the sailor described seemed unthinkable to all of them.

"Why, Mother? Why would he go to Tarshish? What's there?"

"I think it's what wouldn't be there." They looked at me with eyes moist and red-rimmed. "The voice of God."

"I don't understand. He said nothing to you?"

"No. Your father left without a word to anyone that I know of. It…"

"Hurts." Timna filled in the word we all felt keenly.

Adin stood abruptly and paced in small circles, so like his father. He ran his strong hand over his head, combing back the thick black curls. "Maybe God told him to leave."

I smiled as best I could, wanting to believe it as well, that my husband was following the command from heaven and we simply didn't understand the reasoning. I wanted him to be vindicated in the eyes of his children. In my own eyes, too.

"We don't know the ways of the Lord. His ways are higher." It was such a mothering statement, an attempt to dissolve the acrid pain in my children's hearts. I had no other balm.

"Michal."

My father was at the courtyard gate. Behind him were the elders of the city, and Amaziah, the priest from Bethel. So, the news was no longer new. It had followed the sailor and arrived in Gath-hepher more quickly than I anticipated.

I stood and greeted the men, conscious of the fact my tunic was made of soft linen rather than the rough-hewn attire of a woman in mourning. At dawn, I had dressed not knowing I was a widow.

My children filtered among the newcomers, the servants added food to the table, and the priest was taken away to freshen up from his journey. When he returned, the process began again. I repeated the words of the sailor to the nodding confirmation of Amaziah. He told of his own encounter with the man. As we spoke, benches, stone fencing, and floor filled, the news reaching into the city and drawing the broken hearted and the curious.

The news would be repeated as friends and neighbors arrived, the shock reliving itself over and over again around a table of wilting food. The same sorts of questions were asked, and answered in a similar fashion. The same inability to make the pieces fit left a hollow ache in each of us.

As the sun settled, the house was nearly empty except for the mourners who would remain with me for the night. I'd sent the family home, to their own children and beds and comfort of one another. My eyelids sagged, eager for the oblivion of sleep, if it would come. Timna and Adin found me sitting by the window, staring out into the evening sky, down a road that had led my husband away.

"Where's Ethan?" Timna asked, her hand gentle on my head, smoothing the unkempt hair.

"With Lydia."

Timna bit into her lip and shook her head. "I checked. I wanted to bring him here, knew you would want him close. She said he was here when she left for home."

Fatigue was thrust aside as I secured the sandal straps around my ankles. "I'll go to the altar. That's where he was the last time."

"He's not there, Michal. We looked already."

I rose quickly to hunt for my child in the last of the daylight, then just as quickly the darkness came over me and I collapsed into Adin's arms.

PERSIS

"Why are you wearing that old robe? It's not very pretty."

Ba'hiya was the only child who had accurately recited the prayer to Ishtar, one I had been teaching the dozen girls in my charge. The eleven I sent off with another of the wives to practice, while this one I took with me to the streets of Nineveh.

"It will do," I said. "Turn here."

I couldn't make myself dress fully in the exquisite clothing I owned, needing to express pain at the loss of another baby, even if the loss had come by my own medications. The older garment was the closest I could come without anyone taking much notice. A public display of mourning led to questions I didn't want to answer.

"This isn't the way to the temple. Where are we going?" The girl skipped ahead a few paces, knowing I wouldn't reprimand her for acting like the child she was.

"Somewhere you've never been before. A reward for learning the recitation today." A new palace had risen in the heart of the great city, owned by the king yet open to those with privilege. It was a home for his clay tablets and scrolls, written works of the Assyrians and those of other lands. It was a collection of knowledge. A king knew his enemy if he knew the writings of their people, it was said.

My husband didn't prohibit us from learning, an educated wife the sign of wealth, and educated children more profitable in trade. Who else had time to study but those not toiling over their daily bread? I attended lessons with the children's tutor when time had allowed, and had learned the skills required to decipher the inscriptions.

The interior of the spacious building was cool, marble benches and wooden tables interspersed among the shelves. I led a wide-eyed Ba'hiya to a far corner and placed a heavy tablet between us. The foreign words had been transcribed decades ago, the clay stamped by scribes in the Assyrian language.

"These words were written by a man named Job, who lived hundreds and hundreds of years before you were born. His God allowed him to be tormented by an Evil One."

"Who was Job's god? Was it Dagon?"

"No. His God was the Lord, Creator of all. The Hebrew people do not say his name."

In these few dusty tablets, songs of the ancient Israeli king, words of wisdom and history of Job, I had found comfort. Tariq's daughter was to learn only of her father's deities, yet I wanted the Hebrew God to be remembered once my life breath was snuffed forever.

Running my finger methodically beneath the symbols, I read: "If you devote your heart to God, and stretch out your hands to him, if you put away the sin that is in your hand and allow no evil to dwell in your tent, then you will lift up your face without shame. You will stand firm, without fear. You will forget your trouble, recalling it as waters gone by. Life will be brighter than noonday, and darkness will become like morning. You will be secure because there is hope."

Job's troubled thoughts were my troubled thoughts. He wanted answers to explain the circumstances in his life. Parts of his past, his present and his future were ripped away without cause. Was it his fault? Had he made the wrong choice and brought calamity upon himself? Was he so full of pride he was able to dismiss his own sins?

I had asked myself those questions, and had received no answer. Yet on the clay tablet, I found what couldn't be found in the myriad temples and shrines of my great city. For all his opinions and theorizing, Job had hope. He knew the justice of his God would prevail.

Would I see justice? Was there hope for me, hope that reached beyond my sins in this land not my own, and saw who I wanted to be, and not who I had become? Longing for more than freedom, more than placing my feet on my home soil, I wanted to lift up my face without shame.

JONAH

For a moment, I had the sea to myself, standing one last time on the rocky spit where the fish flushed me out as vomit. The breeze of early morning spun off the gray waves and whipped around my face, a brush of familiar comfort I'd found in the last weeks. The air was different than that at home. It cleansed me in a way I couldn't explain. Somehow, I was fortified simply by being on the shore.

I needed that strength for the days ahead.

My time in the village had been one of healing beyond my body, though healing was not complete. The wounds inside me had not been covered in a balm that removed the sting of remembering what I had done. There was no putting thoughts aside as I rested for long hours, no refusing to think about my actions as the dark nights hovered above me.

Unsettled with my past, it occupied my thoughts along with those of what lay ahead. The journey wouldn't be simple. I didn't want to admit it to anyone, but I was scared.

And alone.

Lifting my arms to the heavens, I prayed. "Set my feet on the correct path. Shield me from harm." The words were laced in shame. I should have listened and obeyed the first time. How foolish to believe the voice wouldn't follow me beyond the promised land. How utterly ridiculous to think I could simply run from the Lord and save my people from the hands of the Assyrians. Who was I but dust? God could have sent another in my place.

He didn't.

There was mercy greater than my sins. Lungs full of the salty air proved it.

I looked at the carved image of myself that had been intricately formed by a villager, then threw it into the sea. I was no one to be worshipped, or even respected.

Nothing had changed in God's command because of my flight to Joppa. I was starting toward Nineveh today as I should have been weeks ago. The choice of disobedience, that agonizing conclusion that I had no option, led me to tear down the stones where God was honored. That was rash, done in anger and frustration.

What had Michal thought when she found it?

Leaving without saying anything had been impulsive, and hurtful. She rose in the morning to find me gone. Michal was left alone to tell Ethan, and all the children, that their father had left in the night and she didn't know why. Or where. Or if he would return. I left her with a tremendous burden.

I wanted to explain my reasoning to her. At the time, I couldn't make myself wake her up. Sitting in the shade of the fishing village one night, as the sun dropped under the waves, I forced myself to accept the truth, why I had really pushed her aside before I left. Michal would have convinced me to follow the calling. She would want me, no, expect me, to please the Lord and not be found doubting his intentions.

I hadn't wanted to be convinced, or convicted, into doing what was right. I didn't want her wisdom seeping in and adding to my guilt. I wanted to act according to my own heart, and that was one that despised the Assyrians.

Had the decision not to include her been wrong? Yes, I could see it now, of course. Her heart was softer than mine despite the brutal wars and rampages of pagan nations. There were woman and children to be remembered, she'd say, and hatred solved nothing. Vengeance belonged to God.

Michal would propel me toward Nineveh if that's what I was told to do.

I was the prophet. I was the one with the heart toward God, an ear for his voice and the feet to do his bidding. If anyone wanted to stay on the path of righteousness, it was supposed to be me. Day after day, I went to my place of prayer, I listened to the complaints of the people, I spoke of truth and the ways of living justly. I had done so originally of my own passion, but as the years passed, it was Michal's steadfast loyalty to both me and the Lord that I found reason to continue.

And yet, I had no lasting regrets in accepting the call to be a prophet and carry news of victory to my people. It was a good beginning. I wished I could accept the news I had to carry this time.

Tarshish was across the waters to the west of where I now stood, and Nineveh across the desert to the east. I had been given the opportunity to turn myself around. I had said yes to the Lord and would fulfil the vow. I would go to Nineveh.

Looking at the great waters, peace washed over my spirit. The sea had given me a second birth, a chance to redeem myself before my God. I wasn't the son of Dagon, but I had been reborn. Like a dead man entombed, I had risen anew, bleached white in the fires of rebellion. Outwardly anyhow. I hoped the burning had removed the rebellious sin still present in my soul.

JONAH

The camel was made to kneel so I could climb onto the elaborate saddle, a tiny square room strapped onto the back of the beast. An awning could be raised and lowered so I didn't burn in the sunlight, and there were side curtains for privacy. The caravan master had insisted I ride in the cushioned contraption, not eager to deal with a blistered passenger who was considered part god by the men who paid for the passage. Hairless and pale, I had no grounds to argue.

I gripped the side supports tightly as the camel rose up on legs that seemed too spindly to carry me, itself, and a load of provisions across the desert. The villagers cheered, witness to my ascendancy in more than mere height from the earth. They believed they had saved the child of Dagon themselves, and now would be in his favor. With the first fierce storm to wrack the village, the first withering of crops or locust infestation, I wondered what they would believe of me then.

It was not only my fare that had been covered, the village had supplied me with clothing and ample supplies for the long journey. Covered in layers of loose robes and a turban, with odd skin coloring and riding on plush cushions, I no longer feared being recognized.

And, if all went well, I would be in Nineveh in thirty days.

Then what?

Was I going to simply stand on the street and tell those barbarians they had forty days until the Hebrew God destroyed them? No man welcomes condemnation. Not finding death at the bottom of the sea, I would surely find it on the streets of the wicked city.

The camel fell in line with the dozens of others. Chants of

reverence followed me as the caravan moved away from the coast on a gradual climb. The route would take us over the mountains, climbing and descending, until we reached the sands of the desert. Once across, we'd descend into the valley where the mighty Euphrates carved its way, then on to the rolling hills and fertile plains near the Tigris, where Nineveh flanked the riverbank. It was plenty of time to contemplate where I had been and where I was going, and how I intended to proceed once we arrived.

God wanted Nineveh to receive the prophecy of doom. If the end result was annihilation, no other nation would dare strike up against Israel. Her enemies would fear the Lord God.

I could accept my own death if that were the plan. If the prophesy led to the glorification of my people and my God, I'd feel the honor of righteous duty. There would be no shame. The fact that I left without word would be forgotten in light of the act of heroism. I would be remembered for walking into the jaws of death to save my people.

I adjusted my garments and settled into the cushions lining the box shaped compartment, a sigh escaping. I doubted the obedience on my part would end with Nineveh's destruction. The people might actually listen to me, and repent. Isn't that what God intended when he told me to go and prophesy? He was giving them a chance to live.

All prophets in Israel understood the nature of such a message. The call of doom was a call for repentance. Man provoked God's wrath, and man could revoke it. Mercy was always a possibility. At least, in my homeland. Would Nineveh allow itself to be humbled? Even so, would it matter in a land where God wasn't worshipped? I had no way of knowing. I had never imagined there were second chances for anyone other than his chosen ones.

For all I had experienced, from the belly of a fish to the back of a camel, I still didn't want to go to Nineveh. Being willing and being obedient weren't the same in my heart. I wanted my own people to prevail without the threats of war and destruction that constantly loomed in the shadow of the Assyrian empire.

In obedience to the one more powerful than all gods, I would go and speak, but if there was to be compassion for the people of Nineveh, it would have to be supplied by God. There was none inside of me.

MICHAL

A cool cloth on my forehead helped me wake up. I was on a cushion in the house, Timna hovering above me. I sat up and grabbed her arm. "Ethan?"

She smoothed my hair with her hand, still fragrant with the mint she had pressed into the compress. "Adin is organizing a team to search. You fainted only minutes ago."

I breathed in deeply a couple of times, making sure the blackness was gone, then stood. Timna held my arm until she was certain I wouldn't drop again, then handed me a shawl and tossed one over her own shoulders. She knew I wouldn't remain home if my son was outside alone.

"I want to go to the hill," I said. "I want to start there."

Lighting a lantern, we hurried to the high point and called for Ethan. My voice carried to the hills, absorbed into the fading light without a response. From the land below, Ethan's name rose to me from other voices calling out. Spots of light emerged from homes and spread out, weaving through the fields and pastures. We were searching for my son as we had for my husband. And Jonah was dead. I sat abruptly on a stone as the darkness threatened me again.

I could not lose them both.

Timna's arm wrapped around me, her knobby hand rubbed my arm. "God of the heavens, help us," she prayed. "Bring the boy home."

We remained on the hill, watching, praying. The moon was high overhead when we heard a distant whistle, then saw lantern and torch lights converge towards one point in the valley.

"Home, Michal. We need to go there and wait. If they've found him, they'll bring him to you."

She read my thoughts, knowing I was ready to dash through the night and see for myself. Timna was protecting me from that, not knowing what the men had found. Lion tracks had been observed for several weeks, sheep taken and devoured, and while one cat had been trapped, signs of others remained.

Lydia waited for me at the house. I leaned on her, allowing myself to drop any form of resilience I usually wore in times of trouble. There was no energy reserved inside me to show a strength I didn't feel. I needed Jonah, to hold me and assure me our son would be fine. I needed to absorb the strength of a husband whose own strength came from above. A woman is stronger when fortified by both God and her husband, the strength of the three strands not easily broken. But Jonah wasn't there, and never would be again.

"There they are," Timna pointed to lights coming our direction. She and Lydia ran to the returning search party. Adin was moving swiftly with Ethan cradled in his arms, the other men lighting his way so he wouldn't stumble. I thanked the God of the heavens. My firstborn son wouldn't hurry towards me if his little brother no longer lived.

Adin took Ethan inside and placed him gently on a pallet. "I sent for the physician," he said to me, then softly to my daughter, "Get bandages."

Ethan's eyes were closed but I knew he wasn't merely sleeping. There was a pallor to his skin I'd never seen. He breathed quickly, as if he couldn't get enough air.

Timna and Lydia dropped beside me with rolls of fabric and a pot of water. We unwrapped the blanket that cocooned my son, exposing a long gash across his belly. Blood saturated the blanket and his shredded tunic.

"He was wedged in a crevice of the rock face by the river. I think he was hiding." My oldest son stopped to gauge how I was responding to the report.

"Go on," I said.

He nodded. "A lion or bear, perhaps. Or he may have been cut by a rock. He's lost a lot of blood, Mother."

I sat numbly, stroking my son's forehead as he was cleaned and the gashes, one deep and two superficial, were rinsed and temporarily bound to staunch the loss of more blood. The physician arrived and irrigated the wound again before pulling out a bone needle and hemp threads. The resulting sutures were like mountains on my son's soft belly, an angry range with streams of blood.

We sat around the pallet and watched Ethan's chest rise and fall, rise and fall. Ointments to stave off infection and bandaging worked with the stitching to stem the loss of fluid from his body. His color was no better when the physician stood to leave, but was no worse.

"I'll be back in the morning," the man said. "But send for me if he weakens any more, or if the blood starts running again."

"He won't get worse," I said, to myself mostly. "He will live."

He had to live. I made a promise to his mother the day he was placed in my arms, a promise to protect the child and raise him in the ways of our people. I took him into my heart as my own to honor her as much as save her little lamb.

Brushing his hair back, I traced the birthmark above his eye. With his paleness, the dark mark was obvious. Otherwise, it had faded as the boy grew, blending with his darkening skin. He looked no different than any of my boys, no different than any of the Hebrew children.

But he was. This child hadn't come from Gath-hepher, or any

nearby villages. He hadn't come from the tribe of Zebulon, or from Israel at all. His lineage was one I had never revealed to anyone. Alone when the man arrived with the baby in his arms, I sealed my lips to the full truth of his heritage.

The young foreigner had waited at the door after he knocked, choosing not to leave his cargo on the step and disappear like so many others. He studied my face before he spoke. It was obvious he wasn't local when he did so, unable to disguise his accent. He had not come from the nearby regions.

"Michal, daughter of Zedekiah?"

"Yes, I am she."

He handed me the baby without looking away from the tiny face, then ran a tender finger on its chin before abruptly stepping back.

"Wait," I said. "Please, tell me what the child is called."

The young man paused but said nothing.

"I have bread coming from the oven. Stay, eat and be refreshed."

My requests went unheeded. He said nothing more, returning to a fine horse tethered to an olive tree and galloping away without looking back.

The baby was healthy, and his skin rubbed in perfumed oil, the jasmine scent blending with his baby ones. Covered with a simple cloth, I found an inner blanket made of fine silky linen, embroidered in the winged lions of Assyria. I shuddered at its presence in my home, and burned it in the cooking fires. But my new son, I held to my heart. He knew nothing of the atrocities of his homeland.

Jonah returned from Bethel three days later, welcoming and naming his newest son.

Later, I heard that a young woman had inquired where to find me early that morning, asking a field hand on the outskirts of town. He thought nothing of it, sending her my direction, assuming it was to see the prophet. A small band of travelers were seen leaving Gath-hepher the same day, returning the direction they had come. Their provisions had been replenished, their horses watered and fed, and the group was gone, seemingly without purpose.

Because of their accent, it was assumed they were spies. Assyrian spies. Harsh comments were woven into conversations of the group's intentions. When asked if I had seen the woman or a group of foreigners, I said no. No one asked specifically if I'd seen just one man or if he'd brought me a babe, and I left the information unspoken. The innocent child didn't deserve to grow up despised. He would be considered an enemy though only three or four months old.

Despite the guilt, I didn't tell my husband whose blood coursed within the baby he adopted. Jonah hated the Assyrians, and I feared he would reject the boy because of it. So many infants had been left with us, no one connected his arrival with that of the travelers. Ethan was circumcised and had never been anything but a child of the land of Israel.

It was more than a year later when I made a connecting bridge between my past and the present. At my father's home for a wedding banquet, I was remembering my sister, missing her from a deep place in my heart. Ethan was asleep in my arms, and I wanted Miriam to see this beautiful boy, to know him and love him with me. My mind was jumping back and forth between the two. Her laughter. His cooing smiles. I thought of the blanket. I thought of the raid, the same colors and emblems on the linens as the warriors carried on their banners.

This baby came from the land that took my sister from me, I knew full well. It was those few words of the man at my door that came back as I rocked my son that day. He had not asked for Jonah, the prophet, or Michal, wife of the prophet. He asked for Michal, daughter of Zedekiah. The babe was sent to me specifically, not having anything to do with my husband's status.

I had assumed the mother of the child was among the travelers, that the father was ashamed of the mark over his son's eye. In a heart stopping realization, I wasn't so sure any longer. Perhaps the young woman asking for me wasn't the mother after all, merely a nursemaid for the journey.

It was then my heart shed itself of the black cloak of pain that it had worn since the raid. For all the reasons I knew it couldn't be possible, I believed that my sister was alive.

And the child in my arms, her son.

I had lied to protect this boy and would give my own life to save him now. No, my Ethan couldn't die.

There was nothing I could do for Miriam except that which mattered most. I could protect her child and see him live.

JONAH

Travel on the camel's back was wearisome. Hours of doing nothing but think about my past and my future were harder than those I'd had hauling stones or dredging ditches. Fear, regret, shame, and a homesickness I had never felt so keenly were threads weaving themselves together into one blanket.

As my mood plummeted, I had to force myself to think on the saving mercy of God, and of my children, my wife. I brought to mind the countless hours counseling those who came to me, and teaching about righteousness to those who didn't. Those threads needed to be accounted for to keep me from despair. There was good in my life.

Michal was one of the good decisions. I had never known her to willingly disregard the Laws of Moses. She was as truthful and hardworking as any woman I'd known.

Her sister would have been a good wife, too, although I wondered now if I could have provided the variety in life she so craved. She was enamored by my status and would have found me a disappointment in time, I felt, the tedium of my responsibilities not the adventure she wanted.

Thoughts of Miriam put the Assyrian raiders in the front of my mind, with the anger that always came along side. I failed to save her, failed to defeat even one man. God could have forewarned me. He didn't. I would never understand that decision.

We combed the roads for days afterward, searching for any who may have escaped death, and were injured or hiding. Many good men and women of Gath-hepher had been piled and burned by the retreating warriors, so identifying all the slain became impossible. I used to wonder if Miriam had survived, then prayed that she didn't. I would rather she be dead than in the hands of the Ninevite beasts. She didn't deserve that fate. No one did.

The settling sun allowed me to get off the saddle and walk the last length to the oasis or next camp site. Picturing Ethan in my mind was easy that time of day. He was never eager to go inside in the evening, stones for skipping still held tight in grubby hands. He would drag his feet and find excuses until Michal gave him the mother-eye, then drop his bounty and run into her arms.

Ethan, my delight. It was for him and his children and his children's children that I fled from the Lord. I wanted him to understand my actions, that I hadn't left him for any reason other than my love for him. Preserving Israel was for my family, my name, my nation.

How would he ever know? I doubted I would return from this message of doom.

The boy was given to us by God. A servant girl provided his nourishment those early years, yet the bond between him and Michal was tight. My wife knew Ethan would be her last child to raise to manhood, so she favored him, clinging to him sometimes as if he were made of fragile clay. He wasn't, being a typical boy made of curiosity and quest, and of resilience. He was sure on his feet and quick in his mind. He would be fine without the close tether Michal kept on him. He would be a fine man one day.

And he would be raised without a father.

The thought uncapped my shame once again, the feeling that I had done wrong by my little son. I hoped one day he would understand why I left him, that it was because I wanted him to have life to an old age.

Ethan would grow strong and wise with the help of his brothers. He didn't need me. It stabbed my soul to think he wouldn't remember me at some point as he grew, that I would be a shadow of someone who once tickled his belly and made him laugh. It wasn't something I could change now.

The full moon brought light and shadow to the oasis, dimming the stars. I prayed for my family as I walked among the palms towards the waters. My boy was safe in Gath-hepher with Michal, and for that I was grateful. I was likely walking toward my death at the hands of the Ninevites, but at least I was alone. My family would be fine without me.

MICHAL

Caleb stood outside my house soon after sunrise. His voice carried through the window as he and Timna talked about Ethan's status. Nervousness fluttered in my chest. I hadn't seen him since the day he confessed that it was me he wanted to be near when he came by on some contrived errand all those years ago. It was still me he would take under his wing and protect now.

His Beckah was dead, and so was my Jonah.

I sat at Ethan's bedside and listened to Timna's weary voice, praising God above that my son had managed to live through the night. I hadn't been certain whether either of us would. Had he died, I would have as well. My heart couldn't take another weight without collapsing, crushing me beyond any ability I had to remain strong.

Ethan appeared to be sleeping. His chest rose and fell evenly, his skin no longer a grim pallor. The coolness remained however, and he had opened his eyes only one time in the night, seeing beyond me and everyone else in the room. "Father," was the name he whispered.

Seeing Jonah beyond the grave was more than I could manage. I grabbed Ethan's hands and spoke to him, putting my face so close that all he could see was me, if his eyes opened again. I had not abandoned him, I said. He needed to live, to stay with me and his brothers. I didn't want him to join his father in death.

Timna had pried my hands away. "He's looking for his father in this life, Michal."

I sat back and made myself breathe in the added pain. He wanted his father and his father wasn't there. The one request I could never fulfil.

Morning came and my son was alive. The physician knelt beside him, hands tenderly wiping off dried blood from the little brown belly. The stitches closing the gashes were holding, the oozing less bloody. It was infection we needed to worry about now, and for the days to come. His body was already working to replace the blood it lost.

"He needs water, and nourishment." The old man had been tending to the sick and injured of our village since before I was born. He placed the back of his hand on Ethan's forehead, and held it there, not confirming fever nor denying it. "And a fig poultice over the wounds twice a day."

"Should I try to wake him?"

He shook his head and turned his hand over to stroke my son's cheek. "Not yet. Allow him to sleep for now. If he wakes up on his own, help him drink clear broth. He needs sleep mostly, and prayers."

"Will he be all right?" I had asked that same question yesterday.

The physician didn't mince the truth into acceptable bites that were easily swallowed. "I don't know. He lost so much blood. His insides may stop functioning properly, Michal, and we don't know yet if his mind is damaged. Infection could take him from us even if the wounds heal together again."

I turned from the kindness in his expression.

"I can't do anything more. Send for me if he wakes up, or if there are any significant changes. If he seems to be in more pain, or his breathing is labored again."

"Yes. I will."

He put a hand on my shoulder. "I'm sorry about this, and about Jonah. You need to sleep and eat. And cry. Your family can watch over Ethan for a while." He nodded toward my sleeping child. "He'll need you to be strong if he does wake up. Watch yourself for him, hmm?"

I nodded as he turned and left, feeling like the same little girl he had to bandage a few times in the past, not wanting to sleep and heal while my brothers were scaling rocks and exploring caves without me. I didn't want to miss something important, like discovering fox pups in the pasture or the desiccated bones of some long-dead beast.

Lydia slipped into the room and helped me to my feet, reading my thoughts. "We'll wake you with any changes."

Outside, the weeping of mourners drenched the atmosphere with the grimness of sorrow. Dressed in plain, rough sackcloth, their numbers were increasing. For a moment, I was filled with fury. How dare anyone pronounce Ethan's death while his heart still thumped in his chest? Could they not pray for his life rather than prepare for his funeral?

I turned to ask Jonah to send them away, but he wasn't there. It was my daughter with me and she too was dressed in the garments of grief.

The tirade rising inside my head fell away. They were here because of Jonah. It was the mourning time for my husband.

I had no body for burial.

Jonah's remains were in the great sea, swept into the waters where I would never see him again, never have his bones to bury with his father's fathers.

Lydia took my arm. "Timna will sit with Ethan. I'll help you change."

I allowed her to guide me into the next room, where I took off my crumpled clothing and put on the one made of dark goat hair, stiff and loose, falling from my shoulders in a straight line. A simple woven hemp belt lifted the hem from the earth. I had lost my head covering the evening before, not caring who saw me uncovered, and not bothering now to find another.

My daughter ran a finger comb through my long dark hair with its graying streaks. "Do you want me to cut it?"

I dropped onto a bench and sighed. A sign of my grief, I needed to cut the length by at least half, as was custom for the new widows of Gath-hepher. Half of me was gone, and I would show my sorrow with an exposed head of mutilated and unkempt hair for thirty days. Unattractive and unavailable, without ceremonial cleansing, expectations of me would be limited.

I nodded at Lydia. "Cut it, please." I didn't want Ethan to wake up and see his mother in a state of mourning, in the clothes of death and ashes of sorrow smeared into her skin. I didn't want him to smell the continuous aroma of food as it was prepared and ask why we did so. I didn't want him to hear the wailing that would permeate our walls for the next seven days. His rich brown eyes needed to see beauty and his ears, laughter when he awoke. But that was out of my control. For the next week, the good people of this town would fill my home and be my comfort, following the traditions of our ancestors.

As desperately as I needed Ethan's lashes to flutter open, for him to return to us as he was before, part of me wanted him to remain asleep for a little while longer. There could be peace in oblivion, silence in an atmosphere screaming with grief.

MICHAL

Caleb's head was beside Ethan's on the low bed, his body draped onto the floor in an awkward position. His hand held the boy's in a loose hold as they traveled in dreams side by side. I couldn't help but wonder if my friend already saw this boy as his own.

He had been praying during his watch through the night. Hearing him from beyond the door, I had fallen to sleep on a straw pallet, only a few hours, but without desperate fears awakening me. It was the brightness of a full moon that nudged my eyes open this time, so I got up and tiptoed to my son's side.

I had moved him upstairs to a quiet corner of the house, and allowed no mourners near the room except for the ones maintaining vigil. Flowing in and out on waves of tears, neighbors and family prepared the endless amount of food required to accommodate those who came to sit in sorrow with me. They did the chores, recited words of King David, and slept in the empty spaces of my home. In a few more days, they would be gone. I both welcomed the stillness to come, and dreaded it.

"He's not hot." Caleb's soft comment found me on the other side of the bed, where my own hand was rubbing Ethan's arm.

"Or clammy," I said, not realizing he was awake. My other hand automatically found my head and ran along my chopped hair, self-conscious of its exposure. In the darkness, I knew it was foolish, and I knew my appearance wasn't of any matter. Not now. Not in the present circumstances.

Caleb saw the movements shadowed on the wall behind the

candle light. "I remember when you cut it off before," he said. "I cried when I saw you. Your heart was crushed and there was nothing I could do."

"I couldn't believe Miriam was gone. I wanted to die myself."

"No weddings, no celebrations for months. Mourning affected every home in some way. An entire city in sackcloth."

"I barely remember those days, all the burials. I know I went to them, stood with Mother and held her as she wept. She told me later I was numb, and thought I was lost to her too. I don't recall any details about the mourning."

Caleb shifted his body so he was leaning on the wall. I slid to the floor too, the bed between us. He was quiet, breathing and thinking of those days, I presumed. "We didn't bury your sister. Like your husband, it isn't right," he said.

No one liked to speak about the horror the town experienced. There had been several mass burials where no one was certain who was being committed to the earth. The brutality of the Assyrians made sure of it, the sport of dismemberment and disfigurement their manner of conquest. Along the trail behind the raiders, our men found burning heaps of the dead, and a few others, intentionally left alive with wounds that attracted the lions. In the end, we didn't know for certain what each person's fate had entailed.

Miriam was one of them.

I voiced words I hadn't asked anyone in several decades. "Do you think she's alive?"

Silence, except the breathing of the three of us in the room. I waited for his reply.

"I can't say I didn't think about that at one time."

"Not anymore?"

"No. If she had been able to come home, she would have."

"I asked my parents. Asked the city leaders. They all said she was dead. They said it didn't matter whether or not we buried her body, she had been taken from her people and to us, she was dead. Miriam was never going to return to me and the life she had. Even if we found her, she would have been violated and Jonah would have to break the engagement. Miriam would be worse than dead. That's what they said. Worse than dead."

Caleb breathed in and out forcefully through his nose. "They didn't want you to have hopes that would never be met. Didn't want you to wait for a sister who would never return."

"I don't believe Jonah would have held the rape against her. He would have married her."

"She may have chosen otherwise. And he, well, the leaders of the city might not have allowed him to do so. We'll never know."

I reached my hand to Ethan's side and tucked the hide under a leg that had found its way out. If my boy lived, he needed a father. I didn't want to consider marrying again, yet I might have to at some point, and this friend of mine would be a logical choice. He would provide for us, and welcome us in his home. Caleb would see that Ethan was raised in the ways of Israel's God.

One thing I didn't know. Would Caleb accept an Assyrian child under his roof? He wasn't as vocal of his hatred as Jonah, but that meant nothing. A caldron boiled with or without a lid.

Caleb broke into my thoughts with his own pointed question. "Do you think your sister still lives?"

I bit down on my lip. My feelings had never even been expressed out loud, and I didn't want anyone to invalidate what my heart needed to believe. Somehow, keeping it as my secret made it true.

"Yes." The word came out tentatively, the confession releasing a small measure of pressure.

"You didn't have a body to anoint with spices and wrap in shrouds. That was difficult for you, I imagine, not to have the finality of seeing Miriam without a beating heart, and not to have a tomb to visit and remember."

"Yes. That made it less than real, that I'd never see her again. I saw blood on her scarf. I washed it out, scrubbing and scrubbing until I nearly wore holes in the fabric. But Jonah was bleeding from the wounds he sustained. There was blood on the street. Blood everywhere. I don't know if any of it was Miriam's blood."

"Hmm. She was beautiful. She might have been a captive. It wouldn't have been a good life, and not likely a long one."

It was selfish to keep my sister to myself. I ran my fingertips on Ethan's forehead, her offspring. I had accepted her death for years upon years. Then this Assyrian babe was given to me, specifically to me and foolish or not, I still believed he was the child of Miriam's womb.

Was it a foolish notion to keep her alive in that way? Perhaps, yet I didn't want to be convinced otherwise. No one else needed to know what I believed about the woman who gave Ethan his life. Not even Caleb. Not yet. I didn't want to hear about Miriam being dead to me again, not from anyone.

It had been wrong to keep it from Jonah, I knew. Would love for Miriam's child be stronger than his hatred of the Assyrian blood? In all honesty, I hadn't wanted him to imagine that Miriam was alive. I didn't want to share her with Jonah. As much as I loved my sister, I needed my husband to love me as his only wife.

Ethan moaned softly and fidgeted under the covers. Caleb rubbed the boy's shoulder, soothing him back to sleep. I couldn't help but think about a future that held the three of us as family.

JONAH

The walls to the great capital of the Assyrian empire stretched along the Tigris River in both directions, majestic in themselves, gleaming white in the sun, crenellations capping the top with perfect symmetry to protect the armed warriors on patrol. Buildings were staggered behind the walls, taller than any I'd seen in Israel, windows open to the morning breeze. Some roofs were colorfully tiled, others were topped with floral gardens and lush foliage. Tall palms swayed on the river banks outside the walls, carved boats floated lazily in place, tied to its verdant shores as patrons fished and swam and enjoyed the refreshing flow.

I couldn't pull my eyes from the splendor of Nineveh. It rose from the desert floor as we approached, and I wanted to believe it was a mirage, that barbarians wouldn't have a city so grand, so impressive. How could the ruthless nation live in such a place, breathtaking in its beauty? How could they be so, so – I struggled for the description and settled on the last word I thought I'd ever use to describe Nineveh: civilized.

Its impregnability alone made sense.

The caravan was stopped on the road, in line with others waiting to be inspected and cleared for entrance into the city. Thirty-seven days from the fishing village to the Tigris, I was at the threshold of my enemy. After weeks of prayer and preparation, trying to set my mind firmly on the task ahead, I was still not ready to set one foot inside the massive gate. I deserved death, but couldn't embrace it.

"You sick?" The caravan master had been up and down the row

of camels and merchants in his care several times already, anxious to move ahead now that they'd finally arrived. The brusque man had shed his irritated nature at the first glimpse of the final destination and was now on the verge of being friendly. The journey had been easy, he'd mentioned numerous times along the way. No illnesses of man or beast, no bandits, no foul weather. He gave credit to Baal but I knew otherwise. It was my God who made the passage favorable.

Not comfortable though. I arched my back and stretched out the aches that had had settled into every joint. "No, I'm fine," I said.

"You're whiter than usual, is why I asked."

I pulled up a sleeve and glanced at the sparse, downy hairs emerging in patches on skin that was spotty, like someone started to paint the white with a fine haired brush but left the job incomplete. The evidence of my seclusion within the fish was diminishing, and I hoped I wouldn't stand out as leprous or contagious with an unknown ailment. "I'm fine," I repeated.

"Been here before?"

"First time," I said. "It's not what I expected."

The gruff laugh released a wad of mint leaf. He wiped the remnant from his lips with the back of his hand. "No, never is to newcomers. Even if you hear tales about this place, it's a shock. See why I come here, though? Trading is good. Women are better than good."

"And safe?"

"The women?"

"The city."

The man shrugged. "The women, no. The city, not completely. Mind your business and no one'll bother you." He jabbed a finger at my chest. "Just what is your business here? You going to tell them you're the spawn of Dagon? Might get you in good with the king. Or his harem. They like that fish god here."

Smiling at the man's enthusiasm, I wished I was looking to make my fortune or find some pleasure, anything rather than what I had come to do. "My God sent me."

The man's eyebrows raised up on his forehead. "I thought you said you were one of those Hebrews. That God wouldn't send you here, would he? For what reason?"

"I have a message."

The man peered at me intently with slits for eyes, reading into the words that I didn't say out loud. He shook his head. "They aren't going to like it, are they?"

"No."

He sighed and ran a hand over his scruffy beard. "Should I leave now, then?" His tone was suddenly somber. "Are you going to do something awful inside there?"

"I'm not a god. I can't do anything to Nineveh but speak what my deity tells me to speak."

"Should I leave? I've treated you fairly. Tell me the truth."

The words of God that I tried to drown in the sea came trickling back into my mouth. The impression that burned into my soul was searing my conscience like it had the first time, at the altar. I couldn't keep the message inside any longer.

As I spoke, I knew the days of the Assyrian city were now numbered. "You have forty days. In forty days the Lord my God will destroy Nineveh."

My heart was thumping against my ribs, mouth dry, tears forming in my eyes. I was suddenly overwhelmed with the power of the message, and overwhelmed with my own sin, my own need for repentance and mercy from a God who hates evil and violence. I was overwhelmed with the enormity of my task, and even more so, the enormity of my God.

The caravan master chewed on a gritty fingernail, looking between me and the city walls. I waited for him to speak, to ask about my deity, my people, how I knew what was to come. I had never needed to explain the history of my people and our ways before. Every Israelite knew their origins. How was I going to explain it to this man? Start from the Book of Beginnings? From Adam or Moses, or jump ahead to Abraham? Or David, or just my own history?

He grinned and spit out a ripped nail. "Forty days? So I get thirty nine then I best be getting' my self out of there, huh?"

I released the breath I was holding and punched his shoulder. He believed me with no discourse what so ever. "Be long gone," I said. "I don't know what will happen, how far reaching."

A shrill whistle sounded at the far end of our caravan. The man responded, leaving to move the line forward.

I climbed onto the saddle and pulled the drapery closed around the tiny room, needing this last moment alone to pray for strength and wisdom and the power of the Almighty to help me. As the beast rose and stepped toward the gate, I changed my mind. I didn't want the solitude so yanked the fabric back. I had to see the sky and the trees, hear the river and feel the air on my face. I wanted to taste my freedom, in case I never did so again.

PERSIS

Caravans from the coast of Phoenicia were our favorite. The other wives and I had permission to attend the bazaar alone, without children to teach and train and manage. Our husband won a dozen stallions in a bet and was in a generous mood when he came home in the night, granting the favor for the next day and promising gold coins for each of us. His losses were insignificant in comparison to the ebony beasts he intended to train for chariot races. Mara, his lost gamble, was hauled from her bed and taken away without farewells or the shedding of tears over her change in ownership.

The rest of us forced smiles and coos of affection for the man who so easily traded his secondary wives away. No one wanted to be the next woman to be here one meal and gone the next, the familiar providing a kinder life than one of the unknown.

Tariq handed out his coins and instructions. To one, buy herself earrings of hammered gold. Another was to search for perfume of the Orient that captured the lotus blossom scent, and another was sent to buy herself a hand mirror and Egyptian kohl for her eyes. I was the last one to receive an allotment, more than double that of the other wives. My husband pressed the coins into my hand and didn't release his grip on my wrist.

"And you, dear Persis," he said. "Find yourself the sheerest of the silks, indigo like the sea, and slippers, and something jeweled for your forehead. This will please Dagon."

I forced a smile, fully comprehending the threat. I would be dressed exquisitely for the occasion of my own death, to honor the

246

god and to show off my husband's wealth. Since my beating and his vow to have me sacrificed, I slept fitfully, awake with the torment of not knowing if the threat was an idle one or would seek me out in some unanticipated moment.

Coin purses full and surrounded by guards, we left the estate in a wagon. The chatter was subdued, the gifts a small token of pleasure compared to the loss of Mara. Her name would not be mentioned. There were too many guards on horseback with ears trained to hear and distort gossip. Our friend was another one to be remembered in our minds and discretely searched for in the markets only.

I would be one of those women. A face to be forgotten by the children I bore, a name to be scrubbed from the lips of all who knew me. My life had been of no purpose to anyone. Even the girls I tried to protect were eventually thrust into the sullied ways of the Assyrians. I had saved none, only delayed their fate. I was a pawn in a society despised by my father's god, no matter how I longed to be free of the ties that bound me among them.

A deep sigh escaped my lips, followed by warning glances in my direction. I quickly steered my thoughts to the trivial concerns of the moment. "I do hope we're the first to arrive, before the crowds accumulate. Should we try to stay together or split into groups?" The wives took up the discussion, allowing me to present a mask of interest while retreating to my memories.

I had always loved the arrival of caravans. They passed through my village only a few times a year so it was an event, anticipated and celebrated. Flamboyant traders with faces full of smiles, donkeys stomping up dust, spices of all colors spilling from pots and releasing exotic aromas thickly in the air, barter and delighted squeals of village children wafting through temporary stalls and laden wagons. It's where I touched silk for the first time, heard a mizmar wailing in the wind, and secretly tasted a bite of roasted pig when Mother had her back turned.

The traveling market was dangerous and open ended. Caravan merchants didn't know me, so I could be anyone, infinitely wealthy or orphaned and alone. Blind at one stall, my open hands would be filled with sweets. Limping past another, I'd receive a sympathetic splash of perfume. I used to imagine myself hiding in a wagon and leaving one day, finding adventure beyond the borders of my homeland. Never would I have imagined how much pain would follow me when I was eventually forced to leave.

Mostly, I loved the trinkets offered for sale, the worthless baubles reflecting sunlight or painted in a rainbow of hues. The statues were my favorite, tiny figures of animals and creatures, some half human and half beast, some with multiple arms or too many eyes. I wanted a collection of them to play with, and had been disappointed more than once when told no.

I hadn't fully understood the idols then. As I grew, it became clear, that these miniature figures represented more than mere child's toys. They stood in defiance to the One God of the Hebrews. My father's God had no graven image, and the tiny figures were an abomination to him. When I got caught touching one, I had to undergo the ceremonial cleansing and discipline of my father as if I had actually prayed to it.

So much had changed. I lived among the shimmery, jewel encrusted images now. They towered above the patrons of Nineveh's temples and occupied nooks in every home. Standing, sitting, or reclining on street corners, covering merchant's tables, I was constantly in their presence, and constantly aware of being unclean.

No longer were they beautiful and inviting. I would trade all of them for a dusty street in a small village, where only the Hebrew God was worshipped.

I leaned out of the wagon and looked down the wide paved street that would take us to the heart of Nineveh. The city was immense, requiring three days of travel if one wanted to trace her perimeter. All roads eventually connected to the markets however, the center of commerce and trade. Every sort of patron would converge on the train of camels and canvas covered stalls, all colors of skin and language, all manners and customs and religions.

All but one. Never in the Assyrian capital had I heard the name of the One God spoken in reverence. He was cursed and mocked and questioned, never worshipped.

I would not allow that fact to sully my mood, keeping memories of caravans in the forefront of my thoughts. They allowed a glimmer of joy to poke through. Today's merchants originated at the great sea, so may have passed through my homeland. However unlikely, I wanted to believe the traveling marketplace came with the dust of Gath-hepher on its hooves.

JONAH

Armed guards strode the length of the caravan, searching for an enemy hidden among the crates or a reason to stir trouble. I had been warned not to provoke them, not to give them reason to demand more entrance fee than already required. It wasn't uncommon to be denied entry until bribes or fees changed hands without being officially documented.

It was obvious they weren't interested in picking a fight with our group. Having been forewarned that the son of Dagon was on this particular caravan, the Ninevite soldiers poked at linens and peered into cages as a matter of formality. Slowing as they approached, it was unbridled curiosity cast my way rather than offensive comments. Repulsed and confused by my appearance, they remained civil in case the rumors regarding me were true.

I had no illusions about my humanity but said nothing. For the first time, I recognized the advantage of the misconception. These men wouldn't forbid my entrance to the city if they believed I had powers or connections to a deity of some sort.

We were given entrance into their city after the brief inspection, passing over the Tigris and through the tall gates without harassment.

I sat on the saddle, craning my neck in all directions. The stone and brick buildings were exquisite, architecture unlike any I had ever seen, defying the laws of nature in their height and majesty. Many were temples with carved marble figures adorning the entrance and fragrant waves of incense spilling out the windows. Mansions nestled among the places of business, along streets paved in smooth cobbles. Magnificent gardens and spraying fountains, columned porches with bathing pools and palmed streamside benches, orchards and vineyards, it was unlike anything I'd imagined.

My mind was prepared for simple huts, for bands of barbarians in drunken brawls at all hours of the day and night, for rudeness, and filth, not elegant women in fine linen and children chasing exotic pets.

It took my breath when I recognized that I was the primitive man in that setting. I didn't kill for sport but I had none of the riches that were displayed before me. And this was on the public street. I couldn't imagine the tapestries and artwork and furnishings in the homes, or the numbers of horses and finesse of the chariots in the barns. I expected to feel intimidated by the sheer animosity of these people toward me, not by their standard of living.

Why would any of them listen to me?

The caravan stopped near an open plaza and immediately became a hive of action. Men dismounted and camels were unloaded, crates were pried open and goods displayed. Makeshift tables and tents sprung up around the courtyard with the skill of men who had performed those tasks countless times.

I dismounted and stood in the mix. Once delivered, my voyage with the caravan was over. The payment by the seaside villagers carried me no further than the street where I stood. Other than the clothes I wore, I had only a knapsack with a few remaining garments. I had no plan for obtaining food, no place to sleep, no money to sustain me.

"Need directions?"

I turned to one of my fellow travelers. The merchant had been kind to me the entire journey, himself a nomad with no place to call home other than the place he happened to be. He alone seemed to see me as only a man with one unbelievable story rather than a god of the waters. I wasn't certain he believed any of my history, but we had passed countless hours on the sandy dunes with our conversations, and he hadn't yet ridiculed me.

"No. Or, maybe yes. I'm not sure where to begin."

He had heard my story from the beginning and knew what drew me to this place I despised. He pulled a few small coins from his belt and put them in my hand. "Take these. I'll be here day and night with my jewelry until we leave again, so find me if you need more. You can sleep with us, if you want. It will be safer than any of the inns. Being alone in this city isn't advisable. But, if you anger anyone-"

"I won't bring it back here. I won't put you and the others in danger."

The man's eyes followed soldiers as they passed. "You will draw trouble though, won't you? Whether or not you try to be peaceful. You'll not be well-liked once you start telling these people what your god says to say. They might stone you before the day ends."

I breathed in deeply, well aware of the risks, both of obeying and disobeying God. "Thank you for your concern. I must do what I'm told. I am my Lord's mouthpiece."

"Even here?"

"Yes." I replied. "Even here. I'll be back by nightfall if I'm able."

I left him and walked toward a fountain we had passed a short distance back. On its broad rim, I sat and allowed the spray to cool my face, keeping to the shade and ignoring the stares of those who had followed me. There were several dozen, none daring to speak to me, merely hovering nearby. Closing my eyes, I prayed to my God and asked for his words again to fill my mouth, and the fervency to speak, no matter the outcome.

Feeling nothing but anxiety, I sat and tried to compose a message in my mind. As I did, men and women gathered with the others, subtly pointing and whispering about me. The small crowd drew the interest of city soldiers, who also regarded me from a safe distance. I said nothing. God said nothing.

By the time there were fifty-some people milling around me, a boy about Ethan's age ran up to the fountain and leaned in to splash the water about. He was followed by two men. They seemed not to notice me and continued to debate the terms of a transaction. Money was exchanged and the boy collected, one man giving him to the other.

Then God filled my mouth with fire. He unchained my tongue and didn't need to command me to speak because I was on my feet and eager to let my words be free.

"The sins of Nineveh will be her ruin!" I shouted, and clearly startled the people nearby. "The God of all creation has sent me here. He will destroy this city with all her inhabitants in forty days! Hear the words of the Lord God Almighty!"

I lowered my hand from where I had raised it, pointing at the heavens, directing my condemnation toward the men who stood drop-jawed in front of me. "You are a vile people, wicked by your own choosing and will be wiped from the earth in a breath of cleansing."

No one spoke when I finished. I waited for the soldiers to find their rile, fully expecting to be hauled to prison for disturbing the city with words of destruction. They didn't move.

"Who are you?"

The boy looked at me with the curiosity of my own son, a boy eager for truth and knowledge. "I am a prophet," I said, "Only a man, sent by God from Gath-hepher, the land of Abraham."

"What god?"

"The only God. The God of the Hebrews, of Israel."

The growing crowd gasped as one. Again I waited for the

derision, the stones hurled at my head, the swords to cut out my tongue or cut off my head.

No one moved against me. Sweat trickled down my face as I stood, watching the confusion, the trepidation building.

"A prophet of Israel, and the son of Dagon?" A woman asked.

I shook my head. "Only a prophet."

"A prophet spewed from the belly of a great fish! It was witnessed by fishermen. Listen to him. His god has power."

The crowd became animated, questions tossed around and others answering back, a momentum stirring among them. "Forty days! What shall we do?"

I knew the answer. They needed to recognize the error of their ways, see that it was wrong to be violent against the lands they conquered, wrong to molest their children and offer them to the fire. It was sin before the Creator to worship Dagon and Baal and Ishtar. The Ninevites needed to turn from their wrong doing. Repentance was all my God required. These people provoked the Lord's anger, and they could revoke it. My cry of doom was a warning that, if heeded and repentance prevailed, would come to nothing.

I didn't allow that notion of repentance to come from my lips. It was wrong of me, I knew it full well. I had spoken of the forty days until destruction as commanded. The rest was up to the Ninevites to figure out. I would not go that far to see my enemy spared.

PERSIS

I turned my eyes to the women displayed on stage, being sold to the highest bidders along with beasts and exotic birds in cages. Young, beautiful girls taken from homelands and families, from dreams and hope, made my skin shiver. If any were from my nation, I couldn't tell. They had been dressed for the sale, lined along a wall and told to be silent.

"This is my finest cloth."

I turned back to the merchant, and fingered his fabric without rushing to make a decision. The other wives had moved along the stalls while I pretended to find pleasure in choosing my death shroud. Two of my husband's men stood watch over me, as if I would run. Where could I go? No man would harbor me once he knew who I belonged to, and no woman either if she cared for her life. If I thought I'd be killed for trying to flee, I might have done so, but there were worse fates than death. The Assyrians were infamous in the surrounding lands for the tortures they devised.

My death as homage to Dagon would come by fire. In my exquisite clothing and skin brushed with powdered gold, I would be chained to a pole in the temple courtyard, the image of the god towering over me. Chants and prayers would precede the lighting of the kiln and continue long after I was pushed inside.

If I had opportunity, I'd take herbs to dull my senses first. My hand found the place in my robe where I had tucked dried poppy tears into a tiny pocket, along with the hemlock that would kill me outright if I chose to do so. I hadn't left my room without the secret stash since the day I was beaten.

I chose the most expensive fabric offered, paid the merchant. I had plenty of funds for the other items on my list, so passed the gaudy stands, seeking real treasures. Tariq would know if I disobeyed him and found lesser quality merchandise. A Phoenician jeweler smiled as I slowed to look at his colorful pieces.

"Beautiful jewels for a beautiful woman."

The man said his spiel without looking at me. His attention was down the street, at the back of a small crowd gathered there. I didn't ask what was happening. I didn't care who was pummeling who or what magic tricks were fooling the gullible to part with their money.

He tipped his head toward the gathering, an easy smile on his lips. "Son of Dagon himself over there."

A crescent of gold caught my attention, a piece to drape over my forehead, with tiny dangling chains that ended in teardrops of sapphire. "A god came shopping in Nineveh? Are your jewels truly so fine?"

He laughed at my sarcasm. "Been talking to the man myself. He came out of the sea without a speck of hair on him anywhere, covered in scales like a fish."

"A fishy man-god is good for business?"

The man shrugged. "We'll see. You buying or just trying?"

I placed the jewels on my head, feeling the weight of gold that would melt away if my husband decided to be done with me. "Buying," I said.

The man handed me a mirror. I looked back at the sad woman. She was pretty once, young and innocent. That ended one unforeseen day, shopping in the market with her sister. Buying pastries and cloth, she looked up to see her betrothed watching her discreetly from another table. The heat had climbed up her neck, she remembered, and she had to look away. Then someone screamed.

Of all the memories I wanted to keep, that day in Gath-hepher was not one of them. On the cusp of marriage, the raiders had come with swords, surging from every direction. Scarcely aware of what was happening, I was grabbed about the waist and hoisted over a shoulder. I screamed and fought, beating my fists. Kicking, clawing. One muscled arm pinned me down, the other held a weapon, and it ran with fresh blood. My head covering fell to the ground and I reached for it, and for Jonah, my betrothed. But Jonah wasn't there.

My little sister's terrified screams drew my attention to the ground by a stall that had collapsed. Jonah was rolling the tarp over, and at first, I couldn't understand what he was doing. Then I saw the black hair inside the roll. Jonah hid Michal in the awning.

As my captor took me away, I saw Jonah stand and search frantically, his head swiveling around, looking for me. I called but the noise was too loud. He didn't see me in the chaos, and then he was out of sight, and more raiders were pouring into the street between us. More swords were flashing. More of my people falling. Jonah couldn't save me then.

He couldn't come to save me later.

I held no grudge against him. Not then, not now. The men and boys of my village had all been slaughtered, I was told. Jonah, my brothers and father, all gone in one day. If any of them escaped, there still wasn't enough for an army, not one strong and swift enough to fight the Assyrian hoard. No, Jonah wasn't to blame for my life in this place.

It had not been a mission to collect slaves, but to induce fear. As far as I knew, I was the only captive who survived the entire journey back to the capital city. The others were killed or injured along the way. No good Hebrew would allow his brother to rot on the roadside, and the Assyrians knew this. Leaving a trail of the dead and wounded kept anyone with an interest in revenge too busy to take action.

My innocence was left intact, my skin untouched, a requirement for the auction. No man wanted used merchandise.

The auction house clothed me in delicate garments after cleansing my skin and weaving my hair with beads. My lips and eyes were painted and I was taught how to stand and walk and pose, like all the others being sold that day. I was the only Hebrew among them, yet we communicated with terrified eyes, all of us wishing we'd been killed already.

To my people, I was dead. Taken and married to the enemy, I no longer lived. Having breath and a beating heart meant nothing. From the moment I was whisked away, I knew I would never return to the land promised to my people by God.

My husband called me Persis. I answered to that name and lived in Assyrian territory, but I wasn't one of them. Neither was I Miriam, daughter of Zedekiah. I was far too defiled to be one of the chosen ones any longer. Whatever promises had been made to the people of Israel, they no longer applied to me.

I was no one. My life would soon end, and it had been for nothing.

Avoiding the crowd gathered around the fish-god, we finished making our purchases on side streets. I smiled on the outside as we shared our finds with one another, masking the despair growing in my soul.

MICHAL

I smiled on the outside as I returned to my normal activities, trying to hide the torment settling into my soul. Timna saw right through the mask as she watched my hands pound dough into shape and slap it onto the wooden peel, the loose flour puffing in a cloud around us.

"You must find forgiveness, Michal," she said.

I stopped and looked at my aunt, wondering how I could ever find it in my heart to do as she said. "How? He abandoned us. He put his needs first without thinking of me or his children."

Timna put her hand in the bucket of barley I had ground at the hand mill that morning. The fine powder sifted effortlessly through her fingers, and she gave a quick nod, approving the consistency as if I had not performed the same task many, many times over. She put a hand to her low back as she straightened slowly, then brushed the grain dust onto her tunic. "We don't know his reasons."

"And never will."

"So choose to remember the good," Timna said. "Let the rest slip away. It's only you who will suffer now, for holding on to hurts, and regrets. Jonah isn't here to blame any longer, or here for you to make amends."

"I didn't blame him for anything." The defensiveness flowed readily. "Not until now."

Her intuition was far reaching, spoken without condemnation. "You may not have meant to, but you did, Michal. Whatever it was you hoped for in this life and didn't receive blinded you to Jonah's worth. He's a good husband, a good man."

"Was, and I know, I just…"

"No woman's longings are ever completely satisfied this side of the heavens."

Only Timna could see my heart and flay it open with truth so profound.

"The yearning keeps our eyes looking up, towards the One who knows our thoughts, and comforts us." My aunt ran her bony fingers over my cheek. "Choose to see the good that surrounds you. And forgive him. Forgive yourself."

Staring at her back as she left the courtyard, I knew she was right. As much as I didn't want to admit it to myself, there were dark regions in my heart that needed cleansed. The forgiveness she spoke of was more than my husband abandoning us, more than him running from God and by doing so, drowning.

I rammed the peel into the oven and allowed the dough to slide onto the stone floor, then sat back to watch it brown. The official days of mourning had passed. Resuming the duties of living was taxing, as every room, every corner held memories begging to be remembered and stored in my heart. I was surrounded by my husband, even though he was gone. Any slight noise, a creak of the floor, a branch tapping the roof, made me look to see if he had come into the room. Then I'd remember again that he never would be there when I turned around.

Since his death, there was no preventing my mind from reviewing the life I had with Jonah. It hurt to remember. My own feelings and actions and words rose up with the images and they weren't always a comfort. Yes, I had been a good caretaker of his home and raised his children well. I never brought him shame in this town, never gave his father any reason to regret his decision to bring me into the family. No one had reason to point a finger of blame at me.

Except my husband. Since he wasn't here to do so, I pointed it at myself and cast the stones. I'd allowed a bitter spirit to haunt my heart because he loved my sister before me, because he chose her, then merely accepted me as a replacement. I put Miriam between us as a wall. The fact that she lived on in his memories should have been a blessing, connecting us, not the cursing that I made it out to be.

I knew it was feeble, my selfish heart tethering Jonah and Miriam together when that cord had been severed long ago. I was clinging to a past that was gone like the cold, winter rains. Given the freshness of spring, I had chosen to focus my eyes on bleak shadows instead of the sunshine.

Was it my fault we'd not been bound as one all these years? Could I truly say I loved my husband while doubting his love toward me?

The stench of burning bread spilled from the oven. I watched as the lump blackened and disintegrated.

What I wanted more than any mohar, any glorious betrothal and wedding, was Jonah himself. I had removed the sackcloth, the outward sign of my grief, yet sorrow coursed within me. My hollowed heart ached for something that only he filled and I had been too ignorant to fully recognize it when he stood before me.

JONAH

Seven days stabbing at the heart of my enemy and I was still alive. Each day I walked and spoke the words of doom, each day crowds gathered and stared at me, a pale and hairless sign that they had known was coming for generations. To them, I was more than man, no matter what I said to the contrary. Their own prophets had predicted the coming of one with words that would save them. And I was that one.

The message fell from my lips more easily as the days passed, the condemnation of evil a bold cry. Yet the hatred of the people never rose up against me in the form of violence. Men didn't want to hear me tell them they were wicked, they were wrong, they were the reason my God would annihilate the city. But they listened. Somehow the message was falling on ears willing to hear and I could only give God credit for making it happen. Soldiers with hands gripping swords, men with clenched fists, women with narrowed eyes, children finding stones to hurl – all restrained, all listening, all seeming to search for truth in my prophecy.

Word of my arrival had spread and the number of people finding me, then following me, increased rapidly. The small hoards clogged the streets and limited my travel so I had ventured only a short distance from where I had started. Today I intended to rise early enough to make my way further from the heart of the city before the people penned me in again. I would talk all day, then find a place to stay for the night. Obtaining food and shelter had not been a problem. My needs were met without asking.

Quietly tossing off the covers, I rose and dressed in the near darkness. I was in a modest home by the standards of this city, a palace compared to the home I had built. The floors were tiled with images of flowers and of the great lizards that had been hunted to extinction in centuries past. Tapestries on the walls, urns of imported metals, and vases of fired clay adorned the rooms. Identically clad servants slipped in and out, providing me with food and drink, and sustained glances when they thought I wasn't looking.

The new tunic, long vest, turban and basin of clean water awaiting me hadn't been in the room when I went to bed. I was unnerved that they had been delivered and I had not awakened. On the caravan, my sleep was riddled with bouts of wakefulness. Every hooting owl or rustle of leaves opened my eyes. Here, it was an exhausted sleep I fell into each night, an oblivious one. Anxieties and hours on my feet sapped my strength like no hard, physical labor ever had.

Before leaving the room, I took a knife and made a groove in a strip of leather. This calendar told me what I already knew, it was the eighth day in Nineveh. There were thirty-two remaining before God wiped it off the earth.

If he chose justice.

My ultimate plan wasn't clear. I intended to travel the city and spread my message for at least another week, then perhaps I would take my leave. Then what? I had nowhere to go.

I opened the door from the room I had been provided, one that led into the central garden, hoping to leave the home quietly without disturbing anyone. Instead of solitude, I found a dimly lit plaza full of men.

"He's awake." My host announced the obvious. Two dozen men stood at attention as lanterns were lit and the space filled with light. Most were armed and dressed in the short tunics of soldiers.

So, my days of prophesy were at an end. I lifted my chin to await my arrest.

A man in purple robes and jeweled fingers rose from a cushioned plinth. The other men tipped their heads in deference to the one in obvious authority. "Jonah, prophet of the Hebrews? I am here on behalf of my father, King Sennacherib. He is ruler of this region."

I wasn't certain how I was expected to respond so I lowered my eyes and dipped my head as I had witnessed from the other men.

My actions seemed to satisfy him and I heard no animosity in his tone. "My people have known of the coming of the White Prophet for hundreds of years. You are welcome in Nineveh."

"Forgive me for speaking truth, but I am not the son of your god. I am a man only. Please don't think I've come in answer to some telling of the future by your magicians. I'm here because my God has sent me."

The prince looked at my face intently, the lack of eyebrows seeming to hold great interest. I had to turn away from the scrutiny.

"Regardless of your reasons, you're here, and I'm listening. Tell me what your deity has told you to tell us."

I took a shallow breath and clasped my hands together to keep my trepidation in control. "He has given you forty days warning of your destruction. Thirty-two remain."

"Why does he say this?"

"You are a vile and evil people in his sight." I didn't make an attempt to soften the truth.

The man caught his breath, the soldiers tensed. My host lowered his head onto his hands. I stood absolutely still and waited for a harsh response that never came.

"The master of the caravan sent word to me," the prince said. "You were seen by fishermen, seen emerging from the sea. But you are not of Dagon?"

"No. My God saved me from drowning, preserving me in the belly of a fish for this reason, to stand before you and let you know that he is stronger than all your gods, mightier than Dagon. He alone has power over the seas and skies, and he intends to destroy you."

The regal man pressed his palms together, resting his thumbs against his lips as he thought. The crackle of oil lanterns was the only sound. After a moment, he lowered his hands and pointed a jeweled finger at me. "You were sent to save us. What must we do to appease this God of Israel? How do we stop his hand from striking?"

No disputing the pronouncement of doom. No questioning of motives, or the abilities of the Lord. No anger or weapon raised against me.

I found a chair and dropped into it. In Samaria, I had stood before my own king, terrified and calm at the same time as I told him what God had revealed. My king believed me. Now, facing the leader of Israel's enemy, it was happening again. Requiring more than my message alone, the presence of the divine was in the words that fell from my tongue.

Still, I wanted to clamp my lips together and say nothing more, or lie and tell him I didn't know.

King Sennacherib's son waited for my reply.

"Repent," I pushed the key to salvation into the air, betraying my nation, betraying my king and people. Saying the word gave Nineveh the means to open the door of survival.

Leaning back and closing my eyes, I fought the urge to hit something, to smash an axe into a solid piece of fine furniture or shred a fine tapestry into rags. Every part of me wanted to tell this pagan that there was no salvation for him and his people. And I wanted it to be true. Instead I gripped the edge of the seat and forced myself to be outwardly calm.

Never had I felt so unworthy to be God's mouthpiece. He and I had far different views on how this situation should resolve.

Over the centuries, my own people had willingly turned their backs to the covenant established between Moses and God, then confirmed through Abraham. Worship of gods made by human hands and devotion to the stars were common practice now. Hebrew kings paid for the altars to Baal and the construction of Asherah poles, priests were appointed from tribes other than Levi's. There were profane sacrifices and rituals that mimicked those of the nations around us. Fathers gave their daughters to men who prayed to the moon.

No longer were we on the path to righteousness. The chosen of God were slipping, satisfied to walk in the muck of their sins. The prophets gave warning, and no one listened. We'd never be banished from the earth completely, but discipline was promised.

Our adultery to the One God would not go unpunished indefinitely.

Israel was doomed to face a refining fire. By sparing our greatest enemy from death, I knew that I was the one to light the kindling.

MICHAL

Ethan squealed as he splashed into the pond. I held my breath until he surfaced and shook the water from his face, paddling in place to stay afloat. Meanwhile, his cousin caught the swinging rope and took his turn running along the bank, flying off the edge, then releasing the tether and plummeting into the depths. Over and over the children ran as animals, flew as birds, and swam as the fishes. My child took his turn with the others, though never running as fast or flying so high. The other boys watched him closely as I had asked, and there was no reason for me to hover nearby, yet I found it difficult to leave. Ethan's laughter was a sweet song in the afternoon breeze.

I stood in the shade pretending not to monitor my son's every move. His wounds had closed and healed, leaving a scar striped belly. The physician assured me that the blood he lost had been replaced and there was no reason for him to be excluded from activity any longer. He needed the exercise to firm his limbs and strengthen his lungs again. Outwardly, he looked fine.

Inwardly, he struggled. Ethan's personality was different since the accident. His exuberance for living had diminished, and it took him longer to grasp information and form opinions. The death of his father was the reason given for his demeanor, yet I felt it was more than that. When my son walked past a toad without notice, and hesitated to venture into the pasture unless I held his hand, I realized he wasn't the same confident boy. As Ethan's sorrow sorted itself out, I prayed my life-loving son would return.

Ethan stayed in a restless sleep and waking cycle for four days after the scrape with death. When he opened his eyes fully and looked around the room with comprehension, he cried with agonizing sobs. His father wasn't there. Ethan had gone looking for him the day the sailor came to tell us that Jonah was dead. He didn't believe the swarthy man who brought us the awful news.

I couldn't either sometimes. Jonah left in the night nearly three months ago now, and still, I reached for him in the bed and looked for him in the fields. My heart wouldn't accept what my mind understood.

"He's fine. The older boys won't let him get hurt."

I smiled at Caleb, who had come up the path and leaned against a nearby tree, a grass blade stuck between his teeth. The men of his home and my father's had joined to carve out a new tomb in the face of the rock nearby. I had helped prepare a thick lentil stew to feed them until I couldn't stand being inside and having Ethan from my sight.

"I had to make sure."

"You're less anxious. That's good to see. A few weeks ago, you would have swung with him on that old rope rather than allow him to go alone."

I laughed, not telling him I would have done so today had I not had other duties. "He hasn't complained about a hovering mother yet. For now, he's still my baby."

Caleb spit the grass blade and plucked another. He hadn't mentioned the fact that I was free to marry again, hadn't so much as looked at me in a way to wonder if I was interested. As much as I didn't want to talk of it at first, now I wanted him to broach the topic. It was too hard for me to initiate, as if I was giving up on the love for my husband.

He read my mind. "Michal, have you given any more thought as to what you will do now?"

I wrapped my arms around my waist and exhaled. "I don't know what to do. I can manage the sheep and my home. My boys are close and they'll help. We can manage without payments from the king."

"The sheep will be fine. The fields, the finances. I know this. What about you, Michal? What do you want, or need?"

I bit down on my lip as the sting of tears hit my eyes.

Caleb turned kindly away, his arms crossed over his chest and his eyes on the boys. "That's what concerns me. You, and Ethan."

"He needs a father."

"All your sons can fill that role. He'll learn the ways of a man from them."

"You don't...?"

Caleb found my eyes. "I'd be honored to raise him, already love him as one of my own. But he doesn't need me, not specifically. It's his mother who might need me. Or want me. That's what I'm trying to understand. Michal, do you want to remain a widow or would you like to marry me?"

I didn't want to make this decision. There was no man I'd even consider other than my true friend Caleb, a man with a compassionate heart, and listening ears. A man who loved my children and loved his God, and worked diligently. He was wise, and gave sound council. I could do no better and would be content beneath his roof, and in his bed in time.

And I would be his choice, his first choice. I didn't want that to matter yet it was imprinted on my heart, that this man would have brought my father the finest mohar he could afford. Caleb would have placed a value on my head, a symbol of devotion and respect. I would not have been the logical second choice in a situation gone awry.

I didn't want to be alone for the remainder of my years. I loved

Caleb, and could be a good wife to him. Marrying again made the most sense.

I just couldn't take that step from the life I had known to another. Not yet.

"I..."

Caleb reached out a hand and took mine with a firm squeeze. "The offer isn't limited to any certain time. You don't need to decide at this moment. Just know that I am willing to be your husband, and a father to Ethan. You and I, we've always been good together."

He released my hand and left me with the greatest gift I could have asked for, that of options.

PERSIS

I hid my eyes as the courtyard filled with members of the household. I didn't want anyone to see the fear that was surely evident there, a morsel of pride I clung to for no reason other than I wanted my day of death to be one of dignity.

My indigo garment draped over one shoulder, then cascaded in a waterfall over my hips and legs, puddling at my feet. Golden chains of sapphires draped my forehead and tinkled together as I moved, a merry sound in any other circumstance. No face or body paints had been added yet, the gold dust to be applied by the priestesses who prepared me for Dagon.

In one small act of defiance, I refused to have my hair coiled. I wanted it free, spilling down my back and catching the breeze as it had when I was a child and knew nothing of the life that would eventually be mine.

Running my hands along the woven belt, I checked again for the hidden pouch that bulged from the underside. The medicinal contents would still my heart before the fire could touch me.

The children were in a playful chase, weaving in and out of the women in a game of their own making. My daughter brushed past me without looking up, not realizing why we were gathering. She was maturing into a beautiful girl. We secondary wives weren't permitted to be partial, yet we were. We heaped extra affections on our own children, eyes blinded to their misbehaviors, and favoring their responses to lessons being taught. None of us meant to, it was in a mother's blood to do so, to protect her own.

I had done so with this girl when she was assigned to my care, and with my sons in the short span of their baby days, when I was allowed to tickle their tummies and coo blessings in their ears. Raised by eunuchs after they were weaned, I had little opportunity to pour love into my male children. The boys would be leaders and warriors of this Assyrian land, pagans, and abominations to the God of my father.

All but one.

One son delivered into this world was protected, a risky venture sparing him the life of a brutal killer. I wanted, needed, a child of my womb to find his place among my own people.

When the boy was born, I acted on a plan that had formed in my mind months prior. I had no choice. The healthy newborn had a birthmark over his right eye, a purplish splotch that would have marked him as unfit for Tariq's household. My husband would not have allowed him life. The boy would have been abandoned with the refuse, not even valued as a worthy sacrifice.

Trading rings and perfumes I'd been given over the years, I wrapped my newborn son in fine cloth and gave him to a young couple, Nabatean merchants with the caravan, their youngest still suckling. I asked them to care for my boy, and to deliver him to Michal, daughter of Zedekiah in Gath-hepher. The riches I gave them was far more than they would make in a year selling their wine.

My husband was informed that his newest child was marked by the gods, and had died. The few women who knew the truth had willingly lied to see this one child set free.

I never saw the young man and wife again, although I searched for them among all the wagons and stalls as the traders came to this city.

There are two forms of hope. One is certain, like the hope of a

Messiah to save Israel. It is one that has substance, that can be grasped in the soul and no matter how long the waiting, will happen in the timeline of God's making. The other hope is tethered to uncertainty, a wish, desire, an optimistic outcome. My hope was of the latter sort. I chose to believe my sister was alive, and my son was now her son.

It was home my mind turned to as my husband addressed the family and reminded them of my faults. There would not be a beating, nor farewells. I stared at the sky with my hand on my belted secret.

Michal would raise my child as her own, in the ways of Moses and tradition of the Israelites from generation to generation. I prayed that Caleb's bad leg had somehow spared him from being killed by the raiders, that he had been unable to stand and fight so had survived and married Michal. Together, they wouldn't reject the boy as an orphan, or despise his heritage.

I regretted not telling the traders my name when I paid them, fearful at the time that they would betray me. I wondered if Michal knew anyhow, connecting me to the Assyrian blanket, seeing me in the child in some familiar way. Seven years old, nearly eight now, I hoped he resembled his mother's family.

For all the ways I had sinned in this land not my own, I knew saving at least one child was something I had done right. If the Hebrew God remembered me, I hoped he found a way to overlook my offenses and smile at my attempts to cling to the way of truth.

"Come."

Steered from the garden to a wagon, I looked at no one and kept my tears inside. Four guards were assigned to take me to the Grand Temple of Dagon. Not even Tariq, the man who purchased my innocence at the auction block, would accompany me to my death.

I was so alone.

PERSIS

"Don't touch me." I shrugged off the man's hand and got out of the wagon myself, taking care to gather up the length of silk in my trembling fingers and not trip over it.

A glut of people filled the streets and blocked the way to the temple entrance. We were forced to stop. More curious people followed behind us, and in a short time, we were part of the crowd. Somewhere at the front of the throng was the son of Dagon. Armed soldiers stood among the women and children who wanted to hear him speak. Common men, slaves and business owners had stopped their labors, disrupted their routines to see the anomaly for themselves.

My guards didn't dare return to my husband with a task incomplete. They led me away from the temple, pushing against the flow until we were behind the stagnant mass. From there we took side streets, making our way to the rear of the temple.

The temple building, a massive square structure with images of sacrificial offerings carved into the façade, was surrounded by a wall. Several dozen young men were perched on the top, their attention to the street and the man everyone wanted to see. The path along the wall leading to the temple entrance was blocked with more people.

The men let out a stream of curses. "We'll go this way," one guard said, patting the wall. It was twice my height and not easily scalable, as the stone bricks were smooth and had no footholds.

I was dressed in the finest sort of clothing and jewels worth more than a dozen stallions. My husband held prominence in the city of his birth, and whether or not I believed in Dagon, I was supposed to be a gift to him. A spark of pride rose up and lashed out of me at these men who could so readily hand me to an executioner. "I will not be tossed over a wall like one tosses out his refuse."

"You'll do what I say." The man gripped my arm and yanked me toward the enclosure.

"Tariq will slice your throats when he hears how you handled his offering." There were witnesses all around us and I made certain they heard me. I had the upper hand with a threat that was real.

The men cussed the crowd that now blocked the way we had come. Gathering tightly around me, they pushed forward toward the entrance. "Make way!" A path cleared, people forced to move aside as they were jabbed with elbows.

I was steered toward the arched entrance but couldn't enter into the temple grounds. The son of Dagon stood in the back of a wagon, in front of the gate, blocking it. I flinched at the sight of the man, not accustomed to seeing anyone with an infirmity. The diseased and maimed were hidden away, if not executed, yet with once glance I could see why he garnered attention. He had no fish tail or scales, just unnaturally pale skin, and a face with no hair, not even eyebrows. A turban covering his head had slipped slightly, and there was only splotchy scalp beneath it. Dressed in expensive robes, and intense in his manner of speaking, I understood the fascination.

"Stop!"

The demi-god pointed at me. His eyes were dark and clear, not those of a madman.

The guards holding my arms hesitated.

"Don't you care that you will burn with the fires of Sodom and Gomorrah because of your sins?"

I dropped my head at the rebuke, heat flooding my face as all eyes turned toward me. Anger sparked its own fire. Who was this odd stranger to cast judgment?

"Release the woman. Release your vile intentions. My God will destroy you for that very sort of wickedness within your souls."

My head snapped back up as I realized it wasn't me he condemned.

The stranger recoiled ever so perceptibly when his eyes found mine. In a brief moment, he shook off the startle and pulled his gaze away, yet I could feel him watching me indirectly. He hadn't expected to see the sin in my own soul after demanding my release, I assumed. He knew I was as guilty as the men who wanted my death.

The guards tensed in preparation for a battle of wills. "Stay out of our business!"

The stranger on the wagon didn't yell back. The crowd around us did it for him. "Listen to him. He's a prophet coming to us from the sea!"

I felt the loosening on my arms.

"Who is he to tell us what to do? Under whose authority does he speak?"

"The king has listened to this man from beyond the Tigris," a man replied. "He has ordered the White Prophet's protection. We are to do as he says."

My snares were released.

The hairless man raised an arm to the heavens. His sleeve fell back and revealed a limb as pale and smooth as his face. "Thirty-one days from now every living creature in this great city will pay for the injustices meted out against her enemies. For sacrificing your children to the fires, you will be condemned. For bowing to false gods and prostituting your sons and daughters. For your lack of mercy, you will receive your due."

I caught my breath and held it. Who but the God of the Hebrews had the power to strike this nation? Was it he that threatened justice to my captors?

The prophet's bleached lips proclaimed the impending destruction of Nineveh and no one questioned him. Any madman could say the words he spoke and be pierced through with a sword. Yet the pale man was spared. It had to be the hand of my own God protecting him.

"Son of Dagon." The guard whispered under his breath to the others.

Their attention was locked on the stranger, a man they believed held divine powers. I wanted to stand among them and listen, but didn't.

I took a small step backward.

Then another.

When I was beyond the reach of the men, I turned and forced my way back the way I'd come, then ran as best I could with my clothing bunched up in my hands. I had nowhere to go for protection, so went to the library, where I had often found solace. My native tongue was stamped into tablets there, the words of my God, my hope of the certain kind.

The back corner where I generally found the Hebrew text undisturbed was humming with scribes. Scrolls of parchment were deciphered and discussed, bits of the tablets were read and debated. I sat nearby on the tiled floor, amazed as the hours passed. These learned men were searching for the God of Israel.

"At the next full moon, the entire city is to wear sackcloth and fast for three days. Every man, woman, and child, free and captive. Even the beasts of the land are to fast."

"Does this appease the God of the Hebrews?"

"No one knows for certain. Not even that prophet. His people offer animal sacrifices, and grains, but he says that isn't what is required of us. Our sacrifice is of our hearts. Not literally. He means we are to turn from violence and aggression, from having gods other than the God of Israel."

"Do you plan to leave before the numbered days expire?"

"There's a royal order to prevent any citizen from doing so. Only the caravans and travelers will be permitted to go. The usual inspection for stow-aways will be magnified, and anyone harboring a resident of Nineveh will be imprisoned. I plan to follow the orders of the king and stay, and fast."

"The god will spare us if we conform? And Ishtar won't take offense?"

The depth of devotion to false idols kept these men from truth. I sighed loudly. They turned, noticing me for the first time. I had not yet been painted with the gold dust of sacrifice that would have preceded my execution, so they saw only my expensive adornment. It gave me an air of importance, so they didn't automatically shun me from their presence.

"You must listen to that man." I found a boldness to speak, aware of the fact that I still had breath on a day I assumed it would be taken from me. "His God is all powerful."

"How do you know? Have you met this prophet?"

"No," I said as I stood. "I don't know anything about him. I was taught of his God when I was young. His God was, is my God." The last words I spoke haltingly, fearing the Lord would look at my sins and strike me for claiming him as my own. Instead, a calm fell over me.

"He was spit from the mouth of a great fish before he came to us. You bow to Dagon?"

"No. My God is the Creator of the sea and all its inhabitants, and of the land and the skies. Only he has the power to lay low the great city of Nineveh."

"We should take heed, then. Listen to that Hebrew's words."

My heart thumped at a quicker pace. The prophet was the seed of Abraham. I nodded. "Yes. He is a mouthpiece for the God of the Israel." I said. "What village is he from? Did he say? Do you know?"

"A village of no importance. Gath-hepher."

The blood drained from my face and I had to brace myself against a pillar. I once knew a prophet from there, and believed he was dead.

"What, what is that man's name?"

"Jonah. Jonah son of Amittai."

JONAH

The woman's face haunted me. I tried not to stare as she was drug through the crowd, but I couldn't help myself. For all the nights I lay awake wondering what Michal was doing at that same moment, all the times I felt alone and wanted more than anything for her to be at my side, to hear her laughter, I hadn't expected to see her.

It wasn't actually her, I knew. When the woman looked me fully in the face, I realized my mind was creating a mirage. Michal wasn't there. I turned away, but couldn't keep myself from finding her again. And again.

Now in the darkness, I couldn't sleep because her face returned. It unnerved me, the inability to forget the woman and her striking resemblance to my wife. The two could be sisters.

Sisters.

I threw off the hide covers and bolted to my feet. It wasn't possible. Miriam was dead.

After I hid Michal, I couldn't find her sister. There was chaos in the streets, men falling under the swords of the raiders who came from every direction at once. I fought, never gaining ground, so I couldn't give chase to the hoard as it moved through. In their wake, I found my betrothed's veil, and that was all. I didn't know Miriam's actual fate. How could she be anything but dead?

Thirty days of traditional mourning was lengthened to ninety. By then, we knew no one would return to us. Our city leaders ended the time of outward grief. We needed to return to the living.

It may have occurred to me once or twice since then that she might have survived, and that's all. For us, the captives were dead.

We had no means to fight for their return. And no certain hope that any still breathed. Unless the king called up an army and attacked the Assyrians, we knew any survivors would never be seen again. They wouldn't survive at the hands of the barbarians for long.

And yet, I had just seen Miriam. Hadn't I?

She hadn't recognized me. Of course, who would have? Not with my appearance, not at my age, and certainly not in Nineveh. She hadn't seen me since she was fifteen years old. We both had matured past our prime now. But in the woman's features, the flowing ebony hair and intense eyes, the stance of defiance at some injustice, the quick flash of anger - I recognized the daughter of Zedekiah.

Could it be?

Could Miriam have survived these years since she was taken?

I stood in the window of the house in which I stayed for the night, looking at the stars. The same stars that covered Gath-hepher.

What had she endured? I really didn't want to speculate. She hadn't wanted to be with the men who held her at the temple and had disappeared into the throng at the first opportunity. How would I begin to find her? Any notion I entertained about leaving this place was dashed. There was no leaving now. I had to see Miriam again.

If it was Miriam.

I threw a heavy robe over my shoulders and went out into the garden, fragrant with jasmine and roses. I could find her in any crowd dressed as she was, her garment the color of the sea and head adorned with gems. Would I recognize her otherwise? Up close, yes, the face reflecting her sister's. From a distance? I didn't know. I didn't know if I should even try. But if it was Michal's sister, stolen from Israel and believed to be dead, how could I not?

MICHAL

Timna panted as she ran up behind me. I dropped the basket of wet clothing on the path by the stream to take her shoulders in my hands. "Is it Ethan? What's happened?"

She shook her head and caught a breath. "No. Not Ethan. King Jeroboam. His men."

"Here?"

She nodded. "Here. At the house."

"With a gift for Jonah?" I assumed those would cease to arrive now that he was gone.

"None that I could see. I don't like it."

My knees wobbled beneath me. I found the royal advisors a haughty bunch, and knew they viewed my home and manner of living with disdain. Jonah was the spokesman, and I could perform my tasks quietly, without interacting on the previous occasions. I had no choice but to face them this time.

The lands of Israel had been restored under King Jeroboam's army, as Jonah had prophesied, giving my husband royal favor. Although visits from the advisors had dwindled over the years when no new prophesies unfolded, they continued to ask for blessings on the nation when they came, as if Jonah could control the hand of God and be bribed with favors.

Even in the king's good graces, having those men on my steps was of no comfort. I was always glad when they were gone, tributes to Jonah or not. King Jeroboam didn't fear the Lord our God as King David had, didn't find the worship of false gods a threat to his kingdom. This was an abomination to the Lord. My husband tried to sway Jeroboam's men towards righteousness, with little success. Over the years, that conversation was merely an annoyance, and they waved it off without a thought.

Jonah blamed himself for the lack of conviction. He knew he didn't have the thunder of Elisha. The words of admonition dripped out of his mouth like lukewarm water, not inspiring anyone to turn from their sins, and not offensive enough to make himself an enemy of our people.

I had often wondered if the boldness he desired would come if it was an old mule he rode from place to place rather than the chariot. Black stallions from the royal palace placed a bit in Jonah's mouth, stifling his words and steering him towards compromise. The advisors expected a prophet to speak of the Lord, yet our guests were never pushed beyond their tolerance. Jonah wanted their report to return to the palace with favorable light.

Now Jonah was gone.

"What do they want?"

Timna hoisted the basket onto her hip and started back to the house. "I'm not certain, Michal. They asked for you, though. Not Jonah."

"O God of my fathers," I prayed. "Help me. Help us."

I hoped the men were here to pay their respects for the dead prophet. I hoped they didn't know that he fled from his home on his own accord.

Four royal advisors waited in the shade of my courtyard, sitting on cushions and sipping the wine from my storehouse. Trays of hastily prepared grapes, goat cheese and bread with olive oil were passing among them. Ethan sat nearby, cradling his baby cousin while my daughter Lydia saw to the food. Along the perimeter of the enclosure, armed guards waited for instructions. There were far more than had come on previous occasions.

I bowed my head in reverence. "Shalom," I said, sitting on the stone flooring near the firepit rather than in the midst of the men as Jonah would have done. I was mistress of the home yet I had to heed my position as a woman. I didn't want to cause offense.

Phineas ben Daniel was chief among the men, and had been to my home many times. "We have come on behalf of the king," he said. "He wants to know what has happened to his prophet from your lips."

I was relieved at his tone, not one of condemnation, but of a fatherly concern.

"He's dead. Jonah is dead."

Phineas nodded, his hand stroking a thinning gray beard that fell neatly from his chin. "This we have heard. Tell us the circumstances."

I clasped my hands together to keep them from trembling, and told them of the day he was simply gone, without a word. I told them of the sailor, of the man's report that my husband had been in Joppa and was bound for Tarshish. The fury of God in the storm, the calm of the seas when Jonah was sacrificed, all this I explained. The men listened attentively.

When I finished, I waited for the response. Ethan had heard the same recitation many times and still it brought tears to his eyes. Lydia gathered him up and led him away.

There was no evident grief among the four men. Phineas set his drink aside and leaned onto a cushion. "This is what we were told. We have also been informed that the prophet Jonah is alive."

I snapped my gaze from my retreating son to look at Phineas and the knife he dug into the open wounds of my spirit. "Who has said this? Is there proof?"

Phineas granted me a tiny slice of smile. "No evidence, Michal.

None for certain." He held up his cup to be filled, then continued. "There's a village on the northern shoreline, a small fisherman's harbor not far from the ruins of Ugarit and the trading routes. They claim to have seen a man coming from the mouth of a great fish, spit like vomit onto their land. They nursed him to health."

All eyes were on me, as if to see if I knew this and was holding it back. I shook my head. "That isn't possible."

"He claimed to be the prophet Jonah, of this town."

"No. That can't be. He drowned in the sea."

"According to the fishermen, the man claimed he was saved by the fish. Saved by our God."

Blackness wanted to take me away from the words the man was saying. I put my forehead on my hands until the dizziness abated.

"No," I said in a whisper when I could finally do so. "That's absurd."

"Is he here?" Phineas asked quietly, but he asked as if I was hiding my husband, as if I had been the one to lie.

Blood boiled back up into my head. "No! Jonah is dead. Why are you telling me this? Is your purpose to bring more torment on my home, on my sons and daughters? How can you ask such a thing? Jonah drowned. It was witnessed by a shipload of men."

Phineas linked his fingers and pulled them back until they crackled, then crossed his arms over his chest. "There were witnesses in the fishing village as well. We don't intend to bring dissension. We come seeking the truth."

I didn't at all like the seed of doubt in my mind, the notion that what the men heard had merit. As much as I longed for my husband, handing me false hope now was simply cruel.

"He isn't here. If God did save him, he didn't come home. Go to that village and find him, if you believe the fish tale."

Phineas gave me the sliver of a smile again. "We've been. Your husband has left the coast. He joined a caravan."

I let the air from my lungs out slowly. The men knew more than they had revealed, baiting me piece by piece. "A caravan? He's returning?"

Phineas licked his bottom lip and pulled gently on his beard. "No. Apparently he followed a command of his God to go elsewhere. To Nineveh."

Nineveh?

My mind churned all directions, seeking for any hint of truth. Jonah despised the Assyrians. He wouldn't go there on his own accord. He was on a ship to Tarshish, the opposite direction. The sailors were witnesses.

Unless they had been paid to lie.

And the fishing village? How would they even know the name of Jonah if he hadn't been there? The advisors weren't beyond telling falsehoods themselves, of course, if they stood to profit.

What was real and what wasn't? I couldn't make any sense of it. "Someone isn't speaking the truth," I said.

"It is King Jeroboam's decision to believe the fishermen, at least the part of them meeting the prophet and sending him away on the back of a camel. We see now why the prophesies that benefit Israel have ceased. Jonah ben Amittai has fled to the land of our enemy."

The realization of the man's meaning sunk into my gut. I shook my head. "He is *not* a traitor."

No one seemed eager to contradict me. Phineas cleared his throat and caught my eyes. "Was he headed to Tarshish? Perhaps. Did the prophet drown? Your king thinks not. Jonah schemed with the sailors, he fled this land, trading his loyalties and betraying Israel."

"No! There is no proof to any of it. Jonah would never betray

Israel. Never."

"Nevertheless, the prophet is gone and hasn't been useful for some time. He's deserted us, or dead, or he might as well be." Phineas paused, allowing me to calm a bit and give his next statement full focus. "King Jeroboam will collect his property thirty days from this one."

"His property?"

"All that was given to Jonah will be sold and returned to the royal treasury."

"Take the chariot and horses now. I don't want them. The rugs and such will be stacked in the barn."

The man snickered, waving his hand towards the house and surrounding land. "The king's gifts purchased all of this. All will be sold."

I sprang to my feet. "My husband built this house! He raised the herds and cultivated the soil. They belongs to his sons!"

The advisors stood. The servants and guards drew in closer. I stomped the ground, shook my finger in Phineas' face and said what I believed was just, yet knew wasn't true when it came to the authority standing before me. "None of this is yours to take."

Phineas sighed and stepped back. "You defy your king, Michal? Your children and their children have been spared from rotations of royal service. An unhappy king will see that order revoked."

I turned and fumed, anger too soft a term for the fury of my emotions. With deep breaths, I made myself control the venom of my tongue. "Please. Please don't destroy us. Jonah was loyal to our king."

"Was." Phineas motioned to his guards. Some entered my home, some turned toward the barn, following a plan that had already been set in place. I could do nothing but watch as men exited with possessions in their arms. Sacks on horses were filled with dishes, jewelry and trinkets. The stallions were harnessed to the chariot and driven to the road, it too filled with tools and supplies, leaving barely enough room for a driver. Clothes, small furnishings, even food stores, taken.

Ethan ran to me once the guard ushered him outside, crumpling in fear at my feet, his stability once more challenged. Lydia and the baby fell beside him, all three crying. Timna knelt gingerly and wrapped them in her wings.

I refused to give in to the torrent of despair, standing, keeping my head lifted high and defiant until their task was complete. "May God strike you down," I said, not caring how hateful the words came out.

Phineas huffed and waved it off as he and the others prepared to leave. "The house and livestock are to be sold. We have eyes in this town so make certain your transactions are fair. We'll return for the payment."

"And if it's true that my husband lives, and if he returns?"

Phineas looked at me with pity in his eyes. "He won't."

I collapsed in their dusty wake. I didn't know what to think or feel, but I believed the man spoke truth with his parting statement. Tarshish or Nineveh, dead or alive, my husband wasn't coming back.

PERSIS

I sat alone among tablets of many tongues, tales of gods and creators, histories of wars and conquests, of kings and kingdoms rising and falling and rising again. The laws of Moses, the songs of David, and wisdom of Solomon were a small part of the collection and had held no more importance than any of the religious writings from foreign lands. Now the dust was cleared and the words read with fervency.

The local scholars were trying to accept truth. The Lord Most High had looked upon their city and found it wanting. He would wipe it from the earth.

Knowing that justice was to be delivered stabbed my heart. It didn't please me to think of the destruction, righteous or not. What of the wives I had shared a home with, and our children? The beautiful gardens, the majestic structures, they could be rebuilt. The living souls of Nineveh could not. I didn't want them to be destroyed. Judged and punished, forced to face their sins and make amends, yes. Forced to free the captives and demolish idols, to stop the executions and ravaging of other lands, yes. But killed, no.

As much as I longed to be free of my captive existence, I didn't want it to end in an all-consuming rain of destruction from the heavens. And I didn't want to be counted among the dead.

When I was asked to leave my sanctuary in the darkening night, I discreetly followed the lingering street crowds to a modest home in the heart of the city where the prophet was said to be sleeping. I found a columned porch nearby, where I could watch the entrance from a distance.

The moon rose higher, the crowd grew thinner, and thinner, until I was alone.

Could it be Jonah? My Jonah?

All the able-bodied men of Gath-hepher were slaughtered the day I was taken, no army left to follow and retrieve those of us still alive. That's what my captors had said. I'd seen the horrific slayings as we left the region, and had no reason to doubt their words. I thought Jonah was dead, and my father and brothers.

Now, I wasn't certain. It was a simple lie to tell a terrified girl, one that took her hope and gave her no reason to believe she could ever go home.

If it was Jonah —

My heart pounded at the thought of returning to my native lands.

I hadn't recognized the prophet, his appearance strange and his words piercing. The young man I remembered was gentle when he spoke. He gave words of truth without fire. He didn't point and condemn. He lifted, supported, encouraged, and remained true to the ways of Abraham and Moses. He would have been a good husband, one that saw his sons as blessings, not sacrifices.

I couldn't help but wonder if he thought about me any longer, and who had taken my place as his bride. His life had surely been far different than my own. A righteous one.

Notions of going home slithered from my heart. I was forever unclean, and Jonah could never take me back. How could I allow him to see what I'd become? I was the very essence of what God wanted to destroy. It was better for him to believe I was dead, remembering only the innocent girl with her dreams.

Pressed against the pillar where a passing patrol of soldiers couldn't see me, I was glad I had been given a different name. If Jonah did remember me, he'd never find me. No one knew me by the name

Miriam. I hadn't been the Miriam that he knew since the day I was abducted.

It made sense to leave the prophet alone, yet I couldn't. He came from my city, he knew my family.

I would die soon, once Tariq found me or when God struck the city. On my last days of life, I needed to know what had happened to those who shared my blood. My sister and brothers, my mother and father. And more than anything, my son.

JONAH

Even in the darkness, I knew I was being followed as I walked the street, praying and searching for a plan that made good sense. Without the intensity of the sun on my skin, I moved freely about, grateful for the torches still burning to guide me. Whomever she was, she moved lightly and thought I didn't see the glimpses of her in the shadows. My instincts told me it was Miriam.

At the Fountain of Aserte, I ducked low and made a quick shuffle around the basin, waiting there, crouched until my knees ached. The woman crept from her hiding place after a minute, paused, then moved in the direction she thought I had gone.

Only a few arm lengths away, I stood and whispered her name into the crisp air. It shot across the space between us and hit her squarely in the heart.

"Miriam," the name barely left my lips when she spun to face me.

"No," she said, too quickly, as if she knew her identity was about to be questioned. Her hands flew to her cheeks. "No."

I closed the distance between us and reached out my hand. She drew back from my touch.

"Miriam," I said again.

"No. Don't call me that. She's dead to you."

"I thought she was. I, I looked for you. I didn't know…"

"I was taken. I lived."

I nodded, not knowing where to begin with the questions I wanted to ask, and not certain that I should try to find the answers. "I'm sorry, I wanted -"

She put a finger on my lips, then swiftly drew it away at the

292

touch. Her eyes searched my face, looking for the young man of her past. "I know. I hold no anger. You couldn't have known that I survived, and couldn't have rescued me if you had. It was better that I was dead to you."

I nodded again, my agony fresh once more.

"I thought you had been killed, Jonah. I never imagined..."

She said my name tentatively, my name on her lips rusty from disuse.

"Many died," I said. Already unclean from placing my feet in Nineveh, I lifted my hand and ran a finger over her cheek, wiping away a tear stained track.

Miriam pulled back and lowered her gaze, her hand resting where I had touched her face. "You, I saw you protect my sister. I saw you cover her in tarp. Did she..?"

So much had happened, so much she didn't know. "Michal lives. She's a fine woman."

"My parents?"

"Your mother has been gone many years. Your father lives, and all your brothers but two. One in birth, when you mother died, and Seth succumbed to fever. He left sons and daughters first. You have a flock of nieces and nephews."

"The town survived? Not attacked again? Not destroyed?"

"We have been blessed by God, and Israel's army is strong."

"Your prophecy was proven true?"

"It was. Our borders expanded just as God said."

A smile crossed her face for a moment. "I knew it would."

I couldn't believe this was Miriam and reached out to take her hand, something I had longed to do once before and never could with the eyes of the city upon us, or the eyes of a little sister.

She stepped away. Her eyes filled with tears, tinged with pain.

Miriam of long ago had only laughter in her eyes.

"Please. Sit, and talk." I had no way of restoring what was taken from her, yet I couldn't let her disappear. I patted the edge of the basin where the carved marble goddess poured water into a shell.

Miriam hesitated, then sat with the grace and poise of nobility, staring at the overflowing shell and the fishes swimming nearby.

I remained standing, pacing but never taking her from my sight. "I can't believe it's you."

"Is it true that we will be destroyed? Israel's strong army will come and strike back?"

"Not the army. It was the Lord who sent me here, the Lord who will strike."

"I'm not surprised at his anger."

"No," I said. "Neither am I."

"Why would he send his prophet to enemy lands?"

I sighed and crossed my arms over my chest. "His ways are his own."

She watched my expression, reading the displeasure. "God warns Nineveh through your lips so we have no excuse. We'll perish as a sign to other nations. No one will attack Israel once we're gone."

"We? No, Miriam, I'll get you out. I won't leave you in this place."

The trepidation in her expression surprised me. "I have children," she said.

Seeing her forced towards the temple of Dagon earlier, I assumed she would be eager to put the dust of Nineveh behind. I had to rethink my impressions. This was her home. Miriam was an adult, not the girl of my past. "We'll take your husband, and family," I said. "Anyone you want. The king will permit it, I believe. God will surely make it happen if he refuses."

She nodded slightly, not committing herself. "Can the Lord be appeased? There is a royal command for fasting, a call for repentance."

"I don't know what will happen here."

The splashing of water filled the air as we both grew silent. It was a fresh fountain, clear and without the stench and salts of the fluids I had bathed in for three days. I turned away from it and the fish and looked at the moon.

"Your skin. Your face. They say you are the child of Dagon."

My hands slid across the smooth surface of my scalp where I once had thick rings of hair. "God did a miraculous work. He preserved me in the belly of a fish. If I didn't see my own coloring in the light, I might believe it was a dream."

"A fish, in Gath-hepher?"

I shook my head, not wanting to admit my rebellion, not even to a woman whose heart no longer belonged to me. "In the sea, I should have drowned. The fish brought me to shore so I could come here."

The words between us stopped again, the past and present colliding awkwardly.

"Are you happy, Jonah?"

Hearing her say my name sent a chill along my spine. Miriam, long dead, in my presence and asking what I couldn't answer. "I don't know any longer. I'm not happy to be in this land. I don't know if I can find it at home."

"Who is there for you? A wife? Sons?"

How could I tell her? I sat on the basin ledge and took a breath. "I married a fine woman." I tried to look Miriam in the eye but had to drop my gaze. "I married your sister. Michal is my wife."

The woman beside me gasped, hands flying to her mouth.

"We thought you were dead. It seemed right. We didn't know..."

She exhaled forcefully. "You don't need to explain. I understand. Michal is a good wife to you, then?"

"Yes. Yes indeed."

"And, are there children?"

"Seven sons, three daughters." I tried not to feel the guilt over leaving my youngest without a father. "Most of them have children of their own."

Miriam wrapped her hands over her arms, hugging herself. Her questions were laced with the onset of fresh tears. "Most? Your youngest child, how old is he, or she?"

"He. Soon to be eight."

Her jeweled hand rested on her throat, her voice wavering. "He's healthy, a good son?"

"Ethan is a wonderful child, loves to find trouble and adventure wherever he goes. He was a gift from God."

Miriam nodded and whispered his name with a slight smile. "Ethan. Ethan. Enduring and strong. A good name."

"You'll like him. He makes everyone laugh with his antics. He-"

I stopped my own words, realizing I was committing to leave this city with Miriam and take her back to Gath-hepher. The notion sunk like a stone in my gut. Was I going back? How could I?

Miriam stood abruptly and backed a few steps away from me.

"Don't leave," I said. "I want to help you."

"No. Don't follow me. Or try to find me."

"But-"

"No! I'm not the girl you knew. You can't help me." She turned from me, then stopped and looked back with softer words. "Jonah, prophet of the Lord God of Israel, forget about Miriam, leave her in your past, innocent. And dead."

I watched her disappear into the city with memories crashing into me like the waves that had consumed me weeks before. I had given myself over to God then, and he had saved me. I prayed for God to intervene again. Only he could make the path I was to follow clear. Until then, I knew I couldn't leave that place.

PERSIS

I slipped into the temple of Ishtar and kneeled, head down as if in worship, hoping the priests and priestesses would leave me alone. Only a handful chanted and swung bowls of incense at this hour, and I was the only patron. The admonitions of the prophet Jonah were evident, the carved idols ignored as his words were heard, and heeded.

I could hardly believe I had seen him again, and that God sent him here.

Was I supposed to leave Nineveh? Israel was the only other home I'd known, yet it might not welcome me back. I was wed to a gentile, unclean, and my presence would defile those I touched and the homes I entered. Despite the nature of my captivity, I wasn't certain I'd be allowed in my village. Viewed as a spy? Shunned? There were no guarantees that the priests would ever declare me clean and permit me to dwell freely in the land of my birth.

I had no lasting means of support, and wouldn't receive the assistance of a widow. Even if Tariq fell at the hand of God, technically I was still bound to Jonah. He wouldn't have annulled our betrothal since I was presumed to be dead. Michal, my father and brothers, they would see that I didn't starve but I would be a burden. It wouldn't be fair to any of them. Too much time had passed, none of us the same. It wouldn't be the life I'd known before I was taken.

I lifted my head and leaned against the wall, absently watching the swaying rhythm of the young servants of Ishtar. What happened to Caleb? He adored my little sister and I never imagined she would marry anyone but him.

The flurry of emotions I felt were difficult to sort. Jonah and Michal, married. Relief was primary, that both survived. Then jealousy, and betrayal. These I shoved aside. To the town of Gath-hepher, I was dead. There was no reason for Jonah not to find another bride. He could do no better than my sister.

Still, a hollow ache rested in my heart. Jonah and I both lost our lives that day, I'd thought. He, literally, and me, in spirit. There was a connecting thread between us by the mutual loss, one that I'd never severed. But he had. By living.

Jonah had ceased to be mine the day I was abducted. My betrothed was alive, and had a wife and children. He had not died, and hadn't waited for my return. His life had resumed. Another woman took my place at his side. My own sister. There was a sting to knowing that, no matter how I tried to not let it hurt me.

Was it a marriage Michal wanted? It was a logical decision, one I could see my father's hand in. The mohar was paid, everything for the marriage in place. In a town mourning its losses, I hoped the celebration was a good memory, and not one filled with the wails of the bereaved. Michal deserved happiness.

I closed my eyes as the priestess passed by with her pot of burning incense, seeking the blessings of the goddess Ishtar on the fertility of her womb. Jonah, the young prophet, had probably prayed to his God that way. He had to leave me in the past and step forward into life. It was the way of our people. He had to have sons and I couldn't provide them for him.

Except the one. Ethan, they named him. It had to be my son. I wanted to ask about the mark over his eye, about how he arrived and when, and had he been cared for on the journey. Jonah said he was a gift, but gave no indication he knew the boy's origin. Had they not seen the blanket, not realized I had sent it?

I had wanted my sister to understand, to see the foreign symbols and realize that I lived, and was entrusting my son to her. It was another connection I'd kept tied to my heart, that Michal remembered me, and loved me still. Somewhere in Israel, I hoped I had not been entirely forgotten.

Standing and smoothing my garment, I left the temple and stood in the cooling air, myriads of stars hovering over me. A smile found its way to my lips. Knowing my child had been raised to trust the Lord God, creator of the stars, gave me a long sought-after peace. I had done one thing right in this life, I realized, as I had given a son to my husband after all.

I wanted more than anything to see my little Ethan and hear his laughter.

I never would. I couldn't return to my homeland. My roots had been ripped from the Hebrew soil and transplanted in a land not my own. As much as I yearned for home, it wasn't mine any longer. My sins were far too deep to be cleansed now. The land of my birth would no longer claim me.

In a few weeks, if I survived that long, I would die with the city of Nineveh.

MICHAL

Ethan watched his grandfather tend a calf who had gotten itself wrapped in a thorny vine. He made no move to help, content to sit quietly despite my father's gentle encouragement. In a few days, this would be my home again. I shook off the tears that wanted to cascade in rivers from my swollen eyes. I had had enough of that.

"I don't know of anyone who can afford to buy your house, then give it back to you, Michal. And no one is eager to take the home of their prophet, no matter the circumstances. There's some element of fear going around, that God will be angry about the transaction. It will sell to an outsider, I imagine. You understand, it has to be done. It's no longer yours if the king says it belongs to him. It has to be sold."

"I do understand." I yanked my head covering off and ran fingers through my hair, still unaccustomed to the shorter length. "I still don't like it. Jonah built it for Miriam and it will be hard to see someone else living there. I tried to keep it nice, for her as much as myself."

His tanned face had aged in the past months, the furrows deepening. "I'm sorry that I can't do more."

He, Caleb and my brothers had purchased the livestock already. I wore clothing borrowed from my daughters, Ethan's were from his cousins. "There's nothing more I would ask of you, or anyone in the family. I am blessed to have a home to return to. I'm not ungrateful."

Father cooed to the frightened calf as he pried the vine from her leg, the same secure voice I had been raised with. "It's a time of trial, and transition," he said to the beast, but I knew it was for my ears. "The Lord has not promised a path with no stones. We place our trust in him. He will see us through the rough patches."

"I want to stop all together some days," I confessed. "Let someone else move forward while I rest under a tree. But then the memories come." I stood and wrapped a scarf loosely over my head. "I'm going for a walk," I said. "Ethan, do you want to come?"

He shook his head. "I'll stay here."

My father straightened his back, arching it so that it cracked and popped. "Caleb's home this morning."

I couldn't miss the smirk on his face. There was no attempt to hide the fact that he thought my future was set already. I told him what the king's advisors said about my husband being alive, and like Lydia and Timna, he dismissed the notion as rumor. It was an excuse for the king to justify his greed, as Jonah would never go to Nineveh on his own power.

The town believed Jonah's possessions were taken back simply because the prophet was dead. I had not said anything outside the family to suggest there was more to the unkind action, that my husband was believed to be a traitor.

I knew Jonah wouldn't reject Israel. If he did go to the heart of his enemy, it wasn't because he was disloyal.

When I allowed my mind to put pieces together, starting from the beginning, I no longer knew in the depths of my being that I was a widow. Doubt whispered in my ear, suggesting that the fish tale was true, and my husband was alive.

And my anger whirled about inside me like a seething storm on Lake Gennesarat.

MICHAL

Caleb's laughter came from his belly and filled his home. I stood outside and listened to the happy chaos as he and a handful of grandchildren played a game of lots, the chosen one having to perform some awful task decided by the others. The last girl had to succumb to the relentless tickling of the others.

Leaning on the outside wall, I pictured Ethan among them. It was a good fit. Caleb was a good man. He wouldn't walk away from his home and family without sound reason, and not without speaking a word to anyone.

Why had my husband done so?

Bound for Tarshish, then to Nineveh? Perhaps Jonah did know that Miriam was alive, and wanted to take her back from her captors.

Had he drowned? Had there been a fish sent to save him?

What was true? I couldn't put the story together, but I could seethe in my frustration.

For all the unanswered questions, my husband had walked away from me and for that, he may as well stay dead. If he was alive.

How was I to know and how long was I to wait? Jonah made the choices that put me in this situation, that of no home or resources, no means to care for Ethan.

And if he did return, with Miriam, what then?

I wanted my sister home again. I wanted my husband home again, yet I feared what would become of me if they were. Would he love us both?

I hated the man that I loved. Standing on wet quicksand of

uncertainty, I needed a rock beneath my feet before the anxiety swallowed me up.

There was one option that ensured my future. There was a man willing to open his doors to me and my child. How could I say no?

JONAH

At the full moon, the residents of Nineveh donned the rough garments of sackcloth and began three days of total fasting. They would not eat or drink, nor indulge in any pleasures or worship of any god but to the one true God. Each man, woman, and child was to list their sins and repent of the ways they had disobeyed the commands given to Moses. Even the cattle had a drape of rough-hewn cloth on their backs and were denied their grains. These pagan thugs hoped to bend God's ear and find his favor.

I alone wore standard garments, and ate my meal at daybreak as usual before I ventured out to observe the consequences of my prophecies. My God would listen to the cries, I knew. He would see the repentance and withhold justice.

I drank a full cup of weak wine with the fruits and breads before me, and packed more to take along for later. I would not fast. I had no interest in joining the citizens here in their plea for life. I had followed the commands to warn them and that was all that I intended to do. It was not my decision as to what happened now.

As the sun rose and I walked the streets of the city, I was amazed at the relative stillness of the day. The bustle of merchants and patrons gone, replaced by prayers coming through household windows, requests to a god they knew little about. In the few weeks that I had been on this soil, no one but Miriam had claimed to be Hebrew. If others were out there, they had assimilated into the culture.

Picturing Miriam, I wondered how deeply she had been tainted. On the outside, she was no different than the natives, but her veins flowed with the blood of Abraham. She was an Israelite, no matter where she lived. Covering her hair, removing the face paints, and donning modest clothing, she could be Hebrew inside and out. Miriam's devotion to the Lord God was the one element that might separate her from us. Had she remembered him?

That thought was sobering. My own king bowed to idols made by human hands. The covenant with Abraham was all that spared Israel from obliteration, I imagined. How did I imagine Miriam would remember the God of her youth when surrounded by so many others?

Whomever she worshipped, I hoped Miriam would find me soon. I wanted to locate a caravan and help her depart from the Assyrian territory. She and her family could choose where to settle and start again. Perhaps Gath-hepher would call her home.

As for myself, I didn't know what to do. I desperately wanted to return to the land of my birth, craving the life I had before I fled. Restless, tired, angry, and fearful, I didn't know if I could go back. I was a traitor. But I couldn't remain in Nineveh, regardless of what happened. If not Gath-hepher, or anywhere in Israel, where was I to go?

PERSIS

The estate was oddly quiet, even in the early light of morning. The ovens were cold, no fires to bake breads or pots of meats beginning to heat. No one bustled about making preparations for the meals, and it made my footsteps on the marble floor more evident.

"Persis."

I froze at the sound of my husband's voice.

"You're back."

I turned and faced the man who had sent me to my death. He was clothed in the sackcloth of mourning as the king had commanded. No jewels flashed from his fingers or neck, no oils gleamed from his skin. No weapon was in his hand. It took my breath for a moment, to see him dressed this way, and still to emanate his power over me.

"Yes." I had hoped to delay the interaction. I didn't know how hot his anger toward me still burned. It wasn't a safe place for me to return. Yet I had to. As the city was searching their hearts for ways to please the God of Israel, I had to do the same. By whatever evil means I had arrived, this was my home, and this man, my husband.

My life I placed back into Tariq's hands. I had nothing to lose except a few days, when we would all be served justice. In my death, I would know I had chased after the forgiveness and restoration my God desired.

He looked at me a long moment. "I didn't expect to see you again."

The tone was less than angry. "I escaped."

I said the obvious, at a loss for how to explain why I was alive and why I came back. In his presence, my return felt foolish.

"The prophet of Dagon was at the temple. He prevented your death."

"The prophet, yes."

"What did he say? Why were you released?"

Did I dare speak against the ways of my husband? It had never been tolerated. I bit down on my lip and looked at the floor.

"Speak." He was irritated, but not hostile.

I sucked in a breath and breathed out a prayer for strength. "The prophet spoke against the evil of Nineveh. Against the sacrifices, the human ones." I lifted my head to look into his eyes. "They are offensive to his God. To my God."

His eyebrows raised. "Your God? That of the Hebrews?"

I nodded.

"I suppose I knew that when I bought you. I'd forgotten. A Hebrew captive. He didn't save you then, your God, and you still cling to him?"

"His ways are not the ways of man. Not the ways of my own understanding." Wisdom from my father found the light of my memory. "Who am I to question his plans?"

My husband regarded me with an expression I couldn't discern. His manicured fingers ran a track through his hair, the thinning strands blowing in the breeze that filtered into the room. "My city is on her knees before this God of yours. Pleasing him may save us. Do you remember his ways?"

I shifted from foot to foot. "Some of them. I was young when I was taken away."

He gave me a smile, one of remembering the beauty of my youth, I thought. "It's more than the rest of us know. Change your clothing. Go to the courtyard. I've sent the others there."

I hesitated.

"You aren't to be punished." He turned and left me alone.

Once I put on the proper garment, I made my way to the garden courtyard. The wives, children, servants and slaves were assembled there, sitting on the stone paving, quiet and solemn. Tariq rose and took my arm, leading me in front of the suddenly wide-eyed and nervous group. "She's not a ghost," he said. "Persis will teach us about this new God."

I scanned the group, searching for the children I had delivered from my womb, allowing my eyes to rest on each inquisitive face before I spoke. "It was in the beginning," I said. "In the beginning that God created the heavens and the earth. He isn't a new God at all. He is the One from whom time began."

The sun rose over me, and fell again toward the horizon as I spoke to this family, telling them of the family I had been born to, and of their ways and traditions, and of their God. I answered questions as best as I could, regretting the times I daydreamed on the Sabbath. The words were taken in, not ridiculed or rejected. God himself affirmed them in the minds of the Ninevites.

I had found a purpose.

From somewhere deep, deep within, a cleansing flow sprang free as I spoke unashamedly of the Lord of my youth, flushing out my own sins. We had no Levite priests to offer a sacrifice for us, we barely understood what was required as we addressed our ways, and vowed to turn from all that was evil, yet I knew the Lord my God was pleased.

Pleased with Nineveh.

Pleased with my family.

Pleased with me.

For the first time since I had been delivered to this land of my enemy, I felt forgiven.

Without a ceremonial bath or the ruling of the priests, I was clean.

JONAH

I was told it took three full days to walk the perimeter wall of Nineveh's complex of homes and businesses, fields and estates, military outposts and orchards. The estimate was inaccurate if the citizens believed you were part deity, or were ordered by the king to heed your message. It had taken me weeks to canvass the city, never going any great length in one stretch because the crowds would rise up and clog the arterials.

Carefully counting the notches on the leather strip where I marked the days, I came to thirty-eight.

Had I been here so long? Each day blurred into all the others. As I dressed, I knew it was my day to leave the way I had come, through the gates of the city. The caravan that carried me here was already gone, as were all the foreign travelers who had come and heard the prophecy, leaving as soon as they could gather supplies.

I had no means of transportation since all Ninevite residents were forbidden to leave, including the beasts. Every living creature was ordered to stay and seek mercy from the God of Israel. The king's city would live or die as one.

Including Miriam.

The woman of my home village had not come to me for deliverance. Disappointment within me grew with each day she didn't find me as I walked the streets. Not able to save her years ago, I hoped to do so now. I wanted it for her, needed it for me, and it would please Michal like no other gift I could deliver. My every failure as a husband might be wiped from her tally if I arrived on my doorsteps with Miriam at my side.

Unless she came soon, Miriam would remain in her captivity. I had no time to find her myself now, and hoped she had already found a way to leave the city with one of the many exiting caravans.

Wrapping supplies from the pantry in a knapsack, I heard the owner of the home praying to the God of Israel. There was no place in the near region where men had resisted the call to turn from evil. The word of the Lord had been heeded.

From the moment I was given this task, I knew the city was going to be spared.

I kicked an intricately carved vase and sent it crashing into a wall.

"Isn't this what I said would happen if I came? This is why I fled for Tarshish." I spoke to the heavens, to the one who held the reins. "You are a gracious and compassionate God, slow to anger and abounding in love, a God who relents from sending calamity."

My clenched fist put a hole in the door of a wooden cabinet. My own people had not sought their God like I was witnessing in the streets of this wretched place. What would become of the land of Israel?

"Take my life, God! I want to die rather than be part of this. I can't be responsible for what's happening." I knew I was wrong to harbor the hatred. I couldn't help my torment.

My legs trembled under the eyes of the Lord. I fell to my knees and then to my face, prostrating myself on the floor.

His voice whispered in my soul, not yelling, not berating. "Have you any right to be angry?"

I didn't permit the words to settle. I rose, packed the belongings given to me along with the food, wine, and some tools. The stench of Nineveh was more than I could take any longer. I'd despised them my entire life and now my warning would give them a reprieve. It wasn't fair. How could God forgive them for generations of atrocities?

I walked out the door, and out of the city. The residents followed me in a great throng but I said nothing more to them. Stopping at the great gate, I alone was permitted to leave. It clanged shut behind me.

Across the river to the east, up a hillside, I scabbed together the sticks I could find and built myself a shelter from the sun. I planned to wait out the remaining days to see for myself what would happen.

JONAH

Dry winds whipped the leaves I'd tied to the wooden frame of my temporary dwelling, the intensity increasing as the daylight turned to night. The palms I'd gathered on my way had shriveled and ripped apart, leaving me exposed to the open sky. The moon hung amidst a torrent of stars, a blanket of lights that turned my thoughts to home, where the same moon was with my wife and children. I'd slept very little.

Now the sun was peeking over the far horizon. My pale flesh couldn't tolerate the rays and I was contemplating a return to the protection of the palms near the river when I noticed a finger length shoot of green at the base of my structure. It had not been there yesterday, it's fresh green hue obvious against the browns of the dry hilltop. Not wanting to waste water to nourish the young vine, I thought no more about it. Like everything else around me, it would shrivel and die.

Covering my head in a turban and my skin in the robes I packed, I sat facing the city. It was the thirty-ninth day.

Nineveh remained intact. Sunshine glimmered off its walls as the morning progressed, the brightness harsh on my eyes. It was an opportune time to pray. I tried, and found my heart cold. "Forgive me, Lord," I managed to say. "I want to feel compassion. I don't know how."

I rested my chin on my knees, sweat running a course down my back and under my arms. Periodically I swiped my hand over my forehead to keep the salty fluid from my eyes. I was hot. I was frustrated. I was angry with the Ninevites, angry with God. Angry with myself. Unhappiness was poison to my spirit, and I couldn't rid myself of its effects.

Ready to entomb myself in robes and simply sleep the time away, I again took notice of the vine. It still lived, and had grown remarkably. Standing nearly as tall as me now, it clung to the poles I'd rigged and was spreading itself laterally. No vine was capable of the growth rate I was witnessing, not on its own power. This was the hand of God.

Scooting closer, I found shaded protection from the large fan shaped leaves that filled the span between the poles. I removed my turban and wiped the moisture away, enjoying the cooler interior. A miracle for my benefit, my mood changed course.

Was this a symbol of God's blessing? Not only on me, but on his people? I wanted to believe that the vine protecting me was also a promise to protect Israel. We were not without fault, but we had never been as merciless and tyrannical as the Assyrians. God had to select us over them, didn't he? And wouldn't he destroy them before they could destroy us?

A twinge of guilt entered my thoughts. Miriam would be among the dead if the city fell. I didn't want that outcome. I hoped God would see to her preservation. Like the vine he called to life and the fish that scooped me from the ocean depths, he could protect her from his wrath.

The vine continued to grow, the sound of its efforts dancing off my ears as a soft rustling. I shed layers of fabric. By midday, I was comfortably enclosed in a green oasis. My anger fell with the temperature, feeling quite pleased with the arrangement, and pleased with God for the first time that I could recall in years. I had to believe the vine was a sign, and that he was pleased with me.

As the thirty-ninth day came to an end, I realized the fall of Nineveh might yet happen, and if it did, I could return to my home. The king's favor would fall on me anew, and that of all Israel. My name would endure for all generations. Jonah, the Victor. I fell asleep with visions of my own glorious return, and more importantly, with hope.

Early the next morning, in the smothering blackness before dawn, I awakened and sat up immediately. It was the fortieth day. Dressed in a light under-tunic, my heart pounded in the cool remnants of the night air as I waited for resolution. I was eager for the long months of personal torment to be over.

The first rays of dawn crested, and the city remained standing.

Keeping disappointment from crushing me, I prayed for favor on Israel while keeping vigilant watch on the heavens above and valley below.

The sun continued to rise. The heavens remained blue. The city stood firmly on the banks of the Tigris.

My visions of a great homecoming drained into the dry soil.

The day was only beginning, but I knew that mercy had been poured out already.

Screaming into the heavens, I voiced my displeasure, trying to wake the vengeance of God and stir it into action. And still, the city stood where it had been planted by Nimrod centuries ago. Unscathed. Untouched by the fires of wrath.

I leaned back and closed my eyes, dissatisfied. Intensely dissatisfied. The decision had been made.

I had no means to travel anywhere but back into the city. I would be welcomed. The favor I'd been shown would multiply and my remaining days could be spent in the riches of the land. But I didn't want to be in Nineveh. I wanted to go home. There, I would be considered a traitor, and shunned, perhaps stoned at the king's command.

How would I explain all that had happened to me?

How could I explain the ways of God when I didn't know myself?

I reached for my turban wrap, intending to plump it into a pillow, and found my arm drenched in sunshine. The verdant leaves on the east wall were withering. A quick scan of my shelter and I found they were curling in on themselves all around me. Tracing the thick stem back to the earth where it had first protruded, I saw the worm. It had eaten half the thickness of the vine already. Squashing it now would make no difference.

Whatever favor I imagined I had been shown was disintegrating. The plant would die.

And Nineveh would not.

I stood and faced the city as the sun climbed its walls, spilling light into the streets beneath a sky, clear and cloudless. Near me, a hawk called as it passed over head, soaring on gentle currents to the abundant life-giving river below.

Hot winds whipped up the loose soil around my feet. They grew as the day progressed, and I was forced to cover myself in robes to prevent my skin from scorching and being blasted by debris. In little time, a skeleton of sticks was all that remained of my shelter. God was rejecting me.

I crumbled to the ground, too dizzy from the heat to care anymore about anyone or anything. I was so tired of this journey, so tired of this life. There was nothing I could do to make any of it right. "It's all in your hands," I said to the God I didn't understand. "I'm done."

And that's when my Lord returned, the voice in my soul clear, and tender.

"Jonah, Jonah."

I remained in a heap with the fabrics wrapped around me, frozen as he spoke.

"Do you have a right to be angry about the vine?"

"I thought it was a promise! You're *my* God. Not theirs. What about all I've done for you? Has it meant nothing? What about all they've done against you?"

The patient voice poured out reasoning like a soothing balm. "You did nothing to make this plant live and grow. My hand formed it, and my hand took it away. You grieve the loss of a vine you didn't even tend."

I held my breath in the still confines, knowing he had more to say.

"How much more are the people of Nineveh of worth to me than that vine? The city holds a hundred and twenty thousand people who don't know their right hand from their left, yet you don't grieve for them. They are my creation, and all the cattle of their fields. Should I not care for them? Should I not be concerned about the salvation of that great city?"

JONAH

I remained on the hillside after the voice retreated and the scorching winds faded, unable to move. In the solitude of my garment cave, I had finally seen God's heart.

And despised my own in contrast.

The depth of the Lord's love was fathomless. He could choose Israel, and still have room in his heart for Assyria.

I thought he was ours alone. Although Gentiles had always been welcomed in the land of promise — it was on our soil, and on our terms. That God could love us, *and* these Assyrians, was hard to place in my biased soul.

God's mercy surpassed his judgment.

For Nineveh.

For Israel.

For me.

I had much to think about, my repentance trailing that of the people I was trying to not despise. Their quick obedience brought me shame. I had turned from the Lord and his commands and ran away.

Gathering the few possessions I owned, I sat back down to call on the Lord. He hadn't commanded me to remain in Nineveh, and I wanted to go home. My place was in Gath-hepher, and despite the risks, I wanted to be with my wife and children. "O Lord, help me return to my people," I prayed.

PERSIS

The steep trail led us to a simple open shelter, and there I found Jonah, arms to the heavens in supplication. "Prophet," I said quietly. I hadn't spoken to him since the night I found him by the fountain. From a distance, I had watched him in the streets, feeling the same admiration I'd had when he was a young man. I wasn't permitted to speak to him in public then, and chose not to the past weeks. I fully anticipated I would be dead by the hand of God by this time, and wanted him to forget he'd ever seen me.

In mercy I never believed was so infinite, God had spared the city despite its many gods and vile pleasures. My life had been saved once again.

Jonah looked up, his attention on the dozen armed men waiting beyond his shelter. No longer in sackcloth, they were dressed for travel. "Miriam," he said, the name bringing a sting of tears to my eyes. "Miriam, the city has been spared. God has, has shown his mercies."

I sat beside him, seeing my beautiful city for only the second time from beyond her fortified walls. It gleamed in the brilliant sunshine. "It's a new day, a new beginning for us."

He searched my face intently, his eyes red and swollen. "Us? You said 'us', not 'them'?"

Placing my hand on his, I smiled gently. "I can't go with you, Jonah ben Amattai, Prophet of Gath-hepher. God brought me here. Who am I to question his ways? He didn't promise me a path without stones."

Sadness crossed Jonah's tear stained features before he returned my smile. "You've had boulders, cliffs, and venomous serpents."

I laughed out loud, a sound I hadn't heard in a long time. "Yes, and still I live. You as well. You've had a remarkable season of great adventure. A fish of all things, saved by a fish to save my city."

Jonah squeezed my hand between both of his, the pale splotchy coloring more evident in the daylight than in the night time shadows. "I ran from home, Miriam. I didn't intend to come here. I had no compassion on those - on your people."

"I know. I've heard from others what happened. Your intentions weren't the same as our Lord's and I am so glad he got his way and you didn't."

The prophet chuckled, a happy laugh that made me smile again. "He knew best. He loves this place, these people."

"We have a second chance."

"Will it last, do you think? The repentance?"

I shrugged. "I don't know. I do know I'm supposed to remain, to teach and instruct."

Jonah tenderly kissed the back of my hand. "I want to bring you back to Michal and your father. You deserve to go home."

"I have purpose here."

He nodded. "I could stay, and help you."

"But do you want to, Jonah, man of God? Where is your heart?"

He looked at me with the same deep brown eyes that stared at me in the market, a face displaying his approval. "You've grown up, my betrothed, a beautiful woman, wise and strong." He turned to the city and hesitated, his heart heavy and weary. "My heart, my heart is in Israel."

"Where it should be," I said, slipping my hand from his and resting it on my cheek, where I could feel the heat rising. His simple

321

affirmations had always fed my soul. "Go and speak to the children of Abraham of the mercy that comes with repentance. Tell them how you were preserved from death, how your enemy turned to the true God."

"I'll be despised."

"Indeed. For a time. The people will soften their attitudes towards you when they realize the raids have ceased." I wiped a drop of sweat from my forehead. "And your wife will be your comfort."

Jonah tensed at the mention of Michal.

"What will you tell my sister?"

"Everything." He lowered his head and stared at his hands. "Everything. She prayed for this city while I cursed it, more like God than his own prophet. She expressed compassion for the mothers here, and believed that not every heart was black to the roots."

My heart quickened at his words. Did she understand then, about her Ethan? "She prayed for me."

He nodded without realizing what I meant. "Yes," he said. "I suppose she held on to you, praying that you'd lived all these years."

I wanted to tell Jonah that Ethan was my child, that I was the mother my sister prayed for, but stopped myself. That was Michal's place, not mine. He was her son now. "Tell her that I'm happy. That I have fine sons and beautiful daughters. Tell her, that I miss her. Nothing has replaced my love for my little sister."

"She won't forgive me for leaving you behind."

I stood and shook the grit from my garment. "Then she'll have to come here and fetch me herself. Perhaps, one day…?"

He nodded vigorously. "Look for us. Michal won't be satisfied until she's laid eyes on you."

"She'll understand why I'm staying, and she'll forgive you for not packing me along."

Jonah closed his eyes and took several deep breaths. "I didn't tell her I was leaving. For all she knows, I was eaten by a lion. I witnessed a fierce storm at sea, lived in a fish's belly and threatened my enemy with destruction, yet facing my wife scares me more than any of that. And I don't know what my children believe, if they will hold anger against me."

"Your children will return to you. They're like that, aren't they? Dropping the hurts so they can grasp love. And my sister, she'll find forgiveness for her husband. Start over, if you need to. Pursue her affections again. Live, and be blessed, you two, as our God has intended."

Jonah wrapped me tightly in his arms, hanging on for strength. He was weary of his calling. The prophet of the Most High was drained of all that had kept his feet moving away from his home to fulfil the task he had been given.

I whispered in his ear the words I had memorized from the writings of my home land. "If you devote your heart to God, and stretch out your hands to him, if you put away the sin that is in your hand and allow no evil to dwell in your tent, then you will lift up your face without shame. You will stand firm, without fear. You will forget your trouble, recalling it as waters gone by. Life will be brighter than noonday, and darkness will become like morning. You will be secure because there is hope."

I wished I could send him on the wings of an eagle back to Michal, swiftly and safely. Instead, I pulled away and handed him a sack of coins and jewels. "Come." I started down the hill toward the Tigris below. "The camels are loaded with provisions and these men will protect you. It's time for you to go home, prophet."

MICHAL

Every small bit of what I had called mine was cleared from the house and barn and storehouses that Jonah built. I allowed the broom to fall onto the floor, the echo loud in the empty space. Prying up the stone cap in the floor near the hearth, I took the remainder of my husband's cache of coins. It was a generous sum, not enough to buy my own property, but enough to pay for the additional room my father and Caleb were building.

More of my life had been lived in these walls than any other, and I was sad about leaving it behind. I went to the window overlooking the pastures, a peaceful view in any season. The morning sun came first through this window, where I sat in the awakening day to pray while Jonah did the same on his hilltop sanctuary. All of my babies I had nursed in that spot, and held on my lap when they needed reassurance, and later, advice and council, until they were too old for such things, and sat beside me as a friend, nestling grandbabies in my arms.

From here I could see out into the kitchen, awaiting the aroma of baking bread that spilled inside each day. The song of the sparrows, the banter of sheep, the laughter of a family, whole, and united, floated on the breezes into my ear as I cleaned or sewed or cooked.

It was a happy home. Was. Now it belonged to someone from outside Gath-hepher whose family would make their own memories here while mine were swept out with the last of the dust.

I sighed as I closed the wooden shutters, picked up the broom and closed the door behind me. I refused to cry. I had shed enough tears over what my life was supposed to be and what it really was and what I wanted to happen and what never would. I was blessed to have a home, and to be cared for, to have children and family to see to my needs. I would never be destitute nor would my life be without love and laughter, and all the joys and triumphs of living and breathing beneath the heavens of my God.

I stopped on the road and turned toward the hill, the sanctuary of the prophet. What had happened there? What really made my husband forsake his calling and home to flee from all the good that was in his life? Over and over I had reviewed the details, the facts, the mysteries, speculating and finding no solid conclusions. I didn't know why Jonah left.

For all my harbored anger at the man who married me, I missed him severely. There was an ache for Jonah that I feared would never be eased.

JONAH

My home was empty.

I felt its hollow soul as I approached in the near darkness, the soil of the promised land beneath me, guiding me back to familiar smells and sounds and sites. I was beyond eager to fall asleep in a bed of my own handiwork. But there was no bed.

Dust on the floor was evident as I walked from room to room, stirring up in a cloud. "Michal?" I called out as if she might be there when nothing else was, not even coals in the cooking hearth. The place had been vacated of possessions and of people. Where were Michal and Ethan?

Walking the last hours alone, I hadn't wanted to sleep, and weariness was overwhelming me now that I was here at last, in my own home, in my own town, my nation. Dust billowed up as I removed the pack of gifts and provisions from my back and dropped it to the floor. I slumped against a wall and slid down beside it.

My escorts hadn't wanted to abandon me, having promised Miriam to see me safely home. I convinced them this was better, that they needed to hurry along to Jerusalem to see the temple for themselves, and to rest there before returning to Nineveh. It would be an awkward homecoming for me, no matter how it occurred, and I wanted to make my peace with my family in quietness rather than arrive with an entourage and be a spectacle.

There was a time I would have loved the attention, the honor my escorts wanted to endow. Not this time. The men knew as much about the Lord as I did now, after our month traveling together, and couldn't hear about the whole fish incident enough times. Eager to tell of the events, they would paint me in a favorable light rather than present the true image. Gath-hepher would hear of courage and conviction rather than rebellion and resentment.

For those men, I was a prophet bringing life.

For my people, I was a prophet who ran from God.

I returned a different man, one with passion. With a firmer grip on God's mercy, a clearer vision of his heart, I had a message.

Yes, the Lord loved Israel, but I knew now what I had never believed before. He listened to the cries of nations beyond our own, and forgave when there was repentance. God loved the world and had compassion on all the sons of Noah. There was no limit to the pouring out of his mercy.

I sought forgiveness for my self-righteous attitude again and again as the camels plodded me toward home. Who was I to accuse God of making an error in judgment?

Nineveh didn't deserve the gracious hand of God.

Neither did I.

Laying my head on my knees, I prayed that my children would listen and understand, and learn. I prayed that Michal would find even a tiny portion of mercy for me. My countrymen might despise me, and that I would contend with, even unto death. But I didn't want to try to stand firm any longer without my wife at my side.

MICHAL

Light of the new morning bathed the altar remnants. I wrapped the shawl around my shoulders and tried to pray, finding my thoughts wandering in all directions instead. I'd been coming back nearly every day since moving out of my home a few weeks back, not able to say goodbye to the memories, the hopes that had been born on that portion of land. The new owner was from Damascus and didn't care that the land had belonged to a prophet and might now be cursed. There would be an altar to Baal on this hill before long, and that tore at my heart the most.

Footsteps on the path roused me from my thoughts and from my knees. I stood, assuming it was one of my children. The man that rounded the last bend was old, taking weary steps. With his head down, the hairless scalp was mostly shiny, pocked with scars that were pale and dull. It was an unnatural color, as were his hands, barely tinted beyond white. Rich colorful robes covered the rest of him, fine linen with new sandals on his pale feet.

I held my breath as the stranger approached.

When he finally lifted his head and realized he wasn't alone, he stopped dead still. "Michal."

I knew the voice, and gasped.

Had I not dreamed of that moment after he disappeared? Even later, after I learned of his death? Hearing my name falling from my husband's lips, seeing him before me, not dead, not gone. In my mind, it had all been a mistake and I had fallen into his arms, my anger melting away.

The moment was nothing like my dreams.

I couldn't speak or move, and no morsel of compassion was rising in my heart. Of all the questions, all the fears and anger, all the explanations I wanted from him, "Where have you been?" was all I could finally sputter.

Jonah exhaled and took the remaining steps to me. I flinched when his hand reached out to take mine, not because of the odd color. I didn't want him to touch me, to believe I was still his, simply waiting and forgiving as I always had.

He pulled his arm back. "It isn't contagious," he said. "I'm not leprous, or ill."

I turned away and looked out at the valley and mountains that had been steadfast in his absence.

Jonah stood beside me, his hands clasped behind his back. "God was here," he said, barely above the whisper of the morning winds. "He spoke, gave me a task that I didn't want to do."

I didn't engage in his attempt to get me to interact and ask him what the task was. I was willing to listen, however, needing to know the why's and where's, so sat on a smooth stone with my face to the valley. He sat nearby, beneath an olive tree that he'd planted when he first purchased the land.

Jonah shifted into the shade as it moved with the rising sun, telling me of the call from God, his own heart on the matter and his flight from home. The ship, the storm, the fish. The villagers and the caravan. Nineveh. Nineveh's response to the warning.

It was true then, the rumors of the prophet of God, spit from a fish and going to the great Assyrian city.

I found my voice again when he grew quiet. "They repented?"

He nodded. "And God granted mercy."

"He sent you there. To warn them. To give them a chance to

live." It was not a direction my mind would have ever gone on its own.

"His ways are not ours. God loves the ones he formed from the dust, even those who shun his presence."

"You tried to run." I reassembled all the pieces and took them apart again, processing.

Jonah drew his sleeve back and ran his hand over his forearm. "As if God wouldn't follow."

"You didn't intend to come back, did you? You walked away from us, forever."

From the corner of my eye I saw his head drop. He shook it slowly back and forth. "I was foolish," he said. "It seemed right, at the time. At least, I convinced myself it was right."

I turned to look him in the eye. "Why Jonah? Why didn't you tell me? Why did you leave and not say goodbye?"

It was his turn to hide from my face. He looked at the earth, choosing a stone to hurl into the air and listen as it hit the ground again and tumbled away. "I couldn't. I knew you'd tell me not to run. You'd convince me to obey God. And, and I couldn't. I didn't want to see Nineveh survive."

"We would have worked it out together." I yanked my head scarf free so a cool breeze could blow over me.

"I know that. Now. I'm sorry Michal. You don't know how sorry I am."

Jonah reached his hand toward my hair, then pulled it back before he touched it. "Your hair. Cut in mourning, for me?"

"Yes, for you. We were told you were dead." I allowed it to sink into his mind.

Jonah rubbed his palms over his scalp. "And Ethan? Has he managed, is he alright?"

Not certain where my emotions wanted to go anymore, I pulled away when he mentioned my son. Jonah protected his own interests and survived. But there were consequences beyond his bleached skin. He couldn't simply come home and have his life restored, as if nothing had occurred in his voluntary absence. Nothing was the same.

And my anger was nowhere near being depleted. "Caleb offered to take care of him. Of both of us."

The arrow struck Jonah squarely. He pinched his eyes shut and dropped his head onto his hands. "That's why our house is empty."

His pain was obvious. I did nothing to relieve it. "We don't live on this land anymore. And neither do you. King Jeroboam took all that we had when he found out you were either dead or finding refuge with his enemy."

I stood abruptly and left the hill, not turning back as my husband fell to his face and wept.

JONAH

A man can't expect to flee from God and have no repercussions. Delayed submission isn't the same as obedience. All the same, I felt in my soul that he had forgiven me my trespasses.

Not so my wife. A man can't expect to flee from his home and have no repercussions, either. I disappeared, then was dead. An honorable man stepped in to take my place in caring for her and her child. I couldn't be angry at anyone but myself. Michal had no home, no fields or resources. And perhaps she loved him. They had been best of friends since childhood.

Still, she was mine, and I didn't want her to be with anyone else. I had every right to demand her back, according to the law.

How could I? There was no home to take her to, no income to provide for her needs. The resources from Miriam wouldn't last, if anyone would accept them. I looked cursed, and once labeled a traitor, would have no friends.

My children, except Ethan, gathered in the shade of Lydia's garden to listen to my explanation of the events that took me from them, and brought me home again. The youngest grandchild bounced on my knee, gurgling the innocent sounds of happiness without any judgment against me. She alone held this view. The rest were reserved in their affections. I had broken a bond by walking away without a word, by leaving as I did, choosing my own death rather than obeying the Lord. My family had suffered and mourned their loss and tried to move beyond the grief of unanswered questions.

Now, without warning, I was back among them.

I told the story again, leaving out nothing except the fact that I had seen Miriam. I saved this portion for Michal's ears only. There were jewels and perfumes in my pack for her, gifts that would pale in comparison to the news of her sister. It was a gift I would present before I left Gath-hepher.

I didn't know where I was going to go. Not so far that I couldn't visit my family, not so close that it was awkward for Michal. Two of my sons had offered me a room, but I couldn't remain in this village while Michal was no longer mine. And I wouldn't take Ethan away from her, though I could. It wouldn't be right to either of them. I wouldn't allow my legal rights to override my moral responsibilities.

"I need to see Ethan before I leave," I said. "He needs to hear all that I've told you from me directly."

Adin couldn't hide his jumble of emotions, eyes red from tears, jaw tensed. My eldest had carried a burden in my absence. Resentment poured out of him, mingled with joy and more sorrow. "You know where he is?"

"Yes," I said as I stood and began the routine of covering myself from the sun.

Lydia put a gentle hand on my shoulder. "Father," she said. "Stay with us. Don't leave again."

I thanked her, avoiding the sharp look coming from her husband. He didn't believe that I had been saved from death by a fish, and I couldn't blame him. I wouldn't have believed me, either.

Skirting the main roads, I stood in the shadows outside Caleb's home. It would be easier on Ethan if Michal was with him, assuring my son that I was real, and safe. His anger toward me was to be expected, and already I felt the knot of emotion in my throat. Ashamed of my actions, my inactions and failures, I didn't want to see the hurt in his eyes. I deserved condemnation, but craved the unbounded love this child had always provided.

Mustering resolve, I went to the door and knocked. Facing Caleb without animosity would not be easy, even knowing the man had done nothing wrong. He had my wife, and that was enough.

Caleb opened the door, and flinched at the sight of me, trying to mask his alarm by coughing into his sleeve. "May I help you?"

The words tumbled from my choked throat. "I'd like to see them. Please."

Color drained from Caleb's face as the light of recognition crossed his face. "Jonah."

I nodded, waiting on the doorstep patiently rather than pushing the man aside.

Caleb recovered and opened the door, ushering me to a cushioned mat and providing a cool drink. He glanced at the foot washing basin, then my sandals. He was clearly leery about touching my feet where the nails had never grown back, yet grabbed a towel anyhow.

I stopped him from treating me as a welcomed guest in that fashion. It was more than my pride could handle. I didn't deserve his favor and felt my own shame keenly. God should have used Caleb as his spokesman. He would not have run from any command.

At the moment, the man couldn't have run from anything. He was stunned by my presence, and doing a poor job of trying to appear at ease.

I tried to relieve the tension. "I appreciate what you've done, giving them a home."

"Of course," he said. "We thought you were dead. A sailor came, said you'd drowned."

Squid, no doubt. "He had reason to believe that I did."

"What happened to you, Jonah? Where have you been?"

"Nineveh." I stood abruptly. I wasn't there to explain it him. "Please, Caleb. Where are they?"

"I assure you, they're fine. I've taken good care of them."

Impatience was seeping out of me. "Caleb." I said it with more sharpness than I intended.

Caleb crossed his arms over his chest. "I don't under-"

"I'll tell you everything. Later." With my odd appearance and desperation, I didn't want him to be any more alarmed and send me away. I calmed my voice intentionally. "I won't make trouble. I promise."

He paused, then nodded. "Come then. I'll take you to them."

Neither of us spoke as we left the home and walked the trail towards his fields and pastures, he graciously allowing me to go first. His eyes burned a hole in my back, out of concern for my sanity perhaps, or his own safety. He led me to a stone enclosure and opened the gate.

My eyes searched for a woman and child. I saw only the curly fleece of sheep.

The skin on my neck prickled.

Caleb kept his distance, his eyes focused on me. There was no one else in the vicinity.

Why had he brought me here? "I don't intend to cause trouble," I said, subtly looking for the nearest stone I could use as a weapon of protection.

"So you've said. I believe you," he responded, but I could tell by his tone that he didn't.

He continued, arms crossing his chest again. "I've cared for them well. They're safe and well fed, and you can buy them back when you're ready."

"Buy them back?!"

Caleb raised his hands in defense. "Just take them when you get settled, Jonah. I'm not trying to take advantage of you."

"Where *are* they, Caleb?"

He stared back at me, eyes wide and confused. "Jonah, I don't know what to tell you. Look at them, they're all here. I'll protect your flock until you get settled again, that's all. You can have them back anytime."

My flock? I looked at the sheep grazing lazily in his pasture.

It had been a while since I laughed, and it came out loudly, exasperation notching up the volume.

Caleb took a step back, more uncertain of me than ever.

"No. Not my sheep, Caleb. I came to see my son and my-" I looked away, the laughter fading. "And Michal."

His smile stretched the width of his face. "Oh! I misunderstood. Your family isn't here."

"Where are they?"

He shrugged. "Not at Zedekiah's?"

"I haven't been there yet."

Caleb put his hands on his hips and tilted his head. "You do know they live there now, don't you? The king took your house."

I stared at him. "They don't stay with you?"

"No." Caleb scratched his chin. "Michal moved back in with your father-in-law. I helped add a room for her and Ethan, and one for Timna."

I leaned heavily on the stone fence. "I thought they were here. I thought she said…"

"That I asked her to marry me?"

I couldn't answer against the lump in my throat, hope rising from the ruins.

"I did, Jonah." His voice was quiet. He waited for me to reply.

336

When I didn't, he continued. "She said no. Michal wasn't certain you were dead, and even if she had been, she wasn't ready to give you up in her heart."

Michal hadn't married Caleb. She was still mine. Angry and unforgiving, cold and distant, but mine. I lifted my arms to the heavens and whooped in delight.

"I'm glad you're home, my friend." Caleb said. "We thought you were dead. It hasn't been easy for Ethan, for any of us."

"I know," I said, absently watching the animals graze. "And I'll give you all the details of where I've been, but right now, I just need to hold my son."

Caleb slapped a hand on my back then pulled it quickly away. "He'll be with his grandfather."

"I'm not contagious," I said before I wrapped him up in my arms. Relief was pouring out of me like the surge of the Tigris.

Caleb tensed and immediately pushed me back at arm's length. "Then *what* is wrong with your skin and where are your eyebrows?"

"You won't believe what God has done."

I yanked the pasture gate closed and turned to run toward Zedekiah's when I recalled the advice Miriam had given me. I stopped and took Caleb's shoulders in my hands. "I would like to buy my sheep back," I said. "Do you trade in rubies?"

MICHAL

Ethan's alarm dissipated and joy unimaginable filled its place. Standing in the window, I watched my son forgive his father without a moment's hesitation once he heard the white skinned man call out his name. There was no fear of disease, no pent-up anger to overcome. Just love and open arms. "You're home!" Ethan cried, as if he knew all along that Jonah would one day walk back into his life.

There was a tickle in my heart that had said he was alive. I doubted I'd ever see him again, but I hadn't been able to marry Caleb. My heart couldn't leap the gully that took me from being Jonah's beloved to Caleb's. I was prepared to live in my father's house, or with one of my children, until I died. No one would've blamed me for taking a new husband. It would have been a good life with Caleb, but not the right life. The hand of God held me back from his arms.

Hearing my son's laughter peal from the depths of his being, I realized I had chosen wisely.

It wasn't long before my father returned from the vineyard. He stopped cold on the path when he saw Ethan showing the stranger his collection of skipping stones. The bristling of Father's spine and the tight grip on his knife relaxed when his grandson's excited voice carried to him. It was Ethan from before the accident returning to us.

Once my father recognized Jonah, his anger grew sharp again. I couldn't hear the exact words, but I recognized the wide stance he held, and it was not one of pleasure. They retreated to the shadow of an old oak after a few minutes, Ethan tucked tightly into Jonah's side. They talked. And talked. Talking eventually led to smiles, and to laughter, and finally to a long embrace. My father forgave the man who left me.

It stirred my anger, the three of them happy together as if nothing had happened, as if no one had been hurt. Would everyone forget what I had suffered because of what Jonah did? There was a sense of unfairness in my soul, and one of betrayal.

I wasn't ready to speak to my husband. I wanted to forgive him, wanted to start again on a solid foundation. Holding resentment inside gained me nothing and it wasn't the sort of woman I wanted to be. And yet, anger clung to me with prideful claws.

My husband hadn't left me to search for Miriam. God sent him on a mission that he fought. I understood all that. It was the manner in which he left, the grief that multiplied in the unexplained absence. He had chosen not to confide in me and that pain coursed through my heart. We were supposed to be one another's strength. We were supposed to be one.

Guilt prowled into my thoughts. Had I been honest about Ethan's lineage, my husband might not have hated the Assyrians with the same intensity. Had he known I believed Miriam lived, he may have followed God's command, not tried to flee from it. He might have confided in me and we would have sought the Lord together.

It was past time for me to be honest. And past time for me to hold so righteously to my anger. As much as I wanted to make Jonah hurt because he had hurt me, I wanted him to crush me in arms of affection even more. I wanted to wake up beside him in the night, to feel his fingertips brush against my cheek.

I had a choice, and I decided to allow the ugliness to slip away.

I wanted my family to be whole again. With all its faults and foibles, it was mine, and I was as responsible as Jonah to make it work.

MICHAL

"But the fence is down on the northern corner. I can fix it, you know I'm capable."

I hadn't seen Jonah in more than a week, keeping myself from Lydia's where he was living in the barn, surrounded by a constant stream of the curious, the angry, the repentant. Some believed, some not. Jonah preached on, regardless.

The resolve I needed to speak to him was there, and I felt I could forgive him. When the crowds diminished and he came around again, I intended to do so.

Father patted my shoulder and grinned in a way I couldn't quite decipher. "Yes, of course you can, Michal. We'll mend it later. This morning, we stay home. I was hoping you'd make that rosemary bread like your mother used to do."

After decades of domestic chores, I'd found a new passion in the labors of the land. I understood why my husband had found his comfort there, sweating over a shovel rather than a broomstick. There was a sense of fulfillment in the raising of a wall that I'd never found in the sewing of a garment. I wasn't my mother, and I wasn't Miriam. And that was finally all right. One aspect of my life with Jonah that I hadn't missed was the endless entertaining.

"You would rather I stay here and bake rather than see to work that needs to be done?"

He shrugged, and didn't quite look me in the eye. "I make the rules in my house," he said, barely able to keep himself from laughing as he spoke. He rose and left me at the table with some feeble plan to repair chinking that had just done a week prior.

I stood and peeked out every window, wondering what he was up to. He never let the sun rise over his crops without tending them that late in the morning. The clear, pale dawn gave nothing away, and neither did any of my brothers who lived nearby.

The third loaf of fragrant bread was out of the oven when I heard the din, a sound from my past. It took me a moment to place it. When I did, I ran up the stairs to the rooftop to look down the road.

A dust storm billowed its way toward me. From the midst, the bleats of sheep, the stomping of hooves, the call of the shepherd. Jonah's voice.

I stood at the wall where I stood years ago as my sister's betrothed arrived with the mohar for my father. So ridiculously disappointed when it was for me that he came, it felt so petty now. Hard-hearted and unwilling to forgive, I only hurt myself. Why did I cling to such a grievance for so long?

Members of my family, old and young, ran from where they'd been hiding. My young nieces were first to wend through the maze to reach Jonah and surround him, not allowing him to turn and flee. The boys spread out around the beasts, urging them forward. My father held back, and before he turned to look up at me, he swiped his eyes with the back of his hand. He was smiling so wide when he caught my eyes, I thought his face would break in two.

Then I understood.

My family herded the entire flock of irritated beasts into the pasture as I left my perch and stood at the door of the house. My hands were trembling, my nose burning with the torrent of tears wanting to fall. My heart could hardly contain itself inside me.

This wasn't my husband reclaiming his animals and seeking pastures for them with my father. This is what my heart cried for the day he came for me as a bride.

My betrothed had arrived to claim me, along with the mohar.

JONAH

The warmth of Michal's hand in mine was the best part of the morning. It was the first time she'd allowed me to touch her since I'd been back. Living with my daughter, I was anxious to begin constructing a home again, eager to fetch my wife and son and wake up to their laughter, fall asleep with them in my arms.

Michal and I reestablished our commitment to one another, digging deeply into our souls and purging the ugliness that remained. I didn't have anything left to be exposed, except one great secret that I'd kept inside for the right moment.

The softness of the dawn strengthened me as we walked up the hill to the high place. Caleb used the money I paid him for the sheep to buy back that portion of land so it wouldn't be desecrated. It would no longer have an altar of any sort. The high places displeased the Lord, he reminded me. They had been banned by Israel's obedient kings, and re-established by those who rebelled. I knew this, yet tried to worship there anyhow. It was compromise of my own making. No wonder God was silent for so long.

Why had he chosen me to be his prophet? I couldn't help but wonder again and again as I counted my failures. For some divine reason, he loved me, flawed and cracked as I was. His mercy had been pouring out on me long before he sent a fish to my rescue.

Mercy had in fact flowed from every direction since I returned. Shunned and disbelieved by some, many others embraced their reluctant prophet, a man who tried and fell, and tried again. I was no longer someone they looked up to, no longer above them. I was simply one of them.

On the hilltop, my wife and I worked side by side, clearing all the stones from the original altar. The largest we set aside to use in the foundation. Caleb's gift to us would be the location of a small, simple home. It would be the place of a new beginning, where I could continue to mend what I had torn asunder. What Michal and I had allowed to fall, we intended to reconstruct, stone by stone, prayer by prayer.

I stood and arched my tired spine, eager to give Michal the last and greatest mohar gift. "We should go to Nineveh," I said.

Michal looked at me with an eyebrow lifted.

"I met an intriguing woman while I was there." I watched her face closely, not expecting any understanding.

I was wrong. Her eyes glimmered immediately, the stone in her hands falling to the earth.

"You found her. You found Miriam."

I put the pad of my dusty finger on her trembling lip. "She found me."

Michal dropped onto a bench and pulled me down beside her. "Tell me everything."

I did, not omitting the fact Miriam was being dragged to her death when I first saw her. The heartaches her sister had endured made Michal weep. "She looks like you," I said. "Strong and beautiful, determined to walk the path of righteousness. Nineveh took your sister and hurt her, but it didn't destroy her."

Michal gripped my hand. "You left her there?"

"I didn't leave her. She refused to come. She has children whose hearts are open to the Hebrew God now. She couldn't leave. She said she found purpose, and knew you would understand."

"I do. But, maybe..."

Her imploring eyes said everything. "Yes. We'll go there."

Michal stood abruptly and took in a deep breath. "With Ethan."

"He'll enjoy the camel caravan, and the beauty of the city, that's for certain. We might have to put him on a leash-"

"Not for those reasons." She sat beside me again and stared at her fingers as they twisted her garment. "He needs to meet his mother."

I said nothing for a minute, her words trying to find purchase in my mind. "He's-? Miriam is his mother?"

She nodded.

"You knew she was alive?"

"No. I prayed, yes, and hoped. Not until months after Ethan was delivered, did I even suspect she was alive. He came oiled and wrapped in Assyrian fabric, and, the man said he was to give the baby to me. Not to the prophet Jonah, as all the others. To me, by name. Later it occurred to me. I thought, perhaps she lived. I hoped, and prayed."

"You didn't tell me."

"Ethan was Assyrian. How could I?"

She was right. I would not have harmed the infant, but I would not have taken him into my care, or allowed him among the people of Gath-hepher. I would have found him a home in a distant village. Had I known, my own prejudice would have cost me one of my greatest blessings.

"Did she ask about him?"

"Yes. She cried. I never imagined..."

Michal put her head on my shoulder and I wrapped an arm around her waist and pulled her into me. "Michal," I whispered. "I own nothing, yet for the very first time in my life, I have everything."

THE SAILOR

The pale fleshed man didn't have time to let loose a cry for help as my arm wrapped against his throat. His hands instinctively reached up and latched on to my forearm, to no avail. He was strong, just not as strong as me. I laughed as he squirmed, remembering the first time he and I met, under similar methods of introduction. I wasn't certain then if I wanted him alive, then grieved a few days later when my hands ensured his death Now, the dead man wiggled in my grasp like a carp in a net.

"Never knew I could catch me a ghost, and subdue it with one arm." I winked at the man's wife, and she smiled in return, her initial alarm replaced by amusement when she recognized who was threatening her husband.

"Take everything," she said. "It's yours. Take him, too, just let me go."

Jonah stopped squirming. Michal's tone of voice left no room for any real fears. He tipped his head back against me and relaxed his vise on my arm. "Squid." My nickname came on a breath of relief.

The prophet who ran from his God turned and clasped my shoulders. He was the color and texture of a shark belly. But it was his eyes that had really changed. They were bright, happy reflections of a man at peace.

"You falsely pronounced my demise," he said, the stern attempt to reprimand me negated by the grin.

I hugged him into my chest briefly, still amazed that it was really Jonah standing on the seaside.

"How can it be you?" I asked. "No man could swim that distance, and I saw you sink beneath the waves. You can't be alive."

Jonah grinned wider and pulled Michal to his side. "I have a story you'll want to hear, my friend."

"The storm was gone as soon as you sank. Did you know that? Your God is all powerful." I had studied the Hebrew God since that day and had no other God but him now. It was to the Creator I asked for guidance and safety on the open seas. It was to him I brought a sacrifice when I was near the lands of Israel, and to him I gave credit for the miracle I had witnessed already. Now here was Jonah, another miracle to add to the tale I told over and over as I journeyed. It had not grown stale.

"And merciful."

"I'm eager to hear of it. Are you sailing with me? The Amphitrite is docked over yonder."

Both of his hands shot up in the air as if to protect himself. "No! Never again. I came here to remember, to write down what happened, so I never forget, and so my people won't forget. And to look for you. I have oil and wool for you to carry up the coast, if you will, to the village that nursed me."

"Nursed you? They didn't do it very well. You're the same color as when you were on board my ship, and it isn't a pretty one."

Jonah laughed, the sound of a freed soul. "I have *so* much to tell you," he said as he dropped an arm on my shoulder on one side and clasped his wife's hand on the other. "But first, let's eat! Anything you recommend, as long as it never, *ever* touched the sea."

EPILOGUE

The old woman licked the last drops of broth from her lips with a satisfied smack, then settled into the cushions that kept her thin bones off the floor. She was asleep before I could tuck the hides beneath her chin. Unable to walk for a year now, the tolls of her life were coming due. I brushed brittle tendrils of gray from her forehead with fingers gnarled and tender, both of us an accumulation of time and the trials of living.

Above my head, the ceiling creaked under the weight of the man who walked there, repairing the old roof that he and his father constructed themselves, when God's prophet found his way home. I looked up instinctively, protectively, even though his children had children of their own now.

"Mother?" Ethan called through a finger-wide crack, his face momentarily blocking the stream of sunlight that poured through and warmed the old woman's face. He would always be my baby.

And hers.

Miriam's blue-veined lids snapped open, eyes bright and alert. In unison we answered, "Yes?"

The End

THOUGHTS FROM THE AUTHOR

What parts of this novel are fact?

The Book of Jonah in the Bible is only four chapters long, so I'll refer you there to read what I used for most of the history portion. In II Kings 14:25 you'll find the reference to his prophecy regarding the expansion of his nation's borders.

Some characters in this novel were real and I believe were his contemporaries, such as Amos and Amaziah, but they weren't necessarily acquainted with Jonah. I chose to make them interact. From there I relied on various commentaries regarding the prophet, and resources describing the culture and regions. The remainder comes from my interpretation and imagination of the life and times of this intriguing man and his place in history.

What became of Jonah, the prophet?

We don't know for certain what became of Jonah after his time in Nineveh. He is considered the author of the book bearing his name, so it is assumed he returned to his homeland to write and recount his experience. There are a number of tombs dedicated to him, one in Masshad, Israel, a city associated with the location of Gath-hepher. There was one in Mosul, Iraq as well, the modern-day city on the outskirts of ancient Nineveh. This tomb was destroyed in 2014 by militants.

What became of Israel?

Despite the warnings of prophets before Jonah, and those who came after him, Israel didn't repent. It seems they expected God's mercy, regardless. The prophet Amos was very clear in relating the implications, that the nation would be taken into exile because of their sins. The nation had broken covenant with God and the day of judgment was inevitable. It came about a generation after Jonah was in Nineveh, when the Northern Kingdom was besieged by the Assyrians. In 722 BC, Samaria, the capital city, was captured and the kingdom, destroyed.

Jonah was right in my version of his story. The punishment of his enemy was deferred because they repented, but his own people ignored the prophesies, and their time of mercy expired. By choosing not to follow in the wisdom of their pagan enemy and turn back to the Lord, God allowed them to be taken into captivity.

The southern tribes of Judah and Benjamin remained a nation for another century, until they too were defeated, this time by the Babylonian empire.

It doesn't end there, of course. God remembered his chosen ones, and they have endured, and endured, and always will. His covenant with them stands forever.

For more of Israel's history, read the Bible with a good commentary or two to guide you.

What became of Nineveh?

Repentance in Nineveh didn't last. Known for its persistent brutality and idolatry, the mighty Assyrian Empire was crushed by the Medes and Babylonians about a century after its revival. Prophesies concerning the fall of Nineveh are found in the book of Nahum.

Excavation of the city-site near Mosul, Iraq, has revealed many palaces, including that of King Sennacherib with its 71 rooms, and of Ashurbanipal with a library containing 22,000 clay tablets. City walls were 50' wide and 33' tall. Art, innovation, and wealth were evident.

Is Jonah's legacy as the reluctant prophet deserved?

Well, he did run from a direct command, so yes, he'll have to wear that nametag. I can't say I would have done differently though, so like to give the guy some slack. I believe that God understood Jonah's ultimate-patriot zeal, especially in light of the brutal practices the Assyrians used to subdue their enemies. His prophet just needed a deeper understanding of divine love and grace.

How is Jonah's experience relevant today?

I chose Jonah as the subject of a novel in part because I thought it would be a fun challenge to write about the whole fishy experience from his point of view. I knew one theme would be woven in, that there are always consequences to rebellion against God.

Story threads regarding mercy and repentance emerged, as expected. I wanted to show this in God's response to Jonah's defiance, God's compassion for Nineveh, and also on a more relatable level, Michal's attitude towards her husband. She had her own set of faults, yet in the end, she chose what was right in God's eyes. Miriam did as well, not something originally plotted. When it came time to bring her home, I realized it wasn't time yet. She had purpose on her mission field.

The short book of Jonah isn't a fish tale, or even about the man himself. It's about the heart and character of God. He is all-powerful, controlling the storms and providing super-natural means of salvation. His ways are not ours, and can't be thwarted. He is the righteous judge, condemning evil. And He is the God of mercy.

"Do I take any pleasure in the death of the wicked?" declares the Sovereign Lord. "Rather, am I not pleased when they turn from their ways and live?" This verse from Ezekiel expresses the missional heart of God, and is a model for our own attitudes.

Also of note, observant Jews traditionally read Jonah on the Day of Atonement, Yom Kippur. This is a day of repentance, of turning from sin and seeking righteousness. The book of Jonah is a reminder that God's mercy is available for everyone who sincerely seeks a clean heart, who puts aside the ways of the world and embraces the ways of the Lord.

And lastly, the fish.

Our Sunday School whale is more like 'great fish' in Hebrew. It may have been of a species that is now extinct, or may have been a unique creation for the purpose of saving a wayward prophet. Nothing is impossible with God. I intend to ask Jonah myself one day.

Thank you for reading this book.

The proceeds from my writing support charitable ministries around the globe. You have just fed a starving child, purchased a Bible in an African language, or provided bicycles to protect girls from being kidnapped on their way to school.

About the Author

Rachel S. Neal lives in Missoula, Montana with her husband of more than a quarter of a century. She writes to inspire, amuse, and provide her readers with a mental adventure infused with hope and truth. When not typing, her hands are covered in garden dirt, concrete, paint, fabric, glue, or the makings of something tasty in the kitchen.

Made in the USA
San Bernardino, CA
08 February 2018